Body Count

Thomas Kelly

Published by Thomas Kelly, 2024.

This is a work of fiction. Similarities to real people, places, or events are entirely coincidental.

BODY COUNT

First edition. July 24, 2024.

ISBN: 979-8224250943

Written by Thomas Kelly.

Dedicated to all those in law enforcement who put
themselves in harm's way to protect others.

Lieutenant Robert Tynan stared at the case folder on his desk and let out a loud sigh. The word "CONFIDENTIAL" was stamped in large red block letters across the top of the folder. The New York City Police Department logo and the Internal Affairs' Bureau seal were directly below it. Tynan thought the seal looked pompous. A poor attempt to copy the FBI's seal.

At the very bottom of the folder were two boxes for the dates the case was opened and closed. Tynan wrote July 6, 1993 in the case closed box. It had been six months to the day since the case had been opened. The same day he had arrived in the Internal Affairs Bureau.

Tynan thought back to when he was first assigned to Internal Affairs. He had applied to go to the Detective Bureau but his timing could not have been worse. The Department, after another crushing corruption scandal, had decided the time had come to "shake-up" Internal Affairs. When his application to the Detective Bureau landed on the desk of the review board, they felt his services were better suited for a two-year stint in the Internal Affairs Bureau, or IAB as it was more commonly known.

The unit got a makeover. Most of the career investigators assigned to IAB were gone. Sent on their merry way to other investigative assignments or into retirement. They were replaced by seasoned investigators who had never been in IAB. The Department set up a panel to review all applications to either the Detective or Organized Crime Bureaus, and Internal Affairs got first pick on any applicant. Anyone selected would have to do two years in IAB before they could go on to their original choice.

As Tynan saw it, he was one of those unfortunate souls selected to go to IAB. He made many phone calls to get out of it but no matter who he called, nor how high their rank, the answer was always the same. There was nothing they could do about it. Tynan would have to do his time.

Beside his desk, tucked down out of sight, was his personal countdown calendar. He started every day by drawing a line through the date. At the end of his shift, he scratched another, completing an "X," and wrote how many days were left. It was his way to keep track of his personal purgatory.

He didn't have a problem with corrupt cops being caught as long as it was someone else doing it. The old Internal Affairs had a reputation for missing real corruption and going after cops for what he thought was nonsense. That supposedly changed when the Department created the new and improved Internal Affairs in 1992. But after looking at the case folder in front of him, he had his doubts. He pushed the folder away from him, with a little disgust, much like pushing away a dinner plate after having too much to eat.

Turning his chair around he looked out the window. His office was located on the campus of the State Maritime College. The college rented out one of its "L" shaped dorms to the Department. Tynan had two teams, each occupying one wing.

His office was down one of the halls and had a great view overlooking Long Island Sound. Tynan watched the dozen sail-boats bobbing up and down at anchor in a small cove. Their white, sun drenched, hulls made the water seem bluer. As far as Police Department offices went, this was the best he ever had. He wondered if the location was intended to help offset the poor morale. Somehow, he doubted it. The offices still contained the typical dull green metal desks and cabinets that filled every police station in the city.

He swung around in his chair to get back to the case folder and caught sight of his reflection in the glass. He felt much older than his forty years. His once jet-black hair was now streaked with gray and his face was ruddy, more from drinking than the sun. His back and knees bothered him, reminders of old injuries earned while doing real police work. He stood up and stretched towards the ceiling, trying to get the kinks out of his six-foot frame. "God, I'm getting old," he said out loud.

He opened the folder. Maybe if he tried reviewing it while standing, it would make more sense but he doubted it. The case was an example of what he thought was wrong with IAB. They had spent six months on this case. It should have been closed as soon as it was opened but the higher ups in IAB demanded that all cases be treated seriously. *That was the problem*, thought Tynan. *When everything is serious, nothing is serious.*

He skimmed through the file. He was too familiar with it. He had nicknamed it the "French Fry Connection." Unlike the original *"French Connection,"* there were no kilos of heroin, mob guys or hundreds of thousands of dollars. *This case was just a tad bit smaller,* thought Tynan.

The case involved an allegation that a cop in a Bronx precinct received free French fries when he ordered a hamburger at some greasy spoon diner. Receiving an Unlawful Gratuity is what the New York State Penal Law would have labeled it. Complete bullshit is what Tynan called it.

A simple case like this had required background checks on the officer involved, following him on patrol to see what he did, and then sending an undercover to follow the cop into the restaurant where the ill-gotten fries had been obtained. All this surveillance turned up nothing. The cop had paid full price, including the fries. A month ago, Tynan had wanted to close the case as unfounded but the brass running IAB headquarters at Hudson Street said no. Their orders were clear. Keep following the cop into the restaurant.

That annoyed Tynan to no end. He had tied up both of his teams following this cop. His teams consisted of two sergeants and seven detectives. He had two more detectives who were assigned to administrative duties, just to handle the mountain of paperwork the teams generated. Eleven people, not exactly an army. Tynan thought he had proved nothing was happening but that wasn't good enough.

The second round of surveillances had the same result. The cop ordered his burger and fries at the restaurant and paid full price. Tynan finally called up his superiors and told them that the only thing this cop was guilty of, was working on a heart attack. Reluctantly, they told him to close the case.

He flipped to the last page of the folder, checked the box marked approved, and signed his name. One less case to worry about, and the good citizens of New York could rest assured there was no cop in the Bronx taking free fries. At least, not this cop.

He tossed the folder into the out basket and opened the next case. The phone rang, saving Tynan from having to wade through another pile of useless surveillances that had found nothing.

He picked up the phone, "Lieutenant Tynan, Group 41."

"Hey Lou," said the voice on the other end. "It's Sergeant Spano, how's it going?"

Although Tynan's name was Robert or Bob or Bobby, he, like all the other Lieutenants in the NYPD, had been rechristened upon promotion. From that day forward, he was called Lou. Tynan liked that moniker better than "boss." He never called his superiors boss and he never shortened their titles, but the word "Lou" had grown on him.

"You called me up to ask how's it going?" said Tynan. "Well, I just signed off on the 'French Fry Connection.' If I should die tonight my life is complete. How goes your war on corruption?"

"You ain't going to believe this," said Spano. "I'm out here with Linda on a 'call-out.'"

"I was wondering where you guys were when I came in. Another call-out," sighed Tynan.

Call-outs were the word IAB used when they wanted a team to go out and start an immediate investigation on an allegation. The call outs came from IAB's Action Desk. It was the Internal Affairs equivalent of 911. If the people working at the Action Desk thought the case sounded routine, they shipped the paperwork through channels to the group covering that area. If not, then they called the group to respond immediately.

"Yeah, it came in from the Action Desk, this morning. They were pretty hyped up about it so we ran right out."

"The Action Desk," snorted Tynan. "More like the *inaction* desk. What's the emergency?"

"Get a load of this. The info came in from a federal CI and he says he has info on a 'hit' being put together by a cop in the Bronx."

Tynan sat down and planted his elbows on the desk. *This wasn't your run of the mill call-out*, he thought.

Spano lowered his voice on the phone, "The guy is trying to set up a contract murder. Plus, a whole lot of other stuff. I can't get into all of it right now but we're on our way back. I think it sounds believable. The ATF agent who is handling him says this guy is on the money all the time."

"Alright, I guess I'll see you in a bit."

"You got it, Lou."

Tynan hung up the phone and absent-mindedly fumbled through another bulging case folder. "Contract murders," he mumbled to himself. "I'll believe it when I see it."

It took him another hour to read through two more cases. All the usual boxes were checked and they met whatever standard Hudson Street was looking for. Tynan was never sure if they were looking for thorough investigations or just something to cover their ass.

As he reached for another folder there was a knock on the door. In the doorway stood Sergeant Joe Spano and Detective Linda

James. Spano smiled. With his balding head, pencil thin moustache and small goatee, the smile looked more sinister than anything else. Tynan thought Spano must have modeled for the Guy Fawkes mask.

Spano's thin build didn't allow Detective James to hide behind him, as small as she was. Spano was another draftee into the Internal Affairs Bureau. He was an active sergeant, and opened and closed his cases with refreshing regularity. While Spano wasn't thrilled to be there, he never let it bother him. He smiled and joked like he was polishing a stand-up comedy act. Tynan wished he could be that carefree.

Linda, on the other hand, had spent several years in the unit and had survived the purge, which told Tynan that she was competent. Linda had about ten years on the job with six of them in Internal Affairs. She kept her head down and took her work seriously but was not afraid to speak up and give her opinion, asked or not. Tynan liked that. She was the only black female on the team and didn't mind being used in an undercover role whenever Tynan asked. She was reliable, someone who didn't need to be carefully supervised.

"Ah, it's the two amigos. Okay, impress me with this bolt out of the blue," said Tynan as he pushed his chair back from the desk and placed his hands behind his head.

"Oh, you'll be impressed, Lou," said Linda as she scooted around Spano, stepped into the office, and quickly took a seat. Sitting, her feet barely touched the floor. She motioned to Spano to take the chair beside her. Linda was not impressed by rank, a trait Tynan admired.

"Let's see, where to begin," she said as she thumbed through her reporter's notebook. She let out a soft, low whistle as she finally landed on a page.

"I got a call from the Action Desk saying there was an Alcohol, Tobacco and Firearms agent that needed to talk to us about a case. That's what started the ball rolling. Early this morning, me and

Sergeant Spano headed out to meet up with the agent and his Confidential Informant."

"The CI is really reliable," added Spano.

"Yes, the CI," said Linda slowly as she scanned through her notes. Taking a deep breath, she continued, "His name is Angel Lopez and supposedly is very reliable," said Linda emphasizing her words by tapping on the notebook with her pen. "The CI says that, three days ago, a friend of his named Sammy Lugo was told by the cop to get someone to kill a drug dealer named Miguel Santos."

"Kill someone, just like that," said Tynan in a dull flat emotionless voice. He knew his dead eye stare intimidated people, even hardened criminals. He found it handy in his line of work.

Linda didn't skip a beat as she looked up and down from her notes. She slowly flipped over the pages of the notebook and pressed on with her briefing. Spano sat beside her, nodding, while he looked back and forth between Linda and Tynan.

"The cop's name is Peter Warren," added Joe. "Assigned to the Four-One Precinct." Like all cops, Spano always referred to precincts by their individual numbers. Only civilians would say Forty-first Precinct.

Linda picked up her cadence. "He's been on the job for five years. After the academy he was assigned to that precinct on patrol. He has two corruption complaints, one in 1989, the other in 1990. Both were closed as unsubstantiated. One was for selling drugs and the other for ripping off drug dealers. Other than that, nothing unusual about him, except he has virtually no arrest activity. In fact, he's made less than forty arrests in his career and only three in the last two years."

"Three collars in two years," laughed Spano. "He makes thirty something arrests in his first two years and then goes dead. We know one thing for sure, he's not making collars for dollars. No overtime in his checks."

Tynan didn't say anything. The number of arrests troubled him. What had happened? Did this guy burn out after only three years? Retired on the job as they say? Pretty unusual for a new cop to not be out there making arrests. Most new cops were running around like lunatics locking up anything that moved, but this guy had flamed out early. He went back to listening to Linda.

"...According to the CI, Lugo ran into him three days ago and asked him if he was interested in getting rid of someone for him. Lugo then told him the story about the cop who wanted this guy hit. Supposedly, this guy Santos owes the cop money for cocaine he got on consignment. Apparently, Miguel Santos won't pay up and is threatening Warren by saying he'll turn him in if he doesn't stop hassling him about the money."

"Wait a minute, wait a minute," said Tynan as he unclasped his hands from behind his head and leaned forward. "This guy Lugo asks the CI to do a hit for some cop. How long has this CI known Lugo and why does he wait three days to tell us about it?"

"I'm getting to that, Lou" said Linda, arching her eyebrows, "I'll explain."

"This CI says he has known Lugo for years. They grew up together. Lugo sells drugs in the neighborhood covered by Warren's precinct. Lugo became friendly with the cop after Warren caught him with a load of coke, but he didn't lock him up."

Linda flipped another page in her notebook. "Instead, they went into business together. Warren and his partner, a cop named Ed Wright, started working with Lugo. The CI says Lugo bumped into him several days ago. That's when Lugo asked him if he'd be interested in making some quick money by doing the hit."

Joe now chimed in "Lugo told the CI that his business was growing and that the two cops provided protection for his spots and helped him move drugs between stash houses."

"How long has Warren been running protection for this guy?" asked Tynan.

"You won't believe this, Lou," snorted Spano. "Lugo has been working with Warren for at least two years. Warren runs off other dealers and tells Narcotics about Lugo's competition. This way Bronx Narcotics knocks out Lugo's competition without even knowing it. According to the CI, the operation is expanding. Lugo will take over Santos' turf, and the CI could run it for him."

Linda looked at Spano and said, "Can I continue?"

"Sorry, just trying to cut to the chase," said Joe as he held up both hands.

"Thank you." Linda flipped a page in her notebook. "It looks like Lugo and the cop have been in business for a couple of years but he's not the only drug dealer working with the cop. Apparently, Miguel Santos also sells cocaine and works with Warren. Warren seized a load of coke and gave it to Santos to sell, but instead of paying up, Santos told the cop to get lost or else he'd rat him out to us."

"Okay, makes a little more sense. Why is Lugo asking the CI to do it?" asked Tynan.

"Lugo is afraid he won't be able to kill Santos because he'll be expecting it. Santos knows Lugo is in tight with the cop. That's why Lugo wants to bring in the CI. Santos won't have his guard up and the CI should be able to kill him," said Linda.

"Okay, so when does he reach out to the ATF agent?"

"That same day, but it takes two days for them to connect, and after the agent meets with the CI, he calls the Action Desk and that's when we come in."

Tynan nodded slowly. Looking at Linda, he asked, "And the Agent says this guy is reliable?"

"Good as gold," said Joe. He held up his hands as Linda shot him another dirty look.

"Yes, as some people say," said Linda, pointing her pen at Joe.

Tynan nodded and swung his chair around to look at the bobbing boats at anchor. *It'd be nice to be out there* he thought. Joe was right. This certainly wasn't a case of free French fries or like any of the other nonsense that drifted through the office. This was the real deal.

Without turning around, Tynan said in a low, almost absent-minded voice, "What happened to the old cases on this cop? The cases that were handled by this office?"

"They were both closed out as unsubstantiated," said Joe, shrugging and looking at Linda.

"They didn't find anything?"

Tynan could see Linda's reflection in the glass. She slapped her hands down in her lap and said, "Honestly Lou, we do two or three surveillances on people, and by some miracle, we're supposed to catch them in the act. What are the odds of that?"

Tynan sensed Linda was getting defensive. She was career IAB after all. She took this stuff personally. "Nobody is blaming you or anyone else, Linda. I'm just asking a question, and trust me, the brass are going to ask the same thing. Of course, it's ridiculous. With the amount of time we waste on bullshit, it's amazing we catch anyone."

"Fuck them," said Linda in a whisper. "They're the ones making us run around in circles."

"So, what do you think Lou?" asked Spano.

Not taking his eyes off the boats, Tynan responded, "I think we got a real case."

He swung around in his chair, grabbed a yellow legal pad, and started writing. "Okay, first, I want those old cases pulled. Look them over and see if there's anything in there that would back up the CI's story. We're going to need info on his partner too, like any old allegations, his residence, cars, bank accounts, you know the drill."

Without looking up, he continued writing.

"I want a meeting with this CI. Today. Bring that agent up here with him because I don't want to step on any toes. I'm going to call the geniuses at Hudson Street and tell them what we got. We're going to have to move fast on this."

"What, do you have in mind?" asked Joe.

Tynan stopped writing and looked up. "If this is true, Warren or Lugo might be out there right now trying to get someone else to do the hit. We've got to move on this."

"Talking to others is going to be risky for Warren," said Linda. "I'm not so sure he would do anything until he hears back from Lugo."

"You're probably right but we can't take the chance," said Tynan. He looked directly at Linda. "We need to get this CI to make a call to Lugo today to confirm he'll do the job. Get it on tape. That way we got Lugo in the bag. The tricky part is going to be making the link between Lugo and the cop."

One thing Tynan knew about crooked cops was they weren't like average criminals. They were more suspicious. Making a case against Warren wasn't going to be easy.

Linda closed her notebook slowly, as if trying to work out the plan in her head. Then she said, "I don't see Warren meeting with the CI. He's asked Lugo to do the hit. Even if Warren agrees that Lugo should farm the hit out, why would he ever agree to meet the shooter? He'll meet with Lugo but I don't see him meeting with both of them."

Spano nodded. "I don't see that either. If we get the CI to make the call and then set up a meeting, we got Lugo. But who's to say he'll flip. He may not give up Warren."

"Yeah," Tynan said, "but what other option do we have? We have to show a link between Lugo and Warren. Maybe if we put the squeeze on Lugo, he'll roll and give up the cop, just to get out from under."

"What about a wire on Warren's phone?" suggested Linda.

"I don't see him talking shop on his home phone," said Joe. "Not to mention, we don't have time for a wire."

"Alright," sighed Tynan, "we can wargame this later. For now, let's get those cases, set up a meeting with the CI, and get him to make the call to Lugo. I'll call Hudson Street and let them know what we have. I got to run this up the chain."

"The IAB brass at Hudson Street," laughed Joe. "There you go. They'll have some suggestions. Probably want us to see if we can lure Warren in with some free French fries."

As Joe and Linda left, Tynan reached for the phone. He had a lot of calls to make. As he started to dial, he knew one thing was certain, he never knew what type of reaction he'd get out of Hudson Street.

THE PLAN

It was nearly an hour later by the time Tynan got off the phone. As he expected, it was one call after another up the chain of command to the Chief of Internal Affairs. The calls to Hudson Street had gone more smoothly than expected. There were no suggestions, instead his story was met with silence. His captain thought there should be an immediate meeting with the chief. The chief wanted nothing to do with it, and told Tynan to just keep him in the loop.

Tynan was relieved he had freedom of action. Suggestions from headquarters just added more work and accomplished nothing, but deep down, he knew why there were no suggestions. This was a big case and if it went wrong, someone's head was going to roll. If the brass kept their distance any mistakes would fall squarely on Tynan.

He had been around long enough to know how the game was played. If the case went well, his superiors would hold a meeting with the commissioner. Tynan would be invited of course just to answer any unexpected questions, and the brass would pat each other on the back about the good job they had done. If, on the other hand, the case went in the crapper, Tynan knew there would be a different kind of meeting. One where he would be quizzed and asked how he could be so stupid, incompetent, or whatever word they chose. He'd be transferred, maybe brought up on department charges and the brass would have another meeting with the commissioner where they would pat each other on the back for identifying and getting rid of an incompetent subordinate.

In the rarified atmosphere of the fourteenth floor at police headquarters, people with stars on their shoulders usually didn't have to take the fall. There were plenty of people further down the food chain for that. While Tynan was not at the bottom, he knew he was in the unenviable position of not being big enough to escape the blame but small enough to be a suitable sacrifice.

Tynan got up and walked into the hallway. "Joe! Linda!" he yelled.

Two heads popped out from different doorways farther down the hall. "We'll be there in a minute, Lou," said Joe. "Just got to grab some stuff."

Tynan walked back inside his office. While his view of the water was great, the actual office left a lot to be desired. He looked at the mold that was slowly working its way down the wall from the window. The office had bare walls with peeling, off-white paint and no pictures. His metal desk with a bent leg was supported by a Bronx phone book. A bulletin board with miscellaneous notes and lists of phone numbers hung next to a whiteboard. Green metal filing cabinets made by inmates on Rikers Island completed the look. *Nothing but the finest for the finest,* he thought.

He sat at his desk with its stack of case folders and waited for Joe and Linda. He heard their fast paced, footsteps coming down the hall. They walked with a purpose. Not the casual sauntering of someone going to the copier. Tynan knew that Linda and Joe understood things were about to get very serious.

As Joe entered the office he motioned with his hand towards the hallway and said, "I asked the rest of the team to join us."

"Good thinking," said Tynan. "We're going to need everyone. The conference room would be better but we can all fit in here."

Over the course of five minutes, they were joined by the other members of the unit. A total of nine people squeezed into the office. Tynan, Linda, and Joe were seated and everyone else grabbed a spot along the wall where they leaned with quiet interest.

Tynan motioned to Linda and Joe. "Okay, tell them what we got."

Joe and Linda stood up and moved over to the whiteboard. Linda, looked for a marker she could use to outline the case on the board as Joe, started talking. "It looks like we're going to be busy today and probably the next couple of days. We got a case involving drugs and a possible contract murder."

Joe described all the players and how the case came about as Linda wrote their names on the board and attached their pictures. She drew arrows between the names indicating connections. *It's starting to look like a NYC subway map*, thought Tynan. The other members of the team were no longer leaning on the wall. They were standing straight, listening, their eyes shifting from Joe to Linda's diagram and the pictures of the people involved.

Tynan listened, along with the others, trying to see if something was missing. He was pleased at how much work they had both done in an hour. Pictures of the suspects had been printed out, along with rap sheets on the CI and the other players. They'd pulled addresses, phone numbers, registered cars, anything that might be useful in the coming hours.

Finally, Joe looked around and said, "Any questions?"

Tynan stood up. "You know how I work. This is now a team case. There's no rank in this office right now. If you have an idea, spit it out. If you think something won't work, say so. When we walk out of here, I want everyone to either have had some say in what's going to happen or at least agree with it. Understood?"

"Okay," said Joe, "this is what we're thinking." He turned to Linda, motioning her to start.

"As of now, the plan is to talk to the CI and their agent, get him here and have the CI make a recorded phone call to Lugo, where he'll tell him he wants to do the job. Hopefully, Lugo will say enough to not only incriminate himself but also the cop. Then we set up a meet tonight, where the CI will get some money up front and a gun. The CI will use one of our cars, wired for sound, and we'll also use the surveillance van for video. We are thinking of doing it at the abandoned gas station by the Bruckner. Once the transaction is made, we arrest Lugo, take him back here, and hopefully he flips and agrees to contact Warren for us. Thoughts, questions?"

Bill Russell, the other sergeant in the unit, was now leaning against a filing cabinet. Russell, or Russ as everyone called him, was another draftee. He had been hoping to go to Narcotics but IAB grabbed him. He was gruff but did his work without complaint. Russell shifted his large frame, rubbed his hand across his crewcut, and said, "I don't get it. Let's say we grab this Lugo character and he doesn't flip, Warren is going to find out he got pinched. He's not going to go within a hundred feet of him. Then you got nothing other than the word of this CI. We're counting on Lugo flipping and that might be a bad bet."

Tynan nodded. "That's all true but this is time sensitive. For all we know, our guy Warren is out there right now looking for someone else to do the hit. If we do the usual IAB routine here, we'll wind up with a dead guy on our hands."

"Just asking," said Russell.

"Any other thoughts?" asked Linda.

The room was silent. Tynan sensed they didn't like the spot they were in but nobody seemed to have a better idea, or any ideas for that matter. He waited a couple of seconds before clapping his hands and raising his voice, "Okay, let's put this in play."

He turned to Spano. "Joe, when is this CI getting here?"

"Should be here within the half hour."

"Alright." Tynan felt like he was running out of time. He couldn't stand inaction. *Better to make the wrong decision than no decision*, he thought.

He turned to the team and said, "Let's make sure the equipment in the car and the surveillance van are working. Get someone to take a drive by our abandoned gas station, make sure we don't have Con Edison or someone else tearing up the street over there. Then get the surveillance van out there to find a good spot to watch the gas station. I want the rest of the team, with the exception of Joe and Linda, out at the site waiting, before we put the call in to Lugo."

The team shuffled towards the door as Tynan added, "I don't want Lugo getting there first and watching us setting up. Everyone will be in place before the call is made. Got it?"

"You got it, Lou," said Russell. Once the room had cleared, Tynan looked at Linda and Joe. Linda walked over to the chair and sat down, letting out a heavy sigh.

"I hope this works," she said. "This whole thing is rushed."

"Ah, it'll work," said Joe. "What are we dealing with, a couple of rocket scientists? These guys can't think past the next hour. We'll be fine," he muttered as he walked over to the window.

"Let's see what our CI and his handler have to say about this," said Tynan. "I can hardly wait."

Linda looked down at her watch. "They'll be here soon."

Just as she spoke the loud buzzer at the end of the hall signaled that someone who didn't work in the unit was looking to get in.

"Well, don't just stand there, Joe," said Tynan, "Let in our honored guests."

Tynan heard the heavy metal door at the end of the hallway open and slam shut. Spano's laugh rose over the indistinguishable chatter. The footsteps grew closer, and Tynan and Linda were joined by Joe and two other men standing in the doorway to Tynan's office.

"Lou," this is Agent Kurt Morse with the ATF and Angel Lopez. The agent stepped quickly into the room as Tynan rose from behind his cluttered desk and extended his hand.

"Hi, Bob Tynan, how do you do?" Tynan shook the agent's hand.

"Glad to meet you," said the agent."

Tynan had expected the agent to be bearded and scruffy but he wasn't. Kurt was in his thirties, tall, clean shaven, and dressed in clean blue jeans and a denim jacket.

Kurt turned back to the other man in the doorway, gesturing towards him to come in, "This is Angel. He's been working with us for quite some time. He's quite a guy."

Angel walked up to Tynan and shook his hand. He had a Yankee baseball cap on, pulled low over a pair of sunglasses. He was short and light skinned with a blondish goatee. Tynan wondered if the goatee was dyed. The CI wore a black leather jacket, pressed trousers, and brown dress shoes. The informant was also not what Tynan had been expecting.

Tynan shook his hand. "Nice to meet you, Angel. Why don't you have a seat. Do you want anything to drink?"

"Nah, I'm good," said Angel as he sat down in the chair beside Linda. "How you doing baby?"

"I'm good," said Linda.

"Oh, you're a lot more than good," said Angel as he stroked his goatee.

Linda just smiled. Tynan had seen that smile before. It was definitely a smile, but behind it was the thought of "I'd like to punch your face." It looked like Angel and Linda weren't going to be friends. *Just as I like it*, thought Tynan. *Never trust a CI. They are never your friend and you are never their friend.*

"Okay," said Tynan. "Joe, how about you drag in another chair or two?"

Joe disappeared and quickly came back with two wheeled desk chairs from another office. "There you go," Joe said as he motioned to the agent. Joe jumped into the other chair and wheeled himself back towards the window.

The agent leaned back in the chair, extending his hands, "What can we do for you?"

All business, thought Tynan. *Good.* "Well, how about Angel run through his story again about Lugo and the cop. How about we start there?" said Tynan with a forced smile.

The agent leaned forward, looking around Linda towards Angel. "Is that okay with you, Angel?"

"*Is that okay?*" thought Tyan. *Who cares if it's okay, it's what he's doing.* "Of course, if Angel doesn't mind," added Tynan.

"Oh no. Not at all." Angel stretched his legs out in front of him, cracked his knuckles, and began a rehash of what Tynan had heard before.

Angel was very comfortable with his story. He told it with no emotion. Occasionally, he would shift in his seat as if he were bored. Then he leaned forward and started to gesture with his hands, when he got to the part about Lugo asking him to do the hit on Santos.

Tynan watched and listened to him closely, looking for any sign of nervousness or if any part of the story sounded fake. He couldn't find it. Linda was leaning in towards Angel, staring at the side of his head as he talked to Tynan. Angel never took his eyes off Tynan.

Tynan sat there and took it all in, like he was watching a movie.

Finally, Angel smacked his hands together, and said, "So that's it. That's when I figured I better come to you guys. I called my friend Kurt up and I knew he would have the answer."

"That was very wise of you," said Tynan. He gestured to Kurt with his hand. "I'm sure he appreciated that."

Tynan leaned forward, propped his elbows up on the desk, and brought his hands together. Peering over his fists, he said, "What I don't understand is what's in it for you?"

"What? Are you kidding? I know how this plays out, dude." Angel shaped his right hand like a gun, pointed it at Tynan, and made a popping sound with his lips. "I'm dead if I do this. Lugo ain't going to let me live. He can't. He's smart enough to know that whoever does this has to go."

The CI looked up at the ceiling and put his hands behind his head. "You see, I don't believe Lugo when he says he can't get close to Santos. They do business together, not a lot, but Santos wouldn't have a problem meeting with him. That's all bullshit."

Unclasping his hands, Angel stood up slowly from the chair and stretched. "It's the cop who put him up to it and told him to get someone to do the job. Lugo thinks I'm stupid, but I'm smarter than him and that cop."

Tynan nodded and sat back. "Hey Linda, why don't you take Angel down to the breakroom and get some coffee, okay?"

"Sure. Let's go, Angel. Follow me."

"Absolutely, I'll follow you anywhere, just lead the way."

Tynan watched as they walked out the door. *If this guy keeps talking to Linda like that, he might never make it out of here alive.*

"This is some story," said Kurt. "Can you believe this? This cop is something else. Did you guys know anything about this?"

"No, unfortunately not. We've had cases on him before but nothing like this."

Joe glanced out the window at the boats then turned back to Kurt. "So, Kurt, what's the story with this guy? How'd he become a CI?"

"The usual," said Kurt as he reached into his pocket and came up with a pack of Marlboro's. "Do you mind if I smoke in here?"

"No, not at all," said Tynan.

He looked around as he fished a lighter out of his other pocket. "Do you have an ashtray?"

"No, but don't worry about it, just flick the ashes on the floor. The maid will get it tomorrow," chuckled Tynan. He looked at the yellowed linoleum tile, "In fact the ashes might do the floor some good."

"What's the usual?" asked Joe.

Kurt lit his cigarette with the practiced hands of a longtime smoker and took a deep drag.

"The usual. He got collared trying to sell some guns to one of our guys. He was looking at federal time and he decided to flip. It worked out well, and after that he's been working for us ever since."

"Is he working off time on that old case?" asked Joe.

"Naw, that's old news. We throw him money. I'm sure he figures, if something bad happens and he gets caught up in some bullshit and arrested, we'll come to his rescue."

Tynan arched his back while leaning back in the chair. His old injury was killing him. His spine gave a little crack and he let out a soft "ahh" as he relaxed again. "Is he any good?"

"Better than good, this guy is the best. He's never wrong. Anything he says you can take to the bank. I'm telling you, if this guy is saying there's going to be a hit, it's not a matter of if but when."

Tynan, didn't doubt there was going to be a hit. As he saw it, drug dealers getting shot was an occupational hazard and nothing to cry over. A form of karma or street justice or whatever else someone wanted to call it. He wasn't worried about the hit. His worries were if the cop's role was true, and if it was, how to stop the hit and rope the cop into the case.

Tynan lowered his voice and said to Kurt, who was now busy blowing smoke rings towards the ceiling, "Did you tell Santos, there might be a hit out on him?"

"No, I wanted to see what you guys wanted to do first. If you want me to, I can."

Joe nodded and looked at Tynan, "It might be better coming from Kurt than from us. If it's ATF making the heads up, he might not make the connection to Lugo."

"Plus, everyone takes the Feds seriously," said Tynan. "If you wouldn't mind doing that, it would help us out."

"Sure, no problem, I can do it tonight. What do you want to do with my guy? Any plans?"

"Yeah," said Tynan. "I'm glad you brought it up. We want to make a move on this today. See if your guy is willing to make a call to Lugo and set up a meet. Have him ask for some money up front and a gun. Then we arrest Lugo and put the squeeze on him. What do you say to that?"

"I'm fine with it. I'd like to get Angel's spin on it first. See if he's willing to do it."

Tynan tried not to let his reaction show. *If he's willing to do it? Make him do it*, thought Tynan. He decided to let it go. No sense getting off on the wrong foot with the guy controlling the informant who's making the case.

"Of course," said Tynan. "If he's okay doing it. No pressure, see what he thinks."

"Okay," said Joe. "Do you want me to bring them back in?"

"Yeah, if Linda hasn't put him in a chokehold yet."

Joe laughed and walked out of the office. "Hey Linda, Angel! Break time is over, come on back," he bellowed.

"You got a nice view from your office," said Kurt as he pointed towards the window.

"Yeah, one of the perks that comes with the job. Just one of the many perks."

Linda walked back into the office ahead of the CI. She threw a quick look at the agent to see if he was watching and then glanced at Tynan, rolling her eyes and mouthing the word "asshole."

Tynan wasn't sure if that was directed at him for sending her to babysit the CI or if it was intended for her newfound friend Angel. Either way, Tynan let a brief smile cross his lips. Linda dropped into the chair between Angel and Kurt as Joe took a seat on the windowsill.

Angel looked relaxed as usual. He didn't seem concerned, like someone visiting a friend. *This guy isn't giving anything away,* thought Tynan. *Not a trace of nervousness. He might as well be sitting in the park.* He was about to see just how cool Angel could be.

"Listen Angel, we were talking things over and I wanted to know if you were up to making a phone call to Lugo."

"A phone call about what?" asked Angel.

"You know, a call to Lugo saying you're interested in doing the job but you wanted some money up front and a gun. It would also be nice if you could bring up Warren's name when you make this call. We would like you to meet Lugo today, to get the cash and the gun. Would you have a problem with that?"

Tynan held his breath, waiting for the response. This would be the test as to how much of this story was real.

Angel looked over at Kurt. "I thought I was just going to come in, tell them what happened and that's it."

"Eh, it's not that simple Angel," said Kurt with a smile. "Things are a little more complicated than that."

Angel hesitated, "I could do that. Only thing is, I don't know how easy it's going to be bringing up Warren. Lugo might get a little nervous if I did that. But as for the rest of it, yeah, okay, I guess."

"That's good," said Tynan. Did he detect just a slight bit of nervousness when he mentioned Warren or was it his imagination? "When you call him, you need to say a couple of things." Tynan held up his fist and started counting off with his fingers, "One, you need to say you'll do the hit. Two, you need a gun and some cash up front. Three, tell him where you will meet him. Four, ask him when Warren wants the job done."

The agent leaned forward, looking at Angel. "You could do that," he said, nodding his head.

Tynan continued. "We have a place already picked out. Tell Lugo to meet you there. He shows up, gives you the money and the gun, you drive off, and we take it from there."

Angel rubbed his hand across his mouth. *He is nervous* thought Tynan. The CI repeated the instructions then asked, "You're going to arrest Lugo right after?"

"Yeah, that's right."

"Okay, but then he knows I gave him up."

Tynan nodded. "Yeah, he'll know but by then he's going to have his own problems and he's going to have to give up Warren. If you are worried about a place to stay, we can put you up somewhere where nobody will find you."

Angel pulled his sunglasses down from his eyes. Tynan was surprised they were light blue. Angel stared right at him. "You think Lugo will rat out Warren. But what if he doesn't? Then he knows it's me. Even if he's in jail the word will get back to Warren. Then what?"

"You will be safe either way. I think he'll roll over. Why would he protect Warren if he can get himself a pass? Is he going to do time for Warren, real time?"

"I don't think so," said Angel as he put his sunglasses back on. "But if he doesn't rat, what happens to me?"

"We can move you somewhere safe and you can tell Santos you saved his ass. You'll have a new friend for life. When things calm down, you go back. Santos will owe you. Or, if you want, I'm sure we can move you to someplace else where you can get a fresh start."

"What, witness protection shit?" said Angel, his voice rising.

"No, we don't do witness protection. We're just the city. Maybe the feds could but we can set you up somewhere in the city. I don't think you have to worry."

Linda leaned over and gently put her arm on Angel's. "Listen, Angel, if you are afraid, you don't have to do anything. We would understand. I would understand. It takes a lot of balls to go against Lugo and Warren."

"I ain't afraid of Lugo. I don't give a shit about Warren. I don't care what happens to them."

Linda has made a break through, thought Tynan. Whatever doubts that were creeping into Angel's head were shot down once Linda hinted, he might not have the guts to do it.

Joe got up from the windowsill. "Hey, Angel. I don't think you are seeing this clearly. You make the call, Lugo's going to flip on Warren. After he rats out Warren, how is he going to point the finger at you for being a snitch? Besides, if you don't make the call, then you're a loose end."

Joe walked over to Angel and squatted down in front of him. "You said it yourself. Lugo asked you to do the hit because he is going to off you after Santos is dead. If you don't do the hit, do you think he's going to let you walk around knowing that he set up Santos?"

He pointed his finger at Angel. "You're dead either way. You do it our way and you can walk out of this. But if you don't, you're dead. Lugo can't let you live. Your call."

Angel looked up at the ceiling and let out a long sigh. He looked over at Kurt. "What do you think, bro? Are these guys for real?"

"Angel," said Kurt, "you'll be okay. Make the call and you're done."

"Alright man. I'll do it. But you need to grab Lugo right away and get that other fuck, Warren." He stood up and looked at Linda, "Okay, let's do this shit. Where do I meet him?"

Linda was prepared. She pulled out an index card from her folder, she showed it to Tynan then handed it to the CI. She had written the address down and the words "cash, gun, Warren."

"Want me to let the team know?" asked Joe.

"Yeah," said Tynan. "Let them know. Have them call us when they are set up at the location then Angel'll makes the call to Lugo."

"Come with me Angel," said Linda softly as she pulled on his arm. "We got plenty of time to go over everything." She led him out the door, followed by Joe.

After they left, Tynan turned to the agent. "That went a lot smoother than I thought."

"He's good, he's good," nodded the agent. "I'm telling you, though, he must be afraid of Warren. He was nervous. Normally, he never balks at anything. I'm surprised."

"How deep is Angel into the drug business?" asked Tynan.

"Who knows with these guys. Let's face facts. We always tell these CIs they can't be involved in crime but we all know if they weren't in it up to their eyeballs, they'd be useless to us. As long as we don't know, eh, who cares."

"Yep," said Tynan. "I appreciate your help. This guy Warren is a real problem if this is true."

"Hey, it's true. If Angel said it happened, it happened. Trust me."

"Can I get you some coffee or something?"

"No, I'm good," said Kurt as he fumbled for another cigarette. "What do you want me to do?"

"We'll wire up your guy and let him use one of our cars. The car will be wired too. The CI gets the gun and cash, drives off and we intercept Lugo. Then we pull him in here and see what he wants to get off his chest. We can babysit Angel for the next few days if he wants."

"Sounds good," nodded Kurt. "I'll be in my own car. Near the location. If you can give me one of your portables, this way I can monitor things without getting in your way. I'll have to call into my office to let them know what's up. Is there a phone I can use? Something private."

"Sure, across the hall, there's nobody in that office right now, you can call from there."

The agent headed across the hall and closed the door after him. Tynan sat back down in his chair. They had played the CI but the CI was a player, and that's how it went. It always left Tynan with a slight sense of guilt. He had minimized the danger to Angel and he knew it, but they were acting fast and sometimes you didn't see all the traps when speed was the name of the game. He was pretty sure he had covered everything but he still had an uneasy feeling about this and he didn't know what to make of Angel.

Joe walked back in the office. "Okay, the teams are out. This is the tac plan. We got Russell's team split up. Two in the surveillance van, two in each of the two chase cars. We'll use the van as the 'hospital car.' Hopefully, it won't come to that, and Jacobi Hospital will be the primary hospital in an emergency. Me and Linda will be in one of our cars. Do you want to ride with us, go solo, or go with the agent?"

"I'll ride with you guys. The agent is going solo. After we get Lugo, have Russell's guys pick up Angel and take him up to that hotel we use in New Rochelle. Put him up there for three days and give him some money from petty cash."

"How much?"

"Enough for him to eat and get drunk. I don't want him to think we're cheap. This is New York City's bankroll after all."

"Eat and get high would be more like it," laughed Joe.

"Is Russell going to call in when he's set up?"

"Yep," said Joe. "Then we make the call to Lugo. You want to sit in on that?"

"Are you kidding? Of course I wouldn't miss that."

"Okay, let me go check on things," said Joe as he headed back out the door.

The agent reappeared and he and Tynan sat and talked. Cop talk, complaining about their superiors, courts, the law. Anything and everything they thought was wrong with the criminal justice system. Even though he was a Fed, they seemed to have the same problems. *Same circus, different clowns*, thought Tynan.

Joe stuck his head in the door. "Okay, team's set up. Ready to make the call. We got it wired up. Want to listen?"

The three of them headed down the hallway to a small room. Inside, Linda and Angel sat at a small table with a tape recorder hooked up to the phone. The walls were covered with dirty white soundproofing.

Angel was smoking a cigarette and Linda was sitting beside him with a notepad. Tynan closed the door.

"You ready, Angel?" said Linda.

"Let's do it."

"Okay, let's make the call." She tapped the index card in front of Angel with her pen, "Stick to the script."

Angel dialed and let out a long stream of smoke. "I have to call his beeper and he'll call me back. That's how he does it." Angel dialed the beeper number and punched in the phone number.

They sat and waited. In about five minutes, the phone rang. Linda turned on the tape recorder and the speaker and signaled Angel to pick up the phone.

"Hey, bro. It's me Angel."

"Hey dude. What's up?"

"You know I've been thinking about that job offer you made me. I'm down for it."

"Yeah, I knew I could count on you."

"There's just a couple of things, though," said Angel.

The voice on the other end hesitated. "Like what?"

"I need some money up front and a piece, something..."

"Yo, yo, not on the phone, bro. Come talk to me."

"Yeah, yeah, sure. I got to meet someone pretty soon but how about I see you at Bruckner and Wheeler, by the abandoned gas station."

A longer pause followed, "Okay, when?"

Linda leaned forward in her chair and quickly scribbled, "one hour" then underlined Warren's name on the index card.

"One hour."

Angel took a big drag on his cigarette. "And one more thing..."

The line went dead. Lugo was done talking.

"What the fuck was that?" asked Linda.

Angel hung up the phone and took another heavy drag on his cigarette, "What the do you want from me? You can see he didn't want to talk on the phone. Besides, I'll meet him and set it all straight. You need to chill."

"*You* need to get this guy to say what the job is. A job could be anything. You could be painting his apartment."

Angel dropped his cigarette on the floor and put it out with his shoe. "Don't worry, I'll get it."

Joe Spano patted Angel on the back. "We're not worried, dude. You did good. Now we just need to bring it home, understand? Let's get Angel wired up and test the equipment in the car."

Linda stood up and touched Angel on the shoulder, "Okay, we're good. I'm going to put a wire on you and there's going to be a wire in the car you're going to drive. If you can get Lugo to jump in the car with you, we'll get a good recording. There's a van already there that will hear everything you say."

Tynan opened the door to let the smoke out. "What if he doesn't get in the car?"

"We're good, Lou. Angel's wire will be picked up by the van and we'll have a receiver in our car, so Angel can talk to Lugo anywhere and we'll hear it."

She turned to the CI. "Remember, get the piece, bring Warren into it, and see if he'll front you the money. But you need him to say this is a hit on Santos that Warren wants. Okay?"

Angel nodded and stood up, "I got it, Warren and the hit. I'll put it together. I got to call my woman to tell her I'm not going to be able to meet her." He smiled at Linda. "Maybe I might find a new woman."

"I'm sure you will," said Linda with a smirk.

"Okay, let's get going," said Tynan.

Tynan and Kurt walked out of the small room. "Don't worry," said the agent. "He's good. When he gets there, he'll be a real star. You'll see."

"I'm going to head out with two of my guys. What kind of wheels do you have?" asked Tynan.

"I'm driving a two-door white Lincoln. I'll stay a couple of blocks away. If you can give me a portable or you can call me on my cell, either way works."

"I'll call you on the cell. Our portables are on our own frequency and they aren't all they're cracked up to be. They always work, except when they don't."

"Gotcha," said Kurt as they exchanged business cards. "I'll see you out there."

Tynan walked back down the hallway. He glanced at his watch. It was already four o'clock. *This day is flying by and it is just starting,* he thought.

I t took them longer to get to the gas station than Tynan would have liked. Wiring up Angel, testing the car, checking radios, going over what Angel would say, all of it ate up the clock. Tynan could feel himself tensing up. His back had a stabbing pain by the time he climbed into the front seat. Linda drove and Joe sat in the back working the receiver. As they pulled out of their parking lot, Linda waved to Angel to follow her. They headed over to the location using side streets. It would be quicker than using the highways at this hour.

Tynan called the van on the radio. "Group leader to van. Is the set clear?"

"Affirmative," came the response. "Nobody at the gas station."

"Okay," said Tynan. "When we get there, show the CI where to park then pull down a side street."

As they pulled on to the Bruckner service road, Tynan saw that the gas station was clear. There was one stripped car sitting on cinder blocks beside the old rusted pumps. The boarded-up windows were covered with graffiti, immortalizing some neighborhood tag artist. The street was empty. *Perfect*, thought Tynan. He looked two blocks further down and could see their surveillance van in a parking lot, tucked between a dumpster and a beat-up green van. "They got a good spot," said Tynan.

Linda pulled over to the curb, opened the window and waved Angel alongside. Angel rolled down the passenger window as he pulled up in a red Olds.

"Okay, this is it. Park in the gas station and wait for Lugo. We got eyes on you so don't worry. Once you get the gun and Lugo talks about Warren ordering the hit you can wrap it up. Drive off and pull over four blocks from here. We'll meet up with you. Got it?"

Angel shook his head yes.

"And remember, don't forget to bring up Warren," Linda shouted as she drove off.

"I don't know, Lou," said Linda. "I think my boyfriend doesn't like me anymore."

"Ah well, some people are just unlucky at love. Maybe he'll warm up to you once Lugo is in cuffs. Turn down here and pull over. I don't want to be too far from this guy. I'd like to keep him in sight but three of us in a car has cop written all over it. It will be up to the surveillance van to give us the blow by blow."

Tynan picked up the radio, "Group leader to van. You are going to be our eyes on this. Let us know what's going on."

"Ten-four."

Joe leaned forward from the back seat. "Once the deal is done and the CI is gone, the chase cars will move in and take Lugo. It should go pretty smooth."

"We'll see how it goes," said Tynan. "You know what they say about plans."

They sat for a half-hour. Everyone was lost in their own thoughts. Joe called for a radio check from time to time. Tynan, shifted in his seat trying to get comfortable but it was a lost cause. The slow-moving traffic on the Bruckner Expressway started to ease up. Once in a while a car would race down the service road, trying to bypass the stop and go highway traffic. None of the cars gave Angel's red Olds a second look.

"Where the fuck is this guy?" asked Linda.

"He's on perp time," said Joe. "Five, six o'clock, midnight, it's all the same. In their world, nothing happens until they get there."

"What do you give a shit for? Everyone's on overtime," said Tynan.

"Unlike you two, I have a life," said Linda.

"Sure you…" Joe was cut off by the radio. "There's a dark colored Honda coming down the service road, going slow. It looks like one of the cars that Lugo has."

Everyone sat up straight, waiting for more on the car. "This is it," said Joe.

"Hold on, hold on," came the voice on the radio. "It's driving past. Not him."

They leaned back in their seats. A false alarm. *Waiting for something to happen is always the toughest part*, thought Tynan. It let his mind play with him. All the things that could go wrong started popping into his head. *Focus*, thought Tynan. *Focus on what's going on*.

"What happens if this guy shows up and shoots our guy in the car?" asked Joe.

"That would be so fucked," said Linda.

"What happens? Nothing changes," said Tynan flatly. "Then we'd have Lugo for murder instead of conspiracy to commit murder. Talk about having a hammer over his head."

"That's cold, Lou. Really cold," snorted Joe. "But I agree."

"White Lincoln, driving fast." *The voice on the radio was more hurried now, just a bit louder*, thought Tynan. The Honda driving by must have gotten the adrenaline going.

"The Lincoln just pulled into the gas station."

Joe turned up the volume on his receiver. He could hear street noises clearly. Angel must have rolled down the window.

"What's up?" Angel's voice came in loud and clear.

"Get out of the fucking car. Take off the wire and get out of the car, now!"

"Okay, okay." The sounds of clothes rubbing against the mike drowned out the conversation. The car door slammed and Angel's voice drifted off to nothingness.

The voice from the van was much louder now, almost yelling.

"It's the agent, it's the agent's car. The CI got into the agent's car. They're pulling away fast."

Russell got on the air, "What's going on, Lou? Do you want us to stop them?"

Tynan's back pain and all the things he was thinking could go wrong, vanished. Now he had a real problem. This was his operation and he had no idea what was happening.

"No, stay in position. Don't intercept," Tynan barked on the radio. "Everyone, stay in position. Surveillance van, is the Lincoln off the set?"

"It's long gone. Our car is still sitting there, though. I don't know if it's running."

"Let me find out what's going on," said Tynan. "What the fuck?" He threw the radio on the dash and rummaged for his cell phone and the card the agent gave him. He punched in the number. As it rang, he was trying to keep his temper. *Is this guy kidding me*, thought Tynan. *He pulls this kind of a stunt right in the middle of a meet. Is he nuts?* The phone rang then disconnected.

"No answer, that fuck!" Tynan looked around to see if anyone was on the street. His stomach was tying itself in knots. "Who has the extra set of keys for the Olds?"

"I do," said Linda.

"Good. Linda, I need you to go back there, get that car and get it the hell out of here. The last thing I need is for this Lugo bastard to show up and start poking around our empty car with a wire in it."

Before Tynan had finished talking, she was out of the car walking quickly towards the service road. She turned the corner out of sight.

Tynan reached for the portable radio on the dash. "Okay, Linda's going to get the car and drive off the set. Everyone, stay put." He got out and ran around to the driver's side. A stabbing pain shot up his back as he tried to fit into the seat. He swore as he fumbled with the seat lever to give himself more room.

Not being able to see Linda, made Tynan nervous. Suppose Lugo shows up now. *Relax*, he thought. *Linda's smart, she'll play it off. She'll come up with something.* If not, then he was about to see just how fast he could drive in reverse.

"Can you believe this?" said Joe. He opened his door. "I'm going to follow Linda on foot."

"No, stay here. If this guy shows up and sees a lone female, he won't give it a second thought."

"I don't know, Lou. I think I should follow her."

"She'll be fine." Tynan lifted the radio again. "Do you have Linda in sight?"

"Affirmative, she's heading towards the car, almost there."

"Keep her in sight and let me know if anyone shows up?"

He waited. *She's got to be at the car by now*, he thought as he drummed his fingers on the steering wheel.

"Okay, she's there, she got in." Seconds passed. Tynan clenched his hand tight around the steering wheel. "She's heading out. Driving off the set," said the voice over the radio.

Tynan looked out the rear window and saw the red Olds fly past. *Thank God*, he thought. "Does she have a cell phone, Joe?"

"Yeah, she does. She'll call."

Tynan got on the radio again. "Everyone, stay in place for now, I'll advise."

Joe's cell phone rang. He flipped it open and said to Linda, "Are you okay? Was it something I said?" he chuckled. "Let me find out what's next." He turned to Tynan. "She's fine. She wants to know what you want her to do."

"Nothing. Tell her to head back to the barn. We'll call her if anything changes. No point in staying here. Looks like these guys are gone."

"Did you hear that? Go back to the office, we'll be there soon." Then, "Alright, bye."

Joe hung up. "So, what do you think?"

"We'll hang here for another half hour and see if Lugo shows. Then we head back. After that I have to make a decision."

"What decision is that?"

"Should I kill Angel or that agent first."

Tynan waited another half hour. He hoped that at the last minute either Angel would come walking back or Lugo would drive up to the gas station. His mind jumped back and forth between those two fantasies and a third, where he took Angel up to a roof and dangled him over the edge. What had happened? He tried the agent's phone several times but there was no answer.

As the shadows from the buildings grew longer, Tynan looked at his watch. "Okay, enough of this," he said to Joe. Picking up the radio he said, "Group leader to all units, head back to the barn. The van and intercept cars acknowledged. Tynan threw the portable radio in the seat beside him in disgust. All this for what? He had more questions now than when they started.

By the time he got back, Linda was already sitting in his office, flipping through her case folder. "What was that, Lou?" she asked as he walked in the door.

"I wish I knew. That son of a bitch left us high and dry. Our good buddy Kurt isn't answering."

"He hasn't called? Nothing?"

"Nope."

Joe came in followed by Russell. Tynan held up his hands and rubbed them through his hair. "Don't even start. If I knew I'd tell you."

Russell leaned on the filing cabinet while Joe slid into the seat besides Linda. "What I don't get," said Joe, "is why didn't Lugo show?"

"Hah," said Russell. "He didn't show because that little piece of shit tipped him off. And what's the story with this agent? Whose side is he on?"

Tynan's desk phone rang. He snatched up the receiver and motioned with his finger for the three of them to be quiet. "Lieutenant Tynan, Group 41."

Tynan mouthed the words "It's him," to his audience. Linda and Joe stood up and leaned over the desk, trying to catch some of the conversation. Even Russell moved towards the desk.

"What the hell happened out there?" asked Tynan.

He listened, pushing the phone hard against his ear so he wouldn't miss a word. He could feel the muscles tightening in his jaw. He squeezed the phone in a death grip, his knuckles bulging white. Slowly, he reached for a pen and started jotting notes. His audience of three cocked their heads, trying to read what he was writing.

"Alright, I'll be there ten o'clock tomorrow. I better like the answers I get." Tynan threw the receiver back into the phone cradle.

Linda had practically pushed herself up onto the desk with both hands, "What did he say?"

"That was our agent extraordinaire. He's asking for a meeting tomorrow morning at the US Attorney's office."

Tynan shook his head. "He said the reason he scooped Angel off the set like that was because he got a blistering call from some Assistant US Attorney telling him to take their CI and call the whole thing off. That's why he did what he did. He took our CI to a safe location but he wouldn't say where. I'll get more answers tomorrow from the AUSA herself. That's all he said."

Linda and Joe sat back down. Russell threw his hands up and retreated back to the dingy metal filing cabinet. Joe swiveled around towards Russell, "Can you believe this bullshit? He's taking orders from some prosecutor sitting on their ass in Manhattan."

Russell shrugged. "What do you expect? He's a Fed. Don't trust CIs and don't trust Feds. They will never tell you the whole story. They're always holding back."

Tynan looked out the window. It was getting dark. The boats' white hulls bobbed at anchor in the fading light. He turned and looked at the others, "What about Santos? He's walking around with a target on his back. That agent was supposed to warn him about a hit, but after this, I don't know. We're going to have to do that and do it tonight. We have Santos' address but let's see if we can get any more info about where he hangs out."

Tynan picked up the phone and started dialing. After a few rings, it was picked up. "Sergeant McArthy, Bronx Narco."

"Hey, Jimmy. It's Bob Tynan over at Bronx IAB, how are you?"

"You got me. I confess. I did it."

"Don't be an asshole. I know that might be hard for you but try it for a least an hour. You might enjoy it." Tynan liked Jimmy. He had worked with him before in Narcotics, when he was a sergeant and Jimmy was still a detective. "I got a favor to ask you?"

"Sure, what is it? You want me to stop dating your mom?"

"Okay, you went from being an asshole to a dick in less than ten seconds. That's pretty good. Now let's see how fast you can give me some info about a guy named Miguel Santos. I can give you his NYSID number." Tynan read off the number, "I'm interested in any current info, hangouts, et cetera. I'm not sure how up to date our info is and I figured you would have the latest."

Tynan waited clicking his ball point pen nervously. After a few minutes the clicking stopped and he started writing. "Okay, Jimmy you're the best, you can go back to being an asshole now. I'll talk at you some other time." He turned to the other three. "Russ, you take one of your guys and hit these spots, see if he's there." He turned to Linda, "Give him one of those pictures you got of Santos."

Linda handed the picture to Russell as Tynan said, "If you make contact, make it short and sweet. Tell him you are from Narcotics and you have information his life might be in immediate danger. That's it. Nothing more, nothing less."

"You got it, boss," Russell said as he turned and hurried out the door.

"Meanwhile, the three of us are going to pay a visit to his last known address and tell him the same thing."

"What else are we going to do about this mess?" asked Linda.

"Nothing for now. I'll see what the rocket scientists have to say tomorrow and we'll take it from there. But I'm not going to risk this douchebag getting blown away tonight. At least he can't say he wasn't warned."

The trio descended the steps and got in the car. Tynan winced. His back was killing him. He wanted nothing else other than to be at home in his recliner. The way things were going that probably wasn't going to happen anytime soon. He thought about calling home but figured his wife would be busy with the kids.

He felt guilty. His wife was like a lot of cops' wives. She was a married single parent. Tynan put in crazy hours, came home late and left early. Sometimes he'd go days without seeing his wife or kids. Often, his only contact was a quick glimpse while they were asleep. Today was going to be another one of those days. The job's interference with his personal life infuriated Tynan. *Someday, that'll change*, he thought.

They pulled out of the lot and headed off into the darkness to yet another Bronx tenement, where Tynan would climb the stairs, just like he had hundreds of times before, to talk to someone he wished he had never met.

The street they pulled into looked like many other Bronx streets. Narrow, one way, with five or six story brick tenements on either side. The endless row of parked cars was interrupted now and then by a stripped stolen auto. The canyon of monotonous brick tenements was highlighted with the occasional burnt-out building. The abandoned buildings had sheets of aluminum covering the windows, each painted with venetian blinds, curtains and potted plants. Tynan shook his head. Some genius had figured that such a charade would make people forget these buildings had once been filled with families going about their daily lives. Now they were homes for rats and shooting galleries for junkies.

As their car creeped down the block, a series of whistles could be heard, followed by a couple of shouts of "Five-Oh." The whistles and shouts were warnings to dealers that the police were on the block. *These lookouts were pretty sharp,* thought Tynan. Their unmarked car driven by a black female had fooled no one. Of course, having two white guys with her didn't help much. Tynan didn't care. This wasn't some undercover gig. He wanted people to know the police were in town.

After the whistles, half a dozen people who had been standing in front of one of the buildings stepped off and scattered in different directions. Two guys didn't budge. One sat on the stoop while the other stood next to an open ground floor window. Although it was hot out, the window wasn't open for air. Tynan knew that's where the guns were stashed. If the lookouts had spotted trouble instead of the police, those guns would have been handed out the window to the crowd that had just scattered. *The thin male who is standing his ground by the window is probably the bodyguard and head enforcer,* thought Tynan. And the man sitting on the stoop surveying his kingdom was their guy, Mr. Miguel Santos.

The three of them got out of the car. Tynan gave a quick scan of the rooftop. No sense getting a brick dropped on your head at this point. The day had been crazy enough. The roofline was clear, no heads furtively darting out to see if there was a target. Tynan strolled up to Santos and nodded at the bodyguard.

"Miguel Santos?" asked Tynan.

Santos, smoking a cigarette and with a forty-ounce bottle of beer between his feet, didn't get up. "Who wants to know?"

"Well, we're either the three wise men come late for Christmas or the police, you decide."

"What do you want?"

"Not much. We just came over here to tell you that we have information your life is in danger. Someone wants to kill you."

Santos laughed. "Yeah, who?"

"Let's just say someone who doesn't like you. I know that's hard to believe. I found it hard to believe, but trust me, this info is good. Someone is looking to end your career permanently."

"I don't have a career. You must be getting some bad shit."

"Well, just so you know. Someone wants you dead. Have a nice night," said Tynan as he turned on his heel towards the car and motioned Joe and Linda to follow.

"Thanks man. I can take care of myself. You want a drink?" asked Santos as he raised his half empty beer bottle.

"No, we're good. You take care," said Tynan as he climbed back in the car.

Santos laughed and raised his bottle of beer in a salute. *Not a care in the world*, thought Tynan. Some people lived a charmed life or were just too stupid to recognize danger. He wasn't sure which of these Santos was but he had a funny feeling the guy's days of sitting on a stoop like it was a throne were going to be coming to an end very soon.

Tynan stayed in the office until midnight, reviewing the files on Warren and Wright. He looked at their photos. What made these guys go bad? Did they go bad? There were two allegations against them, both of them unsubstantiated. Reading through the file he could see the investigations into those allegations were just going through the motions. A couple of surveillances, a check on their bank accounts, cars, and property. The usual "lifestyle" type stuff. There was nothing out of the ordinary. From all appearances they were just normal cops. Working class stiffs.

The term for a cop who just showed up for work but avoided police work was going "dead." Why did they go "dead"? Did they get mad at allegations being made against them? Did they just have enough of the revolving door criminal justice system? Tynan couldn't figure it out. But if the CI was right, these guys were flying under the radar and someone was going to have a lot of explaining to do.

He told Joe and Linda to go home. They'd be back in again the next day for the ride into Manhattan to see the US Attorney. The agent made it sound to Tynan like all his questions would be answered then. Somehow, Tynan was supposed to have an epiphany and see the brilliance of whatever it was they were working on. He doubted that.

On his drive home, he could feel his blood pressure rising as he thought about the way they had been left out on the street with no explanation. Things could have gone very wrong. What if Lugo had shown up and confronted Linda? Suppose it led to gun-play, then what? Which led Tynan to another question. Where was Lugo and why didn't he show? Did the CI tip him off or did Lugo just get suspicious?

He still had no answers by the time he got home. It was one in the morning. The house was dark except for the dim glow from the light over the stove. He slipped off his shoes, trying not to wake anyone. He stuck his head into the kids' room. They were asleep. There would be no stories about their daytime adventures. In his bedroom, his wife snored softly. He took off his clothes and slowly crept into bed beside her. He'd be up again in five hours. He closed his eyes and tried to sleep.

It didn't work. Try as he might, the luminescent dial on the bedside alarm clock taunted him as it crept towards five. He couldn't get the questions to stop. They chased each other, never fast enough to leave his head and never slow enough for him to come up with an answer. After a few hours, he gave up. He got up, showered, and got ready for another day. Before he left, he slipped into the kids' room and kissed them on their heads. In another six weeks, they'd be back in school and he'd have even less time to see them. "This job sucks," he whispered to himself. He put his shoes on and headed out the door.

When Linda and Joe showed up at seven, he'd already put down four cups of coffee. He signed off on more paperwork and tried not to look at the Warren file. Linda was the first to peek into the office.

"You're here already?" she said. "Did you even go home?"

"Yep, but I might as well have stayed here."

Joe peeked over her shoulder. "Oh my God, I feel like I never left," he moaned. "Hey Lou, I was expecting bagels."

Tynan shrugged, "So was I. Where are they? You can buy them for us on our way downtown. We're leaving in an hour. It normally takes an hour to get there but with rush hour, might as well figure two hours. We wouldn't want to leave our hosts waiting."

"I'll bring the case file," said Linda.

"Absolutely not," said Tynan. "Those Feds never give up any information. We'll be lucky if we find out a tenth of what they really know, I'm not showing them any paperwork. They brought this to our attention, so let them tap dance for a change."

"Okay, you got it."

The drive was as miserable as Tynan expected. Cars crawled passed fender benders along the FDR Drive. By the time they pulled into the parking area at One Police Plaza, it had taken over ninety minutes.

Kurt stood in front of the federal Building. He walked towards them with his hand outstretched. Tynan wanted to ignore it but decided to be polite and shook it.

"I'm so sorry about this," said Kurt. "This is not what I wanted to happen, not at all. This is not my fault but I apologize all the same."

After the handshake, Tynan motioned with his head towards the federal Building, "Okay, fine, but before we go in there and start talking to a bunch of suits, do you think you could give me some idea about what's going on. Come on, you owe us that much."

"Listen," Kurt took a deep breath. "I'm sitting out there yesterday, waiting for a call from you, but instead I got a call from an Assistant US Attorney. I guess my boss called over there and told them what was going on and they blew a gasket. Turns out they're already working a case on your guy Warren. The US Attorney's Office is working it with the FBI. The minute they heard we were going to try and get this guy Warren, they went crazy. I couldn't hold the phone to my ear. That's how loud the conversation was."

Tynan looked at Kurt but said nothing. He waited for him to continue.

"I had to get in there and snatch the CI before anything happened. There was no time to tell you what was going on. That Lugo guy might have shown up at any minute and then I'd be screwed. So, I swooped in to get him. I would have told you but they said to just do it and say nothing."

"Say nothing?" asked Tynan. "What are you kidding me? I'm just supposed to sit there with my thumb up my ass?"

"I know. But I called them back and told them I couldn't just snatch the CI and say nothing. Finally, they gave in and that's when I called you."

Tynan shook his head. "Thanks, Kurt, I appreciate that. I know you were in a tough spot." Tynan was still pissed about what happened but he figured there was no sense in burning the only bridge he had left. There was still a chance he could use the CI again.

"Let's go see what they have to say," said Tynan. "After you," he said and gestured towards the building.

For some reason, Tynan expected that the meeting would be the usual cordial federal snow job. The Feds would bring a small army to the meeting and they'd schmooze over coffee. Then the Feds would say they were working a case on the same subject and ask for all the information the NYPD had. They would only talk in generalities about their case and never show their cards. You would leave the meeting with nothing.

Tynan had not been to many of these meetings but he'd been to enough to know that's how they went. If you didn't play ball with the Feds, they'd make a call over to Headquarters and tell the Department bosses you were not cooperating. The bosses wouldn't back you up. It was a stacked deck and he knew it.

The minute they stepped off the elevator, Tynan knew this meeting would be different. A short, stocky woman with long brown hair was standing there in the hallway, flanked by two tall men in dark suits. *Probably FBI,* thought Tynan.

"I'm Assistant US Attorney Carol Schmidt," announced the short woman. Her arms were folded across her chest. She didn't extend her hand. Her demeanor reminded Tynan of a flight attendant who had found a passenger sneaking into first class.

"I'm Lieutenant Tynan and this is..." said Tynan as he turned to introduce Linda and Joe.

Schmidt cut him off. "I know who you are." She looked at Kurt. "You can leave."

Kurt said nothing. He just pressed the elevator button. His hand was no sooner off the button than the doors opened and Kurt stepped on. As the doors closed, he looked at Tynan and raised his eyebrows. Tynan sensed the tension in the air.

Now that Kurt was gone, the attorney continued. "You are not to contact the CI, or the subjects in connection with this case. You are not to contact Special Agent Morse. In addition, you are not to go to the residences of or surveil any of the subjects mentioned by the CI, and that includes any officers that might have been implicated. Do you understand?"

"What?" asked Tynan.

"You heard me. I have informed you of this in front of witnesses and you may now leave the building, these agents will escort you out."

Tynan reached over and hit the elevator button. "I have a message for you. You don't pay my salary and you're not my boss. I don't need to be escorted out."

As the three of them stepped onto the elevator, Tynan turned around, waved goodbye with his fingers, and added, "And I'll go where I want, when I want, and talk to whoever I want. And if you don't like that you can take a ride up to the Bronx and try to stop me." The attorney and her matching agents disappeared behind the closing doors.

The elevator was crowded. Tynan said nothing. Linda was about to speak but Tynan looked at her and shook his head. Once they cleared the front door, Linda asked, "Who the fuck does she think she is?"

"I don't know," said Tynan, "but she can go fuck herself."

Kurt was waiting for them outside, his hands thrust deep into his pockets, a half-finished cigarette dangling from the side of his mouth. He shrugged his shoulders. "What can I say?"

"Glad I don't work with her," said Tynan. "She seems a little confused. She's not my boss, and to top it off, she never even hinted at what kind of a case they are working on. Only that somehow, we're supposed to be good little boys and girls and go off in the corner and play with our toys."

Kurt took the cigarette from his mouth, blew out a thin wisp of smoke, and threw it on the ground, twisting it with his shoe. "Listen, if you need my help, I'm willing to give it, but it can't get back to the US Attorney's office, especially not her."

"I appreciate that," nodded Tynan. "I don't want to get you in any trouble with them, so maybe you should stay clear. But I could use your CI. I don't expect you to deliver him to us but maybe a phone call as to where we could find him. That would help a lot. No pressure, though."

"That could be arranged. You might get a call soon from some anonymous source." Kurt stuck his hand out. Tynan shook it then watched as the agent headed back into the building.

"What now?" asked Joe. "Where does that leave us?"

"We're going after Warren with or without their help. We'll start with some surveillances, and maybe we can start a narcotics case on either Lugo or Santos."

"Narcotics?" asked Joe.

"Let's get back to the office," said Tynan as he started walking back towards the car. "We go after either of those two, they can lead us to Warren. Our problem is going to be getting enough weight on them. They are not going to roll because of some dime bag bust."

"Who's going to make the buys? Group 16?" asked Linda.

Tynan wasn't sure just yet. Internal Affairs had its own small narcotics unit called Group 16. They made buys on a regular basis and interrogated street dealers to see if they had information on corrupt cops. Tynan wasn't sure how long they were willing to commit to building a case against players like Santos or Lugo.

"Well, that depends who can help us out the quickest," said Tynan as he picked up the pace. "I'm not sure how much time Group 16 is willing to give us. Bronx Narcotics might be a better bet but it's not their case. I don't know if they'll help or not. I'd have to talk to McCarthy. Not to mention, the IAB bosses will have a canary if we bring in outsiders like Narcotics into one of their investigations."

The three walked in silence towards the car. Tynan still had no answers for himself by the time he dropped into the front passenger seat and slammed the door. "Okay, let's head over to Hudson Street and see if I can get us some help from our bosses."

Joe laughed, "Boy, you really are an optimist."

As they pulled out of their parking spot, his cell phone rang. "Lieutenant Tynan," he answered.

"Hello, this is PAA Brown in Chief Calhoun's office. He wants to see you right away."

"Right away? Where, in 1 Police Plaza or over at Hudson Street?"

"Here at 1 PP, in his office. He'll be expecting you. How long will it take?"

"I'll be there in ten minutes." Tynan closed his phone. "Well, isn't that convenient."

"What was that?" asked Linda.

"Park the car. I've been summoned to the chief's office. Why do I have the funny feeling that he got a call from our new friend at the US Attorney's Office."

"Want us to go with you?"

"Yeah, Lou, we'll go with you. Like backup," Joe chimed in.

"No, that's okay. I think this is going to be a private meeting or at least a meeting where I'll have no witnesses. You guys wait here and I'll be right back."

Tynan opened the door and stepped out as the car came to a stop. He slammed the door and headed towards Police Plaza. Tynan knew the nickname, the "Puzzle Palace" for Police Headquarters was well deserved. Any cop who didn't have an office in the fourteen-story red brick building couldn't make sense out of the orders coming from it. The Commissioner and all the Bureau Chiefs had their offices on the top floor. Most cops never went up to the fourteenth floor during their entire careers. It was a place of mystery and dread.

Unlike the other Bureaus, Internal Affairs had a headquarters of its own on Hudson Street, and the Chief of Internal Affairs had offices in both buildings. Tynan guessed the Palace was the place to be for big shots.

He pushed his way through the revolving doors and up to the security desk. He flashed his ID at the uniformed cops at the turnstiles. They gave him a quick but bored look as he fastened his ID to the outside of his jacket. The ride up to the fourteenth floor was painful. The elevator was packed and it stopped at each floor. As it ascended to the top floor it thinned out until, finally, he was by himself. As he entered the chief's office, he smiled at the receptionist. "The chief's expecting me. I'm Lieutenant Tynan."

The receptionist smiled back. "That was quick." She pointed to the conference room. "He's in there with the others and I don't think he's too happy."

"Thanks for the warning," said Tynan. He adjusted his tie and knocked on the door, slowly opening it. He wasn't too sure what to expect but the group seated around the gleaming mahogany conference table surprised him. The chief, a stern looking, heavyset, bald fifty-year old sat at the head of the table. To his right was

Inspector Riordan, a career Internal Affairs boss who had avoided the purges and was rumored to be the power behind the throne. His gray balding head and pinched wrinkled face struck Tynan as troll like.

To the chief's left was his executive officer, Deputy Chief Klein, a forty-something, up and coming boss in the department. He had a ruddy complexion, a crewcut, and a runner's physique. He was supposed to be in charge of the day to day show over at Hudson Street but Tynan figured a rising star like him probably took every chance he could to rub shoulders with the bosses at the Palace. Tynan had heard Klein was smart. A quick thinker who always thought two moves ahead.

To Klein's left sat a Lieutenant named Sullivan. Her brunette hair framed a face with a permanent frown, and the few times he had seen her, she never said anything. Rumor had it that she was a lawyer who had not spent much time in the street. She sat there, pen in hand and a legal pad in front of her.

The chief waved to a chair at the end of the table. "Please take a seat, Bob."

Tynan wasn't fooled by the friendly gesture. He had seen enough "firing squads" in his time in the Department to know this wasn't a meet and greet.

"I'm sure you know everyone around the table," said the chief as he gestured to the others. "Inspector Riordan will start."

Riordan adjusted his tie. "We got a call this morning, in fact just a few minutes ago, from an Assistant US Attorney saying you were rude to her. She also said you broke protocols regarding the use of a confidential informant and were interfering with one of their long-term investigations."

Tynan pulled his chair closer to the table and folded his hands. "Was that all she said?"

"No, there's a lot more, but that's enough for now," said Riordan in a low voice. "First, I'd like to know who the hell you think you are. We spend a lot of time working closely with our federal colleagues and we don't appreciate our people going into their offices and throwing their weight around. Not to mention, we are not in the habit of interfering with federal investigations."

"Do I get a chance to tell my side of the story?"

"Your side?" said Riordan, growing visibly angry. "You don't have a side. You're lucky you are not being brought up on charges."

"Charges? Charges for what, doing my job?"

Riordan leaned forward and pointed at Tynan. "You broke federal guidelines on dealing with confidential informants and you told the US Attorney that you were not going to comply with their orders."

"I don't even know what the federal guidelines are for informants, and what's more, I don't care. I complied with the NYPD's guidelines on informants. Our guidelines state that if I'm going to use an informant, I have to get the okay from whoever the handler is for that CI. Which I did. In fact, the handler, an ATF Agent named Kurt Morse, came to us with the information and I informed this office of that fact. As for interfering with a federal investigation, I don't work for the Feds, I work for the City of New York. If anyone is interfering it's them." Tynan could feel his face getting hot. He was on the verge of losing his temper.

"Okay, okay, let's all take a deep breath," said Calhoun. "Tell us your side."

Tynan went over what had happened the day before. The call out, the information that Santos was going to be killed, and that a cop named Warren was behind it. He went through the phone call the CI made to Lugo and the meet that never came off.

He tried to keep his temper under control. He clasped his hands firmly to stop himself from pounding on the table. Taking a deep breath, he continued. "Then today, we go down to the USA's office and instead of having a normal meeting to explain what is going on, I'm met in front of the elevators in a hallway by some arrogant piece of shit named Carol Schmidt, and she tells me I'm not allowed to talk to any of the players in the case or be in the vicinity of where they live. Then she tells us to leave the building."

Tynan unclasped his hands and tapped the table with his finger. "Am I missing something? I'm the one who was rude? I'm the one who is interfering with an investigation? I'm not even getting into the most important part of all this. We have a case with an open contract on some drug dealer that's been put out by a cop and we're supposed to pretend like it didn't happen."

Tynan could see that Riordan was about to explode but the chief put his hand out in front of him and said, "Nobody is saying to act like it didn't happen. We're just saying we need to cooperate with the Feds, that's all."

"Cooperate? How am I supposed to do that? I don't even know what type of case they're working on. It must be a real good one if it tops murder. Did she tell you?"

Tynan finally stopped and looked around the table hoping someone would give him an answer. He hadn't noticed but Lieutenant Sullivan was scribbling furiously on the legal pad as she tried to keep up with the conversation.

The chief looked at Riordan. "Go ahead, tell him. He has the right to know at least that much."

Riordan looked at the chief. "Are you sure, chief? I think there's another way to handle this."

"No, go ahead."

"Very well." Riordan cleared his throat. "The Feds are working a case against Warren. They are afraid that your operation is going to jeopardize their case. That is why they are upset and that's why you are here. Although, frankly, I don't see why anyone in this office has to explain themselves to you."

Tynan was trying to hold himself in check. He had to remind himself that everyone in the room, except Sullivan, outranked him by three to six ranks. Speaking too freely wasn't wise but it was all he could do to not jump across the table at this pompous gas bag.

"I appreciate you taking me into your confidence but how come a federal case is going on against a cop in the Bronx and the Internal Affairs Bureau unit that covers the Bronx doesn't know anything about it?" Tynan waited for an answer but Riordan just glared at him.

Chief Calhoun shifted uneasily in his seat. He drummed his fingers on the table. Looking at Tynan he said, "We didn't know about it either. The first we heard of it was this morning. I trust all of my units and if there was a case going on in your area you should know."

Chief Klein spoke up for the first time. "Unless the case was about you and your people."

Klein got a chuckle out of the chief but Tynan felt that maybe he wasn't joking. He knew he hadn't won any friends at this meeting.

"What's the case about? What's so important that they held a case back from us and don't want to cooperate?" asked Tynan.

Tynan detected a shift in everyone sitting at the other end of the table. Klein looked down at the table, Sullivan stopped scribbling and glanced up at the chief. Riordan slouched in his chair and put his hand up to his mouth. Calhoun, shifted his gaze to some point above Tynan's head and frowned. He then looked over at Riordan and nodded.

Looking at the table, Riordan said, "The Feds are working a case involving stolen cars and they believe Warren is the head of the ring. The cars are late model luxury cars, stolen here and shipped overseas."

For a second, Tynan thought he was having a stroke. *Did he just say, stolen cars? That can't be. There's got to be more to this than stolen cars.* He sat and waited for Riordan to say more but that was it.

"I don't get it. Stolen cars? I'm not saying that a cop involved in a stolen car ring is not a problem, but am I missing something here? We have a case involving drugs and an attempted hit and they are willing to let that go, in order to break up a stolen car ring? What did they steal, some Wall Street guy's favorite Ferrari?"

The chief rode to Riordan's rescue. "It's a bit more complicated than that. It sounds like a very involved case, with cars being shipped overseas, and it might involve other cops."

The pieces finally fell into place for Tynan. It was as if he had been stumbling around in a dark room and someone turned the light on. He chuckled. "I get it now. Why take down a cop involved in drugs and attempted murder when you can take him out for stealing cars? Not as embarrassing as narcotics and murdering people. It looks better for the mayor. Much better than a dirty cop who wants to arrange contract murders. Plus, the Feds get some positive press if they can lock up more than one cop."

"We don't know exactly what their case involves," said Riordan. "They didn't give us specifics."

Tynan felt the dynamics of the meeting changing. The smart thing to do now was for him to apologize that he had caused any trouble, get up, and disappear back to the Bronx. Do his time and move on. Part of Tynan's brain was telling him to open his mouth and say, "Oh, now I understand, my mistake." But the other part, the angry part, wouldn't let him do it. He sat there looking at them as the battle played out in his head.

"Do you understand now?" asked Riordan.

The angry Tynan won. "Oh yeah, I understand. We got a possible homicidal lunatic driving around in a police car in the Bronx, maybe running a drug network and trying to put a contract out on some drug dealing piece of shit, but that's strictly small potatoes compared to a half-assed Fed investigation looking to bag cops for GLA. Yeah, I get it."

Riordan bolted upright in his chair. Pointing his finger at Tynan, he said, "That's enough out of you. If it were up to me, you'd be up on departmental charges and looking at a quick trip to the Trial Room and a boot in the ass out the door."

"Easy, easy," said the chief. "Nobody is going to the Trial Room. Nobody's getting charges."

Klein half-heartedly raised his hand like the smart kid in a classroom full of dopes. "I think there is a solution to this problem chief."

"Go ahead."

"Lieutenant Tynan doesn't seem to be able to grasp the sensitive nature of this case, and while I'm sure his heart is in the right place, perhaps we need an investigator who is politically savvy. May I suggest we take this case away from the Bronx and give it to Lieutenant Sullivan." He briefly touched Sullivan's arm as he said it. She stopped writing, looked up at Klein, and smiled.

"Yes, yes," nodded Riordan vigorously. "She'd be perfect for the case. After all, we want this done right."

"Okay," said the chief. "Lieutenant Sullivan, if you wouldn't mind taking this over along with your other duties. And Lieutenant Tynan, I want you to know that this is no reflection on you or your staff but considering the difficulties you had with the US Attorney recently, I think this would be best."

The chief pushed back his chair, stood up, and walked out of the conference room as Riordan hurried to catch up. Riordan glared at Tynan as he closed the door.

Klein turned to Tynan. His demeanor changed. "Now listen to me," said Klein sharply. The soft diplomatic tone was gone. He stabbed the tabletop with his index finger as he rattled off his points.

"You will bring the complete case folder down here to Lieutenant Sullivan by the end of the day. You will not have anything to do with any police officers implicated in this case nor interact with any of the other players that you are aware of so far. Any information you receive on this case will be immediately turned over to her. Do you understand?"

"What about..."

"You are off the case. That's a direct order. If I find out you did anything involving this case from this point forward you will be suspended on the spot. Got it?"

Tynan's face was red hot by now. Riordan was a sneaky little weasel from the Palace but he was nothing compared to this guy Klein. Deputy Chief Klein was dangerous.

"I got it." Tynan looked over at Sullivan. "I'll have someone bring down all the paper on this case today. If you have any questions, you can call me."

Sullivan gave a half-hearted smile and nodded.

"Now get out of here," said Klein as he pointed towards the door.

Tynan didn't hesitate. He got up and walked out. He passed the receptionist and she raised her eyebrows and said, "Have a good day, Lieutenant."

By the time he got down to the car, Tynan didn't know if he should be grateful or mad that he lost the case. He had pushed it to the limit in the meeting but he was out of his league. This was the Palace Guard. They were professional politicians more than cops. He was just a slight bump in the road and he knew it. He hadn't brought up his contact with Santos but he guessed Sullivan could read about it in the case file.

He opened the car door and sat down in the front passenger seat.

"So, what happened?" asked Joe.

"Well, the good news is that my head is still attached to my shoulders."

"And the bad?" asked Linda.

"We're off the case. We're to have nothing to do with this case from this minute forward. I need you guys to finish off whatever paperwork that has to go into the case folder and bring the whole thing back here before 1600 hours. Give it to Lieutenant Sullivan in the chief's office. It's her case now."

"What?!" exclaimed Joe.

Linda started the car, "You've got to tell us more than that, Lou. What the hell happened up there?"

Tynan adjusted the air conditioning to blow on his face. "I'll tell you the long version on the way back to the Bronx. The short version is the Assistant US Attorney we met this morning made a call because she didn't like my attitude. Anyway, it turns out they have a stolen car ring case going against our guy Warren so we are supposed to sit this one out. The powers that be felt the case would be in better hands if it was run out of their office. We're out. That's it."

Linda was quiet as she drove the car. Joe sat in the back and laughed. "Run the case from their office? Who are they kidding? They ain't running shit. The Feds are running it."

"It is as the chief says, 'complicated,'" said Tynan. "Maybe there's more than he's telling us." He stared out the window at the East River. A red tugboat pushed a garbage barge through the green water. Tynan pointed at it. "I wonder if they have one of those just for the Palace." There was no response.

As embarrassing as it was, Tynan told them all the details about the meeting in the chief's office. He thought they had a right to know. They were in this as deep as he was. Linda stayed focused on driving, although Tynan noticed she was driving a lot slower. An occasional chuckle or a "what the fuck" came out of Joe but aside from that he was quiet. Tynan had finished the blow-by-blow description of the meeting by the time they pulled into their parking lot.

"So that's that. End of story," said Tynan.

"Why do you think they're doing this?" asked Linda.

"Who knows for sure but I have a couple of theories. First of all, the bosses in this organization got to where they are by not rocking the boat. They're looking to get another promotion or find themselves a nice job when they retire. They won't get either by fighting with the Feds."

Tynan continued. "Look at Riordan. He's a washed-up prune, who knows he isn't getting promoted again but maybe he can land a cushy federal job. Maybe in the US Attorney's office. The chief might get another promotion and Klein probably sees himself as the future commissioner."

Linda shook her head. "All bullshit. What about Warren? He's involved in drugs and looking to get someone killed. Isn't that a priority over keeping the Feds happy?"

"There's a scandal either way," said Tynan. "Which sounds worse to you, cops stealing cars or a cop involved in drugs and murder? If you're a chief, which sounds easier to explain to the mayor? Do you think building a drug and murder case against Warren is going to help get these guys promoted? They don't want that plastered all over the paper. It's easier to let the Feds take Warren. He'll get arrested and fired. Then he's not the Department's problem."

She turned off the engine and opened the door. "Unbelievable."

When he was back in his office, Tynan stood looking out the window. The same boats sat at anchor as yesterday. They never go anywhere. *Just like my career*, thought Tynan. He walked over, sat in his chair, and put his feet up on the window sill. He turned the case and the meeting over and over in his mind. The more he thought about it, the more it didn't add up. Was Warren a drug dealer or a car thief? Doing both didn't make sense.

Tynan didn't know much about organized auto theft but he didn't see a guy involved in drugs branching out into stolen cars. Then there was the meeting in the chief's office. The chief and Riordan had their offices there and another at Hudson Street. But Klein was a Hudson Street guy. Why was he there this morning? Had he just happened by? There was no way he got from Hudson Street to Police Plaza in the time it would have taken for the US Attorney to make a call to the chief.

Tynan tried to wargame it out in his head. Suppose they were all there this morning. It was just a big coincidence. Right away Tynan didn't like this theory. He had been a cop long enough to know that there was no such thing as a coincidence. As far as he was concerned, coincidences were like the abominable snowman, talked about but never seen. He decided to play out the theory in his head anyway.

The chief gets the call right after he gets thrown out of the federal building. By the time he walks back to the car, the chief knows everything about the Fed's case. He knows what happened and knows that Tynan is a problem. He just so happens to have Klein and Riordan sitting there. He has to tell them the story. Then he has the receptionist make the call for the meeting.

"No fucking way," Tynan said out loud to himself. The more he thought about it the more he realized they knew a lot more than they were letting on. They probably got a call from the US Attorney last night and the meeting was prearranged. That sounded more like it.

Tynan got up, stuck his head out the doorway, and yelled, "Joe, Linda, come here." He paced back and forth in his office, his hands thrust into his pockets. They appeared in the doorway.

"When you drop that case off, go down to personnel and pull Warren's file. I'm interested in knowing if he had any experience with cars before he came on the job, like he worked in a tow business, something like that."

"Why do we care about Warren?" asked Joe. "He's not our problem anymore."

"Just humor me," said Tynan. "Take a peek and see if there is anything like that or if he's had any relatives with criminal backgrounds."

"I don't believe this," said Linda. "Lou, you heard what they said this morning."

"Yeah, yeah, don't worry about what they said. If anyone says anything, you didn't know about this morning's meeting and you were following orders from me."

"I think you're playing with fire, Lou," said Linda.

"Let me worry about the fire."

After they left, Tynan decided to settle down and tackle some of the paperwork on his desk. Joe and Linda didn't have the only case in the Group. There were worksheets from other cases. He also knew that his unit was behind on Integrity Tests. Every unit in IAB had to perform Integrity Tests every month. Some were random, targeting no particular cops; others had specific targets in mind, usually cops who were the subject of allegations. The targeted tests required a lot of planning, and Tynan wasn't sure they were effective.

Some of the tests they had done in the past required renting an apartment, setting it up to look like a stash house or a drug spot, then luring cops there. Inside, there would be simulated drugs and a lot of money. The entire apartment was wired for video and the idea was that honest cops would find the money and drugs and voucher it at the precinct. Crooked cops wouldn't. IAB had scored some "hits" on these tests but for the most part they went off without a hitch.

Tynan's superiors wanted lots of tests, the more elaborate the better. The IAB bosses at Hudson Street thought the reason most cops did the right thing and turned in the drugs and money was not because they were honest but because they smelled a trap. Tynan thought the bosses had lost touch with reality. He believed most of the cops out there were doing their jobs and the rogue cop was the exception.

He picked up a request for a random integrity test by Russell's team. Since the test wasn't designed to catch a particular cop, it would be easier to do and it would raise the total number of tests for his unit. Tynan read through it.

It was simple enough. They were going to stash a bag of crack on top of a tire of a parked car. Then after they put the crack in place, Russell would call in a job to 911. He would say that someone was selling drugs at the location and were stashing the crack on the tire. When the cops responded, Russell's team would have them under surveillance. If the cops, found the crack and vouchered it, everything was good. If they found it and didn't, then things would become a lot more complicated. Not vouchering drugs resulted in an immediate suspension and termination from the job.

Tynan picked up his phone and buzzed Russell's office. When he answered, Tynan asked, "Hey Russ, when do you want to do this integrity test?"

"I was hoping to get it done this week but I know things are kind of busy right now."

"Well things just got a lot slower, so we can pull this off today if you guys are up for it. Tomorrow at the latest."

"We could do it today," said Russell. "I have the crack, the spot picked out, and I got four people working so it won't take long."

"Good, let's try and get out the door by 1500, okay?"

"You got it boss."

Maybe the test would take his mind off things. He picked up some worksheets out of his in basket. Tynan just skimmed them. Most were routine. He initialed them and threw them in the out basket.

After an hour of half-hearted reading and initialing, Tynan heard the buzzer for the front door. He could hear sneakers squeaking on the floor as someone went to see who it was. There weren't too many visitors to Bronx IAB. He heard the door slam shut and muffled voices. Then followed the slow walk of leather dress shoes down the hall. As the footsteps got louder, Tynan realized he might be having a visitor. One who wore dress shoes, probably a suit, probably a boss.

The sound of the steps stopped in front of his door. There in the doorway stood his Captain. Captain Rogan was about five and a half feet tall. He was in his fifties, with a brown and gray receding hairline. He wore glasses, which made his brown eyes look bigger. He stood in the doorway with his hands jammed in his pockets. His tie was crooked and the top button of his shirt was open. Rogan was not what Tynan would call a snappy dresser. He liked Rogan because he stayed out of his hair, didn't say much, and had a good sense of humor. Rogan didn't seem to fit in IAB and Tynan didn't know how he wound up there. It didn't matter.

"Captain Rogan, to what do I deserve this great honor?" asked Tynan as he stood up. "Come on in and have a seat. Do you want some coffee?"

"No, thanks," said Rogan. "I just came to visit. I wanted to see if you were still here or if you were packing your bags."

"I guess you heard about my meeting this morning." Tynan sat back down.

Rogan slumped down in the chair and laughed. "Is that what you call it, a meeting? Sounded more like an ambush to me. I heard all the big guns were there."

"Yeah, you could say that. Although I would have another word for them," said Tynan.

Rogan pulled his right hand out of his pocket and waved it in the direction of Manhattan. "Ah, bunch of suck asses. I wish they had told me about the meeting beforehand. I would have liked to have been there but I guess that's why I wasn't told."

"You bring up a good point. Were you at Hudson Street this morning? Did you see Klein?"

"Nah, he wasn't there. I didn't see him at all today. He called me after you left. He wasn't happy." Rogan chuckled. "Although I don't know what would make that scumbag happy."

"What did he say?" asked Tynan.

"That you were an asshole, didn't know how to talk to anybody. That you had pissed off the US Attorney and had almost wrecked the case they were working on. He said you should be thrown out of IAB and sent to Staten Island on patrol." Rogan laughed out loud.

"So, what do you think?" Tynan leaned forward on his desk.

"I think they are lucky to have you. You're one of the few guys who know what the hell he's doing around here."

"But what do you think about what I did?" Tynan respected Rogan and wanted to know what he really thought. Maybe they were right and he was off base.

"I think you did the right thing. You got some information that needed to be acted on right away and you acted on it. What else were you supposed to do? Wait for this guy to turn up dead and then say what? "'I was busy, I didn't have a chance to get around to it.'"

Tynan leaned back. He felt better. He wasn't some loose cannon after all. He clasped his hands behind his head. "What do you think about their case?"

"Eh, you never know. This guy could be mixed up in several things. I would want to know why IAB didn't know about this earlier and I also would want to know why we're not moving ahead with this supposed hit. That's the better case and it would be pretty easy to prove."

Tynan smiled. "Okay, so why do you think they don't want to move ahead with our case about the contract killing?"

"Simple, they don't want to ruffle any feathers at the US Attorney's office. They got no balls. How's that for starters?"

Tynan agreed with that but he wondered what Rogan thought about the whole auto theft case. Did the brass at IAB not know anything about it? He wasn't sure if he should bring it up but figured Rogan was on his side.

"Do you think the chief, Klein, and Riordan didn't know anything about the Feds' case?"

"I don't know. I never heard anything about it. It's possible they didn't know. But who knows with these guys? They love their little secrets. They think they're in the CIA or something."

Maybe he's right, thought Tynan. *Maybe I've become too jaded. Everything isn't a conspiracy.* "Are you sure I can't get you anything?"

Rogan shook his head. "I'm fine. I just drove up here because I wanted to see how you are doing. That's it. Don't worry, this will blow over. The Feds will get their headlines, the chief and the other meatballs at Headquarters will stand there at a news conference and talk about how it was a joint operation, blah, blah, blah, then they'll forget about it and go on to the next thing."

"I guess you're right."

With that, Rogan, got up and headed towards the door. He called back over his shoulder, "Remember, this is just a temporary assignment for you. Do your time and move on. It's not worth worrying over."

"Okay, Captain." Tynan listened as Rogan's footsteps echoed down the hall. The heavy metal door creaked open and slammed shut. Tynan felt better. At least he wasn't totally alone in this. He went back to his paperwork. Time passed. Before long, Russell was in his office. It was time to go do an integrity test.

Russell showed him the simulated crack. There were ten vials, wrapped up in cellophane. "What did you use for crack?" asked Tynan.

"Simple. Little bits of soap. It looks close enough. Unless they open the cellophane and then the vials, they'll never know the difference."

"This is just a random test, right?"

"Yep, no real heavy cases in that precinct that we are working on right now. So, it should go quick and easy."

"Alright, let's go."

Tynan rode with Russell to the location. Russell brought four other detectives. Two in a van and two in a separate car. The car stayed three blocks away, out of sight. The van was already at the location. Russell checked on the radio to see if everyone was set. Then he drove up to the intersection.

For a weekday afternoon, the street was pretty quiet. One end of the street came off Jerome Avenue and disappeared into a tunnel under the Grand Concourse. Two abandoned buildings stood at the intersection, and two empty lots occupied the other corners. There was little chance they'd be interrupted planting the crack. Russell pulled up to the curb. There was an old faded blue Chevy parked on the corner by the abandoned building.

"Perfect," said Russell as he pointed to the car. "That's where I'll put it." He jumped out of their car and jogged across the street, looking around to see if anyone was coming. He knelt down as if to tie his shoe by the front wheel and placed the bag on top of the tire. He dusted off his pants and walked back to their car. "Easy as pie."

Russell picked up the radio and called the other car. "Go ahead and make the call. Stash is on top of the tire of a blue Chevy sitting right at the corner. Make the description of the dealer as a light skinned female with long hair, wearing red pants and a green tank top."

"Red pants and a green tank top?" laughed Tynan. "What, did you use to work for a woman's fashion magazine?"

"No, but it's perfect. Nobody is going to walk up fitting that description. The last thing I want is some bystander getting nabbed for selling drugs."

"I doubt that will happen around here," snorted Tynan.

Russell turned up the volume on the radio to monitor the precinct's frequency. It wasn't very busy. After about five minutes, the dispatcher broadcasted the call in a monotone voice. *They must be near the end of their shift,* thought Tynan.

"Four-Six Eddy, respond to a report of drug sales at the corner of East 175 Street and Walton. Subject is a light skinned female, with long hair, wearing red pants, green tank top. Drugs are stashed on the wheel of a blue chevy parked at that location."

"Ten-four," responded the sector car.

Russell drove down a block and parked in the tunnel. Waiting and watching for whoever was riding in Four-Six Eddy. Before long, the blue and white police car rolled slowly down the street. The patrol car stopped and two cops got out. One was older, heavy set, with gray hair. The other was young, with a shiny gun belt and shoes. *He looks like he's right out of the academy*, thought Tynan. The young cop started looking under the car. Finally, he came up with Russell's bag.

The older cop walked over and stared down at the bag in the other cop's hand. He looked around, then took the bag from him. He held it up to examine then, started walking towards the sewer on one of the corners.

"No, no, no," whispered Tynan.

"I can't believe it," said Russell.

The older cop got to the sewer. He stopped, turned, and tossed the bag to the young cop. They got back in the car. A voice came over the radio, "Four Six Eddy to Central. That dealer is 90Z, gone on arrival, and we're out to the house to voucher found narcotics."

Tynan and Russell both exhaled at the same time. "Thank God," said Russell. "For a minute I thought he was going to chuck it down the sewer."

"So did I," said Tynan.

"Hey Lou, what would you have done if he did?"

Tynan looked at Russell then looked out through the windshield into the tunnel. "To be honest, I don't know. He didn't take it. If he threw it down the sewer, I'm guessing he figured the dealer lost his drugs and there was no sense tying up a police car vouchering ten vials of crack. In a way, he'd have been saving the city money and keeping a patrol car on the street where it might do some good."

"Would you let it go?"

"I don't know." Tynan thought about it. "I guess I would. We'd have to say the test never happened."

Russell nodded. "I got you."

Tynan took in a deep breath and said, "Yeah, I'd let it go. I've seen worse things lately."

When Tynan stepped out of his house the next morning, the sun was just coming up. He climbed into his department-issued car and headed towards the Saw Mill Parkway. He would be in before anyone else, which was fine with him. The day before had almost turned into a nightmare with the Integrity Test. He went home right after it was over. That had been a close call. Tynan took it as an omen. The last thing he wanted was to bust two cops for throwing drugs down the sewer. Maybe they wouldn't have lost their jobs because they didn't take it but they would have definitely lost a month's pay. If the younger cop was still on probation he would have been fired and that would have bothered Tynan. That's not what he signed up for.

The traffic had not reached its sluggish early morning commute stage. It was just starting to get heavy but still moving and he was at his office in less than half an hour. He hoped today would change things around. The past few days had made him think he might not be able to last the two full years in Internal Affairs. He thought about that as he climbed the stairs to his office. *Would that be all that bad?*

He flipped on the hallway lights and went to the breakroom to make coffee. Within the hour, others would arrive. The smell of the coffee and the silence of the office was both reassuring and strange. Grabbing the mug of coffee, he trudged down to his office.

The early morning sun had a red glaze to it. The same boats nodded at anchor as if they were saying good morning. He sipped the black coffee and looked out at the water. He told himself to think positive. Placing the cup on his desk, he looked at his personal calendar and drew another diagonal hashmark through that day's date. *What a terrible way to go through life,* he thought. Marking time, scratching days off a calendar.

He sat down and looked out the window. At first, he thought about reviewing more worksheets but the early morning sunlight changed his mind. He was going to enjoy the silence for a change. Before long he heard the office door opening and footsteps coming down the hall.

Joe stopped and leaned against the door jamb. "Well, good morning, Lou. You were gone by the time we got back yesterday."

Tynan nodded, holding his mug with both hands. "Yeah, I figured you'd miss me. How did your trip to the Palace go?"

"A lot more boring than you would have thought."

"Well, grab a cup of coffee and fill me in."

Joe disappeared for a few minutes and came back with his own cup in one hand and a notepad in the other. He blew on the coffee before taking a sip. Balancing his coffee and pulling one of the chairs aside with his foot, he sat down.

"To be honest, Lou, I thought you were nuts yesterday. But you know me. The good soldier that I am, I followed orders. First, we dropped off the folder to Sullivan. I think I have a nickname for her. Are you ready? The Ice Queen. Would it kill her to smile or even say thank you?"

"Why would she talk to some lowly sergeant from a field office? She probably thinks people like you shouldn't be allowed in the building."

"After that, we headed down to personnel. You didn't tell me that we'd be sitting in a room with no windows. Thanks for that. We got a lot of strange looks but when you say you are from Internal Affairs people just give you what you want and hope you'll go away."

"Did you find anything interesting?"

"The only thing I got was a blinding headache. There's no record of Warren having any background dealing with auto mechanics or autos. He had a job as a manager in a supermarket. He doesn't list any relatives with a criminal history. We went over it with a fine-tooth comb and made a copy. Nothing there indicating he knows anything about cars."

Tynan rocked back and forth in his chair for a moment, saying nothing. What were the Feds looking at? What's the connection between Warren and a stolen car ring? Maybe the Feds had reliable information and were seeing something he couldn't.

"I'm guessing we're not going to be doing anything with the Warren case," said Joe. "Ahem, like we we're told."

Tynan smiled. "Thanks for checking. I was just curious if there was something in his past life that explains the Fed's case. Now I'm going to behave myself."

"You think the Feds have a good case?"

"Beats me. Even a broken clock is right twice a day."

The door at the end of the hallway opened and closed a few more times as more people drifted in for the day shift. Now it was Linda's turn to stick her head into the office. "What? A meeting and nobody called me?"

"Not quite," said Joe. "You know what they say about the early bird getting the worm."

"Yeah, Sarge," huffed Linda. "You know what they say about the brown noser."

"I hadn't heard that one Linda. You're going to have to tell me some time," chuckled Joe.

"I guess you told the boss about what we found yesterday."

"Come on in Linda," said Tynan. "Joe was just filling me in. Sounds like you two had an interesting afternoon."

Linda stood in the doorway. "It was interesting, if you like flipping through a mountain of paper looking for who knows what. Please tell me you are not going to pursue this."

"As a matter of fact, I'm leaving it in the capable hands of Lieutenant Sullivan and the Feds. They can build the biggest stolen car case ever seen for all I care," said Tynan. "Although, I have to admit, I am really curious as to what they are up to and I'm still more than a little furious they are operating in the Bronx and leaving us in the dark. But who am I?"

Linda looked relieved. She sat down next to Joe. "I'm glad it's over. I don't care about the case. It's not ours. It's not our problem. And to be honest, I was a little worried about looking at Warren's file. You know if they found out, we'd be screwed."

"I told you," said Tynan, "it was my order. It's on me. But rest easy, that's the last thing I'm going to ask you to do on this case. We're out of it."

"Good," sighed Linda.

"Just forget about it. Keep working on your other cases. I'm sure we have no shortage."

"You can count on us, Lou," said Joe with a smile, as he stood up and motioned Linda to follow. They disappeared down the hallway.

Tynan knew he'd be crazy to keep pushing on this case. He could see Linda wanted nothing to do with it. Joe didn't seem to care one way or the other. But this case had grabbed a hold of Tynan like a mad dog with a bone who wasn't letting go. He wasn't sure if it was his bruised ego or just his curiosity that kept bringing him back to it. If he was smart, he'd forget about it. What could he do anyway? If Klein or Riordan found out he had checked Warren's personnel folder, they'd suspend him. He knew he would take the weight if it came to it but there was no guarantee that Klein wouldn't go after Joe and Linda anyway and take everyone out with one swoop.

He had to let it go. Tynan gulped down the last of his coffee. *Stop being an idiot and just do your time*, he thought to himself. Why would he work on a case that wasn't his? He wasn't calling up Brooklyn and asking to work on any of their cases.

"Fuck it, it's their problem now," he muttered.

The phone rang. Tynan looked at his watch. *This can't be good*, he thought.

He picked up the phone and a woman on the other end said, "I've been told to tell you that a friend of yours is staying at the Throgs' Neck Motel. He'll be there for a couple of days, in room 111, if you are interested in catching up with him. A mutual friend of ours trusts you will keep this confidential."

Before Tynan could say anything, the woman hung up.

END OF THE ROAD

Tynan knew what the woman on the phone was talking about. The agent had promised him that he would put him in touch with the CI again and he had kept his word. But as he hung up the phone, he didn't feel grateful. In fact, he felt a little surge of anger. He was almost at the point of letting the case go. He thought he had put it in the rear-view mirror. The phone call took the case from the rear-view mirror and splattered it all over the windshield like some huge bug on a hot summer day. That's what annoyed Tynan now. The case was back in the front of his mind.

He looked at his watch. It wasn't even eight a.m. That motel was not far away. He wondered if the agent had put the CI up in that hotel because it was close. *He wants me to go see the CI,* thought Tynan. Another thought loomed up. *How did he know this wasn't a set up?* He wouldn't put it past someone like Klein or Riordan to put in a call like that and see if he went to the motel. He dismissed the thought almost as quickly as it appeared. Not that those two weren't capable of something like that, but how would they know about the agent's promise?

Tynan got up, grabbed his suit jacket from the back of his chair, and looked down the hallway. Nobody was coming. Walking softly, he bolted out the metal door. He was almost jogging by the time he got to his car. Starting it up and popping it into gear, he felt the doubt starting to creep back into his head. Why was he doing this? If he was smart, he'd let it go.

He pushed the doubts back down and in twenty minutes he was pulling into the parking lot of the motel. He looked around. It was a typical one-story hot sheets motel with about twenty rooms, all facing the parking lot. It was the kind frequented by cheating couples and the occasional drug dealer. Everything looked quiet.

Two women from housekeeping were setting up their carts, getting ready for the day.

Tynan left the car and slowly closed the door. He walked directly to the room. If the CI was like most criminals, he'd still be sound asleep. The CI's day probably didn't start until noon. He glanced at the two women. They hadn't noticed him. He knocked on the door to the room but there was no answer. Knocking louder and tapping his car keys on the window finally brought the sound of rustling from behind the door.

A grunt more than a voice came from the other side of the door. A hand slowly parted the window curtain. The face that went with the hand was still in the shadows. The door opened. There was Angel, standing in his underwear. He was squinting. He smelled of whiskey, and the pungent odor of stale cigarettes wafted from inside the room. Angel didn't say anything, but he turned around and left the door open. Tynan glanced around the parking lot one more time and stepped inside, closing the door quietly behind him. "We meet again, old friend."

Angel groaned. He looked hung-over. He walked over to the bed and sat down. Tynan pulled up a chair. "Looks like you had a rough night Angel," Tynan said. Tynan looked around the room and noticed a half empty bottle of scotch and an ashtray of cigarette butts. He also noticed one more thing: a 9mm pistol on the night-stand beside the bed. He got up and in two quick strides had the gun in his hand before Angel had finished wiping his eyes.

"Now, now, Angel. I would be willing to bet that you don't have a permit for this."

Angel slowly shook his head, "Nope."

"I'll hang on to it for now. It'll just be our little secret, okay."

"Okay," said Angel as he pulled the sheet around him. "What do you want? How did you find me?"

Tynan walked back over to the chair and sat down. He dropped the magazine out of the pistol and ejected a round from the chamber. "Well, that's what we do. We find people." *No sense in giving up the agent*, thought Tynan.

"So, what do you want? I know you're pissed at me but I'm telling you I had no choice in leaving you there. No choice, man. Go ask Kurt."

"I know you didn't. If I thought you left me there like that, you'd be in cuffs right now. So, relax. I'm just here to see how you're doing."

Angel reached for his cigarettes, took the last one out of the pack and lit it up. "Yeah? You want to know how I'm doing. Look around, how does it look like I'm doing?"

"How come Lugo never showed up?" asked Tynan.

"Because I reached out to him. Kurt let me call him. I had to call him. If he showed up and I wasn't there, I wouldn't be here right now. I'd be laying out there somewhere in a garbage bag. What do you think? You don't stand a guy like Lugo up. No way."

"What did you say to Lugo?"

"I told him that I thought I was being followed and for him not to meet me. I told him I'd be in touch with him."

"Did Lugo buy that?"

Angel exhaled a long stream of smoke, "He bought it. He was cool with it. Me making that call shows him I'm not a dumbass who is going to let the cops follow him to a meeting."

"Isn't Lugo going to be suspicious of you now? After all, you got cops following you."

"Nah, he thinks he's being followed half the time. If you don't think you are being followed sometimes, you're going to wind up in a cell out on Rikers or worse. Someone is going to put one in your head." Angel looked at Tynan directly for the first time. "Look, what do you want? I tried to help you but they said no."

"Who said no?" asked Tynan.

"I don't know. Some woman. Some lawyer type." Angel was fumbling around for the words. "Some DA bitch."

"How long are you going to be camped out here, Angel?"

He shrugged. "I don't know. Not much longer, I hope. I've got shit to do. I ain't getting enough money from Kurt to be doing just this. I got things to do."

"Have you talked to Lugo since yesterday?"

Angel shook his head. "No and I got to reach him soon because the longer I wait, he's going to get it in his head that I'm not right. Like maybe I've been grabbed by the cops. And then he won't talk to me. He's smarter than that. I should talk to him today to make sure everything is okay."

"I'll leave that up to you and Kurt. Eh, another thing," said Tynan slowly. "What's the story with this cop and stolen cars? What can you tell me about that?"

"Oh, listen man, I got to take a piss and shower. Can we do this some other time?" said Angel.

Tynan looked at him and nodded. Angel had his sympathies. Tynan knew what it was like to wake up with a hangover. It was tough enough trying to function without some asshole sitting there firing off questions. "Sure, go take a shower. I'll wait. No rush, I got all day."

Having me wait for him was probably not what Angel had in mind, thought Tynan, *but that's the best he's going to get.* Angel got up, half staggered over to a gym bag and got some clothes. He went into the bathroom and closed the door. The sound of Angel peeing was followed by the splashing of water from the shower. Tynan looked over at the pistol. He picked it up and noticed the serial number had been filed off.

A felon in possession of a defaced firearm. The charges were starting to add up. For a brief moment, he thought about arresting him. That wouldn't help their relationship but it would give him more leverage. Kurt would probably be pissed as well.

That thought was quickly replaced by another more disturbing scenario. Tynan arrests the CI, Klein, Riordan and everyone else down in the Puzzle Palace go completely apeshit. Tynan gets suspended and the charges against the CI are dropped. The only trial that takes place is when Tynan is sitting down in the Department's Trial Room fighting a losing battle to keep his job.

The idea of arresting Angel disappeared. Tynan had already crossed the line and he knew it. His job was hanging by a thread the minute he knocked on the motel room door. What he was doing was definitely insubordination. Now he was going to give Angel a pass on having a gun. *The shit was getting deeper,* he thought.

Tynan sighed. "If I'm going down this road, might as well play smart," he mumbled to himself. He stood up, grabbed a corner of the bedspread and wiped the pistol down. *No sense proving I was here,* he thought. The loaded magazine got the same treatment. Before he laid them on the dresser, he took a look at the pistol. It was a Colt 9mm. Angel wasn't carrying crap, that was for sure. Whoever had erased the serial number had gotten a little carried away, leaving a deep scratch through the trademark Colt horse on the pistol. Now the horse looked like a unicorn. *Guess they're not too worried about resale value,* thought Tynan.

He sat back in the chair and waited for Angel to reappear. Angel finally came out of the bathroom looking more presentable. At least, he didn't look like he might pass out and keel over. Tynan wasn't going to give Angel a break. He started right in as Angel looked around in his bag for more cigarettes. "What do you know about Warren and stolen cars?"

Angel pulled a fresh pack of cigarettes out of his gym bag, pounded the pack in his hand, and opened it. "Warren and stolen cars? I don't know much. What's that got to do with anything?" He took a cigarette out and let it dangle from his mouth. "All I know is I heard he might be involved in some stolen car shit. They steal the cars and sell them overseas."

"Who did you hear that from?"

"Some guy. Why are you bothering me with this shit? That's what I told the Feds. They are interested in that. What's it got to do with you? Besides, I was told not to talk to you and definitely not about Warren and cars."

"Why didn't you go to the Feds with the Santos hit? You were already working with them?"

The CI rubbed a hand across his face. "Because they are slower than shit and when I told Kurt he said I should talk to the local police. That's why I came over to talk to you about the Santos hit. The Feds take forever to do shit. Trust me, I know."

"Does Kurt know about the stolen car ring?"

"No, he's only interested in guns. I just told him I had information about dirty cops with stolen cars, and he gave me a number to call. I'm working with different Feds on that and they're always busting my balls. They don't understand, getting information takes time."

"So, Kurt was in the dark about Warren and stolen cars?"

"Yeah," said Angel. "The only time Kurt heard about Warren was when I told him about the hit on Santos. That's when he took me to you guys. If you want, I can find out more about the car thing, but it won't be free. I expect money for that information, especially after they told me not to talk to you."

"That won't be necessary," said Tynan. "You should get in touch with Kurt and find out what he wants you to do next with Lugo."

"Yeah, I'm going to do that."

Tynan got up and opened the door. He stood there in the doorway and looked back at Angel, shrouded in smoke and squinting from the daylight. "Alright Angel, you take care. It's been a pleasure doing business with you."

Walking back to his car, Tynan wasn't even sure why he had come here. Maybe he wanted to confirm the agent's story or perhaps his visit was driven by something simpler and a lot more juvenile. He'd been told not to do something and he couldn't resist ignoring the order. It was his symbolic finger to Klein and company. As Tynan got into the car and started the engine, he looked back at Angel's room. He may not know why he really came over to talk to Angel but now he was sure his part in the case was over. He was finished. Too much downside and no upside. *Good luck Angel*, he thought, *you're going to need it.*

After his visit with Angel, Tynan's life fell back into its normal routine. He signed off on his worksheets, approved the closing of cases, and spent a lot of time looking out the office window. The daily grind was both boring and comforting. He scratched off more days on the calendar and, before he knew it, a week had passed since Klein took his case away.

He was sitting at home watching the news and drinking his morning coffee. Tynan liked these types of days. He was scheduled to do a four to twelve shift. He liked working the evening hours. At heart, he was a night person. Today, he'd take the kids to the park and hang out with them until two, then head into work.

The phone in the kitchen interrupted his news show. His wife grabbed it. "Hello," she said. There was a pause. "Uh, okay, let me get him." She stuck her head into the living room, covering the phone's mouthpiece with her hand. "It's some chief on the line. Wants to talk to you."

Tynan frowned, got up, and went over to his wife. She mumbled, "These people," and handed him the receiver.

"Hello?"

"This is Chief Klein. We got a problem."

Tynan's stomach briefly rolled up into a knot. Had he found out about his meeting with Angel?

"Santos is dead. Someone shot him late last night."

Tynan relaxed. His stomach unwound. Suddenly he realized that for the first time in a long time he had the upper hand. "*We've* got a problem?" he asked.

"Didn't you hear me?" asked Klein. "I just said Santos is dead. You know. The guy who had the hit on him?"

"Sounds to me like *you* got a problem, chief," said Tynan slowly. "Don't you remember, I was taken off that case by you. So, I don't have a problem. I might be wrong but I think anyone who knew he was going to get killed and didn't do anything, *those people*, I think they definitely have a problem."

Tynan could almost feel the anger coming through from the other side of the phone. He was sure Klein was livid, but more importantly, Tynan sensed that Klein was afraid. Klein's decision to take the case meant a dead drug dealer could be laid at his doorstep. To make matters worse, there were plenty of witnesses, including Tynan, who could make the connection.

"You're back on the case. It's your case now. Deal with it. I want you in to work right away. Start by going to the crime scene and then get your toadies to come down here and pick up the case from Lieutenant Sullivan. I want this wrapped up. Do you understand, Tynan?"

Klein hung up the phone without telling him where the crime scene was. For Tynan, he didn't need any more proof that Klein was shook up. Tynan would call Bronx Detectives and find out all the details about the homicide. It didn't matter. That phone call was the best news he'd had in a long time. When he looked at his wife, his feeling of joy quickly turned into guilt. He had been planning on a morning with the kids. That wasn't going to happen.

"Sorry, I got to go in."

His wife, didn't say anything. She walked back into the living room. Her silence said it all. Once again, the job had interfered with his home life. For a job that Tynan had come to hate, he realized how much of his life was consumed by it. He wanted to follow her and try to explain things but he knew that conversation would go nowhere. Instead, he turned towards the bedroom to get dressed.

On the way in, he called Bronx Detectives and found out where the homicide had taken place. Santos had been shot at two in the morning on the same steps where Tynan had last seen him lifting his bottle of beer in a toast. A drug dealer getting shot was all part of the game. Normally, Tynan wouldn't have felt any emotion about it but he had a brief personal connection with Santos.

Tynan had told Santos that he was in danger but he hadn't prevented it. He didn't want to dwell on whether he could have handled things differently. He pushed it to the back of his mind, where it rested along with the guilty feeling about not taking his kids to the park. *Pretty soon*, he thought, *there isn't going to be any more room in there for the guilt.* His mind was becoming as cluttered as his garage, except instead of tools and half-finished projects, it was full of broken promises and missed opportunities.

Tynan pulled up in front of the crime scene. Like he thought, the black and yellow crime scene tape was already balled up in a corner on the steps. All the uniformed cops and detectives were gone. Santos' corpse was lying in a freezer in the morgue. He got out of the car and walked up to the steps. There had been no whistles or shouts of "five-oh" when he pulled into the block. The front of the building was empty. Even the window that was open the day he visited Santos was closed. Whoever was supposed to hand the guns out through the window didn't do their job right last night.

There was still a pool of congealed blood on the top step. Nobody had bothered to clean it up yet. Tynan scanned the roof. Nobody was looking over. He did catch the movement of a curtain at a first-floor window. He walked inside the building. The lobby was cool. The light shining through the door made the rest of the lobby dark, even though it was early morning. Sounds of daily living echoed down the staircase. People were going about their lives. Another day, another murder.

Tynan wanted to talk to whoever was in the first-floor apartment. They had seen him pull up. More than likely it was one of Santos' crew. He went up to the door and listened. It was quiet. He knocked. Creaking sounds from old hardwood floors told Tynan that someone was coming to the door. He heard the metallic click as somebody looked out the peephole. Tynan reached into his pocket and held his shield up. "Police."

The two deadbolts on the door snapped back in quick succession. The door opened a crack and the tall guy who had been standing with Santos peered out. "What do you want?"

"Not much, just wanted to talk about last night. Mind if I come in?" asked Tynan.

If this guy was Santos' bodyguard, he had not only failed miserably but now he was out of a job. The life of anyone working for Santos had become one big mystery. Would this guy move up and become the new Santos or would someone else take that spot? And then what would become of the bodyguard? *Not exactly like he's got a good resume,* thought Tynan.

Tynan was surprised when the door swung back. The bodyguard motioned him to come in and Tynan stepped in quickly. The door shut and the deadbolts snapped back into place. The living room was sparsely furnished. A beat-up couch and a couple of easy chairs adorned the room. There was a kitchen chair by the window that overlooked the steps where Santos held court. Anyone sitting in that spot got a good look at the steps leading into the building.

"Did you talk to the police last night?" asked Tynan.

"There was nothing to say."

"Well, how about we start with your name."

"Jaime Aponte."

"Hi Jaime, what's your date of birth?" Aponte gave it and then sat down in one of the recliners. Tynan opted to stand. He didn't want to get too comfortable.

"So, what happened last night?"

"I told you. I don't know what happened. I was in here sleeping when I heard the shots."

"How many shots did you hear?"

"I don't know. Three or four. Like I said, I was sleeping. I heard the shots, got up and looked out the window. My man was laying there."

"What did you do?"

"I ran outside to help him but he was gone. They got him in the head and the chest."

"They? More than one guy?"

"I don't know, when I got outside, they were gone."

"You keep saying they. Were there two guys? Three? What?" Tynan was getting impatient.

"I told you. I don't know. The only thing I saw was a car driving away. I guess there must have been at least two. One guy did it and the other was driving the car."

"What kind of car?"

"I don't know, dark, maybe a Lincoln."

"Maybe a Lincoln? A Lincoln looks pretty distinctive. It's not a Toyota."

Jaime threw his hands up. "What do you want me to say? It might be a Lincoln but I'm not sure. I had just woke-up and my boy is laying there dead."

"Did you call the cops?"

"No, I just tried to help him but it was too late."

Tynan wondered if Jaime was in on the hit or not. He's supposed to be the bodyguard but he's not there when his boss gets clipped. Somebody should have been there.

"Listen Jaime, let's cut the bullshit. Who do you think shot your boss?"

"You're asking me?" Jaime smirked, then pointed at Tynan. "You're the guy who said someone was out to get him. Maybe you should be asking yourself, dude. Why are you acting like you don't know?"

"Because I don't. I'm looking for some help here. I want to get whoever did this?"

"Bullshit," said Jaime. "You don't give a shit about who did this?"

"The other day I was here, with two other detectives. What I didn't tell you then but I'm telling you now is that I'm not the regular police. Not Narcotics, not Detectives."

"Then what the fuck are you?"

"I'm from Internal Affairs. Do you know what we do?"

Jaime shrugged. "No, you tell me."

"We investigate cops. We arrest cops who break the law. I think maybe a cop had something to do with this. Do you want to help me or not?"

Jaime pushed back in his chair. Tynan could see he was thinking. He knew that Jaime had no interest in helping the police. If there was going to be "justice" it was going to be the kind where Jaime left someone else laying in the street with a bunch of bullet holes in them. But Tynan knew that while Jaime might not help him catch someone else in the drug business, he might be willing to help the cops catch a cop. There was no loyalty there.

"Help you? You knew Santos was going to get killed and he's dead. How'd you help him?"

"That was different. We didn't have the case then, but we do now, and with your help, you can do the right thing by your boss."

Jaime smirked and looked away. It didn't look like he was buying it and Tynan could see why. They hadn't done much for Santos when he was alive. He reached into his jacket pocket and took out a business card. He put it down on the arm of the chair and walked towards the door.

As he let himself out, Tynan stopped and called back to Jaime, "If you don't want to help us, that's fine, but you might want to think about where you stand. Your boss is dead. If you had nothing to do with it, I'd be willing to bet that whoever killed him is not interested in you sticking around. Best case for you? You're out of a job. Worst case? You'll be laying down in the morgue with your buddy before the week is out. You might want to help yourself. Give me a call if you change your mind."

Tynan walked out. He was pretty sure Jaime was not in on the hit. But there are no friends in the drug business. Loyalty is based on money and that's it. If he didn't have anything to do with the murder, then Tynan was sure Jaime's days were numbered. Tynan's next stop was the Precinct Detective Unit.

The precinct was a relatively new red brick building. Like every precinct in the city, parking was a mess. Tynan was lucky and found a spot. He was running through his head whether he knew anybody here at the Four-One Precinct. Nobody came to mind.

As he climbed the stairs and pulled open the main door, he bumped into two cops he knew of but never met, Warren and Wright. They were coming out the door and Tynan held the door open for them. "After you, gents."

The cops nodded in return. Warren was taller than Tynan had imagined. He had black hair and a big moustache that made his face seem paler. Wright, was shorter, balding with brown hair. Warren was wearing a long sleeve uniform shirt but the top button was open and his navy-blue clip-on tie hung to the side. Tynan wasn't sure what he'd expected. They didn't look any different than other cops. He didn't stare. He just walked into the precinct, flashed his shield at the sergeant on the desk and yelled, "Going up to the squad." The sergeant waved and went back to writing in the logbook on the desk.

Tynan knew that when you were visiting a precinct, you were normally well received. You might meet somebody you had worked with, but even if you didn't, the reception was cordial. Once Tynan got into Internal Affairs, all that vanished. The reception was as cold as a midnight in February. The minute you announced where you were from, everyone's demeanor changed. They tensed up, looking at you with a mixture of fear and contempt. Drafting people into Internal Affairs might have taken some of the edge off those encounters but only if the people you were dealing with had worked with you before you went to Internal Affairs. Those people usually shrugged and said to those around them, "'Ah, he's alright.'" Not knowing anyone in this precinct wouldn't help.

He climbed the unswept stairs to the Detective Squad's office. Walking in, he flashed his shield at the nearest detective and said, "Is the boss in?" He was pointed towards a small office at the back of the open bay, which was crammed with desks. The detectives working at their desks gave him a quick look and went back to their paperwork.

As he walked into the office, there was a lieutenant sitting at the desk. He was heavyset, white, with blond hair, in his forties. "Hi, I'm Lieutenant Tynan from IAB," said Tynan as he approached with an outstretched hand. The lieutenant looked up from his paperwork, made a half-hearted effort to stand, and shook hands. "Hi, Lieutenant Morris. What can I do for you?"

This was where it was going to get difficult. Tynan didn't know for sure that Santos had been murdered on Warren's orders. Nobody, not even the all-knowing Deputy Chief Klein, knew that. This case belonged to the Four-One Precinct Detective Squad but Internal Affairs had an interest in what happened. At the very least, Tynan and his Group would be riding shotgun on the case. Tynan was sure Klein would have no problem taking it away from the Detective Bureau if he had to. There'd be fewer people asking embarrassing questions.

Until and unless IAB took over the case, Tynan knew he had to tread lightly. He needed the cooperation of the Detective Squad without coming across like a heavy-handed scumbag while at the same time, not giving them any information. A week earlier he had been in the same spot with the Feds and he didn't like being left in the dark. Now he'd be doing the same thing to this Lieutenant.

"Yeah, you guys caught a homicide last night. Victim's name is Santos. We have an interest in the case," said Tynan in a low voice.

"An interest," chuckled Morris. "I've got an interest too, another unsolved homicide."

"We might be able to help you with that."

"Really? Tell me you got the guy who did it. That's all the help I need."

Tynan closed the door to the small office and sat down in front of Morris' desk.

"For starters, we're going to need copies of all the paperwork associated with the case, including crime scene photos, lab requests and results, ME's report, everything."

"I thought you said you were going to help me. Sounds like more work, not less," said Morris.

"It is for now. If this goes the way we are expecting it to, we might wind up taking the case off your hands. I'll take the case off your hands right now, if I get the green light from downtown. But, in the meantime, we're going to have to play nice in the sandbox."

Tynan saw the frown crossing the lieutenant's face and quickly added. "I can send people over to help make the copies and I can give you manpower to help interview witnesses or do any canvasses, if that would help."

He could see the wheels turning in Morris' head. Tynan knew exactly what he was thinking. Having extra bodies to make copies, do reports, and knock on doors would definitely help, but did he want IAB assholes hanging around his office. Tynan wondered what Morris would decide.

"Nah, that won't be necessary. We can make all the copies you need and keep you up to date."

It seemed Morris had decided he wasn't interested in IAB hanging around his office. That was okay with Tynan too. What he really wanted was to take the case away from the squad but he needed muscle to pull that off. That kind of muscle was only available on the top floor of the Puzzle Palace.

"What do you know about this case?" asked Morris.

"I know there was someone looking to kill this guy, Santos."

"A cop?"

Tynan didn't say anything.

"Gotta be a cop. You wouldn't be here if it wasn't."

Tynan sighed. "Let's just say that we're not saying the shooter was a cop but there may be some police involvement, according to info we've received."

"Then if a cop isn't the shooter, it must be a cop involved in drugs," said Morris, still probing.

This guy Morris was no dope, thought Tynan. He knew how the job worked and he knew IAB wasn't usually going around offering to help Detective Squads. Morris had put together that this was a "drug related shooting," as the Public Information office liked to say.

"Hopefully, it's neither," said Tynan. "But you agree this is a drug shooting."

"Of course. According to Bronx Narcotics, Santos was a player. He gets blasted early in the morning, sitting at his usual hangout."

"Do you have any witnesses?"

"None of any real value," Morris said. "A woman from across the street was up. She heard the shots but by the time she got to the window she only saw a car speeding away and the victim lying on the steps."

"Did she say what type of car?" asked Tynan.

"Yeah, a black Lincoln. That was it. Didn't see who got into it or who was driving it or if the shots came from it. Based on the ballistic evidence at the scene, this wasn't a drive-by. This was an up close and personal. They blasted him. Four shots, two in the chest and two in the head. The ME said one of the shots to the head was a contact shot. They definitely wanted him dead."

"What did they use?"

"The usual, nine-millimeter, gun of choice recommended by criminals all over America," chuckled Morris.

"Shell casings?"

"Four. Sent to the lab for prints and to see if the same gun was used in any other shootings. Maybe we'll come up with a hit. This guy or guys might be smart enough to get rid of the gun but you never know. We're not dealing with brain surgeons here. There's always a chance we get lucky," said Morris.

"Anything else?"

"We're going to go back over later and do another canvass. Knock on some doors and maybe turn up someone we didn't speak to before. I have a call into Narcotics to start asking anyone they lock up in that area for information. Hopefully, some street dealer might be willing to swap info for a get out of jail free card."

"Does Narcotics know about any beefs in the area? Any turf disputes?" asked Tynan.

"No. This guy Santos had a lock on the area. Looked like he was an up and comer. Maybe he was branching out and somebody didn't like it. He's been arrested for drugs before. He's no stranger to danger."

"If I find anything out, I'll get back to you," said Tynan as he got up and opened the door.

"Well thanks, you've been a wealth of information," chuckled Morris. "I can get you those copies if you hang out for a few minutes. We're still waiting on lab reports. The ME is doing the autopsy today."

Tynan felt embarrassed. He'd done nothing but drain Morris for information and had given him nothing in return. He didn't like being a user. "Okay, thanks. I'll hang out for a bit for the copies and I will see if we can't take this off your hands altogether. No promises."

"If you can do that, I owe you one. It's not like we're short of homicides here." Morris shook Tynan's hand. "Good luck. As much as I'd like to lose a case, I hope you're wrong about this."

"So do I," said Tynan. "But I've got an uneasy feeling that I might be right."

RETURN TO THE PALACE

After gathering up the copies from the Detective Squad, Tynan decided to head downtown and pay a visit to the chief. Usually when he went to the Palace his stomach would be in a knot. Not this time. He knew he had the upper hand at the moment. The Palace was political. Most of the brass that scurried around its hallways were never really street cops or if they were, they had forgotten what it was like in the street. Tynan felt comfortable in the street. He was out of his element in Headquarters. He understood the street. To him, even drug dealers and snitches were more trustworthy than a lot of the people walking around Headquarters with gold stars on their shoulders.

Tynan picked up his cell phone and called the office. He needed to put things in motion while he was visiting the Palace.

"Hey Joe, I've got some good news and bad news for you."

"Hi Lou. I'll save you the trouble of asking, I'll take the bad news first."

"The bad news is that Santos is dead."

There was a pause on the other side of the phone. "Holy shit," said Joe in a low voice. "When did that happen?"

"Last night on the late tour. Shot to death on the same steps where we last saw him. Looks like he took two to the head and two to the chest."

"Wow. Turns out the CI was right. I guess they got someone else to do it."

"That could be the case but it's not like drug dealers getting killed never happened before in the Bronx."

Joe chuckled. "True enough. What's the good news?"

"You guys are back running with the Warren case."

Joe laughed. "Nooo, tell me it isn't so! I thought you said you had good news. That's just more bad news."

"Hmmm, well get a hold of Linda and you can share your bad luck. Then grab Russell and some of his people and go over to the scene of the homicide. Canvass the building and make sure people know you are not from the Detective Squad. No reason to hide where you work. Let them know and bring plenty of business cards with you. They might not want to talk right away but they could change their minds. And another thing, give copies of your worksheets to the Four-One Squad. They have been pretty helpful so far and I don't want to look like we're a bunch of one-way fucks, even though we are."

"How much do they know about the Warren case?" asked Joe.

"Nothing and they are to know nothing. You just give them any information you gather after your canvass of the buildings at the crime scene. But if someone gives you something that talks about cops, hold that back from the Detective Squad."

"Oh," said Joe. Tynan could hear the disappointment in his voice. "We're working together except when we're not working together."

"Sorry Joe, that's how it goes. You know the deal. I'm headed downtown to get the folder. See you later."

During the entire drive to the Palace, Tynan daydreamed about rubbing Klein's and Riordan's noses in the dirt. He'd been right and they were too busy playing politics to see the obvious. The hit on Santos was the priority, not some auto theft ring. He felt giddy by the time he got up to the fourteenth floor and strode into the chief's office.

Tynan greeted the receptionist with a big smile. "Good morning. I'm Lieutenant Tynan and I'd like to talk to the chief."

"I know who you are. You keep coming down here and we might have to get you a desk," joked the receptionist. "Let me see if he's busy."

While she was on the phone with the chief, Tynan looked into Riordan's office. As soon as their eyes met, Riordan jumped up and came out from behind his desk. He walked up to Tynan and said in a low voice, "Are you here about the thing?"

"The thing?" asked Tynan as he furrowed his eyebrows like he didn't know what Riordan was talking about. He relished the moment.

"Oh, *the thing*," said Tynan as he snapped his fingers. "Yeah, if you mean by the thing, that giant cluster-fuck with the Feds, yeah, I'm here for the thing."

Riordan looked deflated. He leaned into Tynan and whispered in his ear, "Listen, there's no sense going over that again. We have a job to do."

"Absolutely boss." Tynan had never used the word "boss" when talking to a superior but now he did. He'd never consider Riordan or Klein his superiors. They might outrank him but, as far as he was concerned, they should both be selling hotdogs in Central Park.

"I was doing my job when suddenly I was told to stop but no sense crying over spilt milk - or dead drug dealers for that matter," whispered Tynan.

The receptionist hung up the phone. "The chief will see you now."

Tynan went to the chief's office with Riordan in tow. He knocked and opened the door. The chief sat at his desk. Behind him was a bank of windows looking out on lower Manhattan. All over the wall across from him were various pictures of the chief with politicians and plaques given by one organization or another. To Tynan, the pictures and plaques screamed a warning to anyone in the office, "Don't fuck with me, I know a lot of important people."

Tynan saluted, even though he was in a suit and not in uniform. "Good morning, chief. I'd like to pick up that case we handed over and talk to you about it."

"Good morning, Lieutenant. Have a seat. Would you like some coffee?"

"No thank you, chief," said Tynan as he dropped down into one of the chairs in front of the chief's desk. He noticed Riordan took the other one without asking.

"Deputy Chief Klein will be joining us in a moment. I believe he has what you're looking for. Tell me what's going on."

"Well, after I got the call this morning, I went over to the crime scene. I talked to a friend of the victim but he didn't give me much information. The victim was shot four times. Two in the head and two in the chest. One of the head shots was done at close range. The ME will tell us more after the autopsy."

Chief Calhoun nodded. He picked up his cup of coffee and sipped from it slowly, never taking his eyes off Tynan.

"I got copies of the paperwork from the Four-One Squad. They don't have any leads and no witnesses that can add anything other than a black Lincoln was seen leaving the scene. For now, we don't know how many shooters. It wasn't a spray and pray drive-by. Whoever shot Santos wanted him out of the picture for good. My team is on the way over there now to do another canvass and see if we can turn up anything. Bronx Narcotics has been advised of the homicide and they will be questioning anyone they pick up from that area."

"Good. Good." He pointed at Tynan and looked over at Riordan. "See, I told you he was good."

"Of course, chief, he's one of the best," Riordan said as his head nodded like a bobble head doll in the back of a car window.

Tynan continued, "As for future steps, I would propose the following. We need to get back in touch with the CI and see if he can gather any information for us. We don't know for sure if this was a hit ordered by Warren but the quickest way to find out is through the CI. I know the Feds are against that but I think they already blew their hand. Now it's our turn."

"Okay, let me think about that one," said Calhoun.

"Our problem is that Lugo might not talk to the CI about the Santos murder. Just in case, that's why I'd also like to get IAB's narcotics unit or Bronx Narcotics to try to make a drug case against Lugo. If we can buy weight from Lugo, he's more likely to flip. Either way, I'd also like to put up a pole camera at the spot where Lugo hangs out the most. Maybe we'll see something interesting, like who he hangs out with. Who knows, maybe even Warren might show up."

Calhoun nodded approval. "We could do the pole camera. Inspector Riordan, could you get in touch with Tech Services and tell them we want a pole camera at whatever location the lieutenant is able to come up with? We need it done ASAP. And let Chief Klein know as well."

Tynan took a deep breath, "I'm also going to order phone records on Santos and Lugo. I'd ask for a wire on Lugo but we don't have enough for that just yet."

Calhoun nodded. "Anything else?"

"We'll follow up on any leads that might develop from the canvass but I think getting that CI working for us is the key. In the meantime, we'll do a full workup on Warren with a lifestyle check and heavy surveillance. For that, I'm going to need the cooperation of the IAB surveillance unit. They have the people and the vehicles to do it. I'd also like to do an integrity test on him."

Riordan seemed to come to life for a moment. "An integrity test? What's the point of an integrity test? The murder investigation should be the focus."

Tynan didn't look at Riordan. He was just a loud fart in a bathroom stall. All wind, no action. "We will do an integrity test because if we get really lucky and he fails, then he's suspended, put on the fast track for termination, and when the murder charge comes down, he's an ex-police officer, not a current one."

"Yes, yes," said Calhoun as he turned to Riordan. "That's a very good idea. Notify the surveillance unit as well. They are completely at Tynan's disposal until further notice."

"Excellent. Good thinking, Tynan," added Riordan.

There was a knock at the door and in walked Deputy Chief Klein. Lieutenant Sullivan was two steps behind him, carrying the case folder. Calhoun waved both of them towards his desk. "Come on in, pull up some chairs, we were just going over Lieutenant Tynan's plans. He seems to have hit the ground running. Is that the case folder?"

"Yes, chief." Sullivan took a few cautious steps towards Tynan and held out the folder. "Here you go."

Tynan opened it and noticed that not a single worksheet had been added to the folder since it was dropped off. "Is everything in there?"

Sullivan, nodded and pulled up a chair. *This wasn't the ending she imagined when she took the case over*, thought Tynan.

Calhoun ran down the actions that Tynan had proposed. Klein sat and listened. He didn't look at Tynan and never acknowledged his presence.

"Chief, if I might make a suggestion," said Klein.

"Of course."

"I think it best if we resurrect the connection with the CI." He pointed to Tynan without looking at him, "He could do that by contacting the agent who brought him to our attention."

Calhoun nodded in agreement. "Yeah, I wasn't sure about that but I guess it's the way to go."

"Well, if there is nothing else that needs to be discussed, then I think we shouldn't delay the Lieutenant," said Klein, almost in a whisper. "He's a busy man and probably should be spending his time up in the Bronx bringing this case to a rapid close."

Tynan took the hint and stood. As he headed towards the door, he stopped and turned around. "Oh, I almost forgot chief. This case belongs to the Four-One Detective Squad. I think it would be best if we took over the case. I know I can't order them to give it up and we don't want to step on anyone's toes. Maybe you could talk to the Chief of Detectives and he could have them refer the case to us. This way we're not bumping into each other out there."

Tynan knew Klein wouldn't be able to let that go by without a comment. Klein finally turned in his chair and looked directly at Tynan. "Taking a case away from someone? I can't believe it. Didn't you sit here a week ago complaining about that very thing?"

Tynan wanted to run over and punch Klein in his smug face. Tynan knew that Klein had to give him some grief before he left the office. "Oh, that's quite a bit different Chief Klein."

"Different? How's it different?"

"I already talked to the lieutenant in the Detective Squad about this very thing and he'd be more than happy to give it up. I'd never suggest taking it away from him if he wanted his guys to run with it."

Klein turned back in his chair and looked at Calhoun. Calhoun just smiled and took another sip of coffee, "Don't worry about it, Lieutenant. I'll talk to the Chief of Detectives right after you're gone. The case will be handled by your Group. Thanks for coming down. I'd like daily updates on this case."

Tynan closed the door slowly behind him. As he walked towards the elevator with his case folder, he wondered what they were saying. He had scored some points against both Klein and Riordan and he knew they would remain his personal enemies. The case was back in his lap but Klein wasn't stupid. Tynan knew why Klein wanted him to get in touch with the CI. That way, their hands were clean. If the

Feds pitched a beef, they could deny they had anything to do with it. It would all be the fault of that rogue lieutenant up in the Bronx.

As he rode down in the elevator, Tynan thought about the CI. He'd get in touch with him, with or without the agent. Things were going to get complicated. He had his case back but the folder he had under his arm might as well have been a bomb. If he failed to wrap it up, it would be his fault, and how Santos got killed would be lost in the fog of Tynan's incompetence. He may have won the latest battle on the fourteenth floor but he might just lose the war. Solving this case was not only the right thing to do but the only thing to do, if Tynan wanted to save his career, if not his job.

When Tynan got back to the office it was empty. Everyone was out doing another canvass of the neighborhood. He hoped they'd come up with something because, as of now, they had nothing. With all the car services in the Bronx using black Lincolns, saying the getaway car was a Lincoln was like saying there's sand on the beach. He needed a lot more than that.

Tynan decided to try to go see the CI. Maybe he'd be lucky and he was still in the same place. If not, he would have to contact the agent. He'd have to be a little careful making that call. It would have to be from a pay phone and with someone else doing the talking. Tynan thought he was becoming paranoid, but the way this case was going, he didn't want to take more chances than absolutely necessary. He also didn't want to get the agent in trouble. "Nothing in this place is simple," mumbled Tynan.

He headed back over to the motel. This time he didn't care who saw him. Even Klein wanted Tynan to use the CI. That was the only downside he could see. If Klein recommended something, there was a catch. "You're losing it," said Tynan to himself as he walked towards the room. *Everything is not a set up*, he thought.

He knocked loudly on the door and waited. Angel's face peeked out from behind the curtain. He unbolted the door and pulled it open. "Hey. I wondered when you'd come back."

Tynan stepped in and looked around the room. No booze this time and no gun either. He gave Angel a quick scan, looking for the imprint of a gun under his shirt. He seemed clean. Tynan wasn't going to insult him by giving him a toss but the idea crossed his mind.

"Yep, I'm back. I think we've a lot of catching up to do. You look to be in better shape than the last time we met."

"I'm doing good but I have to get out of this place. It's driving me nuts."

"What happened to your gun?"

"Oh that. I got rid of it. I figure it might just be more trouble."

"Got rid of it. How'd you do that?"

Angel made a motion like he was tossing something, "In the river, man." He walked over to the edge of the bed and sat down. "I got some news too."

"What's that?" asked Tynan as he sat down in the same chair as last time.

"I got in touch with Lugo. Everything's cool. I told him I had to lay low for a while, to make sure nobody was following me. But you know what he told me?"

Tynan shook his head, no.

"Fucking Santos got popped. He's dead. I was all set to try and talk to Lugo about it, just in case you wanted me to meet him, and he told me that Santos got killed last night."

"When did he tell you this?"

"I called him again this morning around ten, just to stay in touch, and he told me."

"Does he know who did it?" asked Tynan.

"He didn't say, but he wouldn't tell me if he did."

"Did he say anything else?"

"Nah, it was pretty quick, you know. He doesn't like talking on the phone. Like I said before, Lugo's pretty smart."

"I'm sure he is," said Tynan. He pulled a notebook out of his jacket pocket. "What telephone number did you call Lugo at?"

"Oh, actually I beeped him and he called me here."

"Alright, then what's his beeper number?" snapped Tynan. Angel rattled the number off like it was his own. *That's interesting,* Tynan thought. *This guy must beep Lugo a lot.* He jotted it down with a question mark next to it.

Tynan stood up and walked over to the window. He pulled the curtain aside and looked out. "I'm thinking it's time for you to talk to Lugo about you and him doing some business."

"What kind of business?"

"You know, drug business. Like maybe you could introduce him to someone who might want to move some weight. Something like that."

"Hey, I'll help you out. I could see about doing that but first I'd have to meet Lugo alone. If I show up with some dude he's never seen before, he's going to know something's wrong. I could go alone, feel him out, and then maybe bring in someone else. He might be willing to do something like that. I could see Lugo wanting to move into Santos' spot right away. But I'd have to check him out first."

"Okay," said Tynan as he let go of the curtain and looked around the room. "I think it's time you moved out of this shit hole. We can set you up in an apartment. A place that nobody would think to look for you. Then from there we can see about you making a move with Lugo. What do you think about that? Are you up for that?"

"Sure, when?"

Tynan had studied the parking lot. There was nobody sitting in any of the cars. If he was going to make a move, this would be the time. "How about right now?"

Angel shrugged. "Okay, let me pack my shit. Should I say I'm checking out?"

"Who's paying for this dump?"

"Ain't me, bro."

"Nah, don't tell them you're leaving. We'll keep this place, just in case."

It didn't take Angel long to pack. Tynan still didn't see any gun. He wondered if Kurt had taken it from him. He didn't believe Angel threw it in the river. He'd sell it before he'd throw it away. Tynan was sure Angel loved money. When Angel had his gym bag packed,

Tynan opened the door and gestured towards the parking lot. "After you."

As Tynan walked into his office, Captain Rogan greeted him with a loud "There he is." He was rocking slowly back and forth in Tynan's chair. "I was wondering when you'd get back."

Tynan turned to Angel, "Why don't you go get some coffee in the breakroom." Angel nodded to Rogan, and stepped out. Tynan pointed Angel in the right direction, "It's down the hall to your right."

Tynan, closed the door and whispered to Rogan, "That's the CI." Then he picked up the phone and buzzed the administrative office. "Hey, I just sent an informant down to the breakroom. Could you keep an eye on him for me? Thanks." Tynan turned back towards Rogan.

"I heard you are back in the game," chuckled Rogan. "Good. It'll teach those shit-birds a lesson. They should have never taken you off the case. How's it going so far?"

"I was down at Headquarters earlier, talking to the chief."

"I heard. Heard you brought shit sandwiches for Klein and Riordan." Rogan slapped his thigh, laughing out loud.

"I don't know about that. But we got the case. The Four-One Squad is out. It's all ours."

"Of course it's all yours. This whole thing is a big stinking mess. You think they want that case sitting in their office. If this gets out, they could have a lot of explaining to do. Now that you got it, a little bit of the pressure is off them. If things don't work out, it's because you screwed up. See how that works?"

"I kind of got that feeling when I left. They aren't doing it because it's the right thing to do, they're doing it because it helps cover their asses and gives them a scapegoat."

Rogan nodded, the smile still on his face. "So, tell me what you got planned."

Tynan went back over what he had told the chief. As Rogan listened, his smile disappeared, replaced by a slight frown. His rocking back and forth in the chair slowed, and finally stopped. Tynan wasn't sure if Rogan approved or not, but he knew Rogan, would tell him if he thought he was going off the rails.

"That sounds pretty good. I see a couple of problems with it."

Tynan pulled up a chair and sat down. "Like what?"

"You have to get this CI to find out if Santos was killed on Warren's orders. Lugo may not want to talk about it. Then the CI is going to have to introduce one of our undercovers to buy weight off of Lugo, hoping he flips when he's charged with selling A-1 Felony weight. He might not."

"Yeah. I don't disagree with you on any of that," shrugged Tynan. "What other choice do I have?"

"Maybe your guys will come up with a witness on the canvass. That might take things in a different direction. If they get some leads, I'd let the drug angle go and just keep working it like a regular homicide. Get whoever shot Santos and they might flip on Warren. The shooter isn't going to take the fall all by himself."

Tynan nodded. "That would make things easier, but I don't want to wait. I want to go ahead with buying drugs from Lugo. If Warren takes the fall for drugs instead of a homicide, does it make a difference?"

Rogan shrugged. "No. He's gone one way or the other. If he was behind the shooting it would be nice to get him for that, but either way, he's off the job and in prison. Did the chief like your ideas?"

"He seemed to. He didn't say no to any of it."

"I'll bet he didn't." Rogan raised his eyebrows. "Do you think he'd rather Warren goes for the drugs or the murder?"

"Drugs. No doubt about it. Murder is a lot worse. Bad publicity. Not that a cop being involved in drugs is good publicity but it's happened before. Murder, that's a tough one. People might start asking questions and it could lead to some embarrassing answers," said Tynan.

Rogan stood up and slowly nodded his head. "It sure could. Something to keep in mind. If you have any questions or problems, you know where to find me. Good luck."

Rogan left. Tynan liked talking to him. He thought Rogan had a lot of insight into the politics of the job. He'd been around longer and he knew that just doing your job wasn't always enough. The political angle was always in play, maybe not in the street but certainly down at the Palace.

He was about to head down the hall to find the CI when suddenly there were a lot of voices and footsteps as people came through the front door. The teams had returned.

Joe, Linda, and Russell barged into his office. Tynan transferred over to his usual seat, vacated by Rogan. He tried to read their faces but couldn't. "So, what gives?"

Linda and Joe sat down, while Russell stood, leaning on the filing cabinet as usual. Linda motioned to Joe to go first.

Joe flipped through his notebook. "We covered six buildings. Almost all of it was a goose egg. Nothing. But we did get some info. We talked to the woman who called 911. She saw a black Lincoln driving away from the scene. She heard the shots but by the time she got to the window it was all over, nothing new there. A lot of other people heard shots too but they were either asleep and were woken up by the shots or they were awake and too slow getting to the window. The number of shots heard varies from two to four."

"Come on, you're burying the lead," said Linda as she rolled her eyes and smacked Joe's arm with her notebook.

"You'll love this," chuckled Joe. "Remember the guy who was standing there the night we went and saw Santos?"

"Yeah, I saw him again too," said Tynan. "He's hiding in that first-floor apartment."

"Exactly. He said he saw you this morning, even showed me your card. Then he added some things that he left out when he was talking to you."

"Some things?"

"Like the fact that he was standing outside when the black Lincoln pulled up. Like the fact that when the car pulled up, someone in the back seat rolled down the window and stuck a badge out the window."

"Someone in the car tinned them when they were on the stoop?" asked Tynan. He sat up straight and leaned forward. He had hoped Jaime would change his mind but he didn't think it would be this fast.

"That's not all. Santos told him to go inside. By the time he goes inside and gets to the window, the guy in the back seat is out of the car and standing beside Santos. That guy pulls out a gun and shoots Santos three times while he's sitting on the steps. When Santos falls back, the guy leans down and puts one more in Santos' head for good measure."

"That's a lot different than what he told me this morning."

"Yeah, well I guess he had a 'come to Jesus' moment after your little chat earlier."

Then Joe leaned in towards Tynan and whispered. "He can ID the shooter."

"Why didn't you say so at the start, instead of all the bullshit? Where is he now?"

Russell spoke up for the first time. "Two of my guys took him over to Bronx Homicide to look at some pictures. That's where they are now."

"Did he see the driver of the car?"

"No and he's not sure if there was anyone else in the car besides the driver and the shooter."

"Alright, let's see if he can pick out the shooter. In the meantime, start writing up those worksheets. I think we have a long night ahead of us."

The three of them got up and left the office. Tynan slowly walked to the window. He looked out at the sailboats. Things were beginning to look up. This case might go a lot quicker than he thought.

Tynan didn't want to go home until he heard from Russell's guys about whether or not Jaime could identify the shooter. He knew of a lot of cases where people said they could identify a perpetrator until they actually sat down in front of the computer screen and started flipping through pictures. It was amazing how many people actually looked alike.

If this guy could pick out the shooter, then things were going to get busy very fast. Rather than go through worksheets, Tynan picked up the phone and called Sergeant McCarthy.

Tynan knew he could trust McCarthy. He also knew that IAB was not a big fan of bringing in outside units. They liked to think they could do it all on their own. The IAB narcotics unit operated citywide. Bronx Narcotics knew the Bronx. They knew the players and Tynan figured they could swing into action a lot sooner.

"Sergeant McCarthy."

"It's your favorite cheese eater," said Tynan.

"We have to stop talking to each other so much. People might get the wrong idea. Like I work for you."

"You should be so lucky," chuckled Tynan. "I have a big favor to ask and you will probably need to clear it with your bosses."

"Okay, what is it?"

"I need you to put some drug buys into a guy we're looking at. This guy might be connected to a homicide in the Four-One."

"Sounds like you guys are doing real police work. What? Did you catch all the dirty cops or are you tired of swimming in the gutter?" asked McCarthy.

"Nah, we're still in the gutter, and that's where the secret part comes in. This guy we're looking at is not only a possible subject in a homicide, but supposedly the guy who ordered the homicide is a cop."

"Get the fuck out of here," whispered McCarthy.

"Nope, that's what this is all about. I can meet you and give you more details. This dealer is named Sammy Lugo. Supposedly he's a player, so you probably know him already."

"I can meet you tonight if you want. Let me see, how about eight? Does that work? I can come over there or you can come over here, whatever works."

"How about you swing by our office? Who knows, maybe you'll like it so much, you'll leave narco and come over to the dark side," said Tynan.

"I doubt it but I'll see you then."

That was the easy part, thought Tynan. If the bosses went along, that was another story. McCarthy's bosses might balk because they were already up to their eyeballs in cases, and Tynan knew his bosses wouldn't like letting Narcotics into their world. *Too bad,* he thought. *If they hadn't screwed it all up to begin with, this wouldn't have to happen.*

The phone rang and Tynan picked up on the first ring. "Group 41, Lieutenant Tynan."

"This is Deputy Chief Klein."

Tynan had grown to detest Klein's voice. He had a calm, smug way of speaking. It was as if Klein thought he was doing you a favor by acknowledging your existence.

"Yes, chief?"

"I'd like to know what is going on so I can brief the chief. Hopefully, you have made some progress since our meeting."

Tynan loved the way Klein wanted the info first so he could brown-nose Calhoun. The other part of the message was the snide way he implied that Tynan needed to act more quickly. Tynan had just talked with Klein a few hours earlier. How much did he think had happened?

"We had positive results on the second canvass. We found someone who can 'ID' the shooter. The witness is a drug guy. He is probably the muscle for Santos, so his world is in flux right now. Losing your boss to a shooter isn't exactly a selling point in the bodyguard business. He's going through pictures, and if we get a hit, we'll go out and pick that guy up."

"That's good. Let me know right away if he picks someone out. Anything else?"

"Yeah, we've been in touch with the CI. We're planning on making an intro to Lugo. Best case scenario, Lugo incriminates himself. Worse case, we have to do a drug buy into Lugo and get some weight on him, hoping he'll flip. I've reached out to Bronx Narcotics already. They are going to run it up their chain of command."

There was a long silence on the other end. Tynan knew what Klein was thinking. Would working with Narcotics on an IAB case hurt or help his career? Finally, Klein said, "Okay, I guess you have to do what you have to do. Not a big fan of this. Why not use our own guys?"

"I will if the Bronx balks at the idea. I know the sergeant involved. I've worked with him before."

Klein let out a long sigh, "Working with someone in the past is not the same as now. If you swear by him that's fine, but I just want you to know if anything leaks out or the case goes sideways, it's your ass."

"My ass? If things don't work out, it'll be more than just my ass," said Tynan.

Klein ignored the remark. "Tech Services and the surveillance unit have been told you have a top priority case. Pole cameras, any technical support you need, you have. You are to keep me in the loop." Klein hung up.

"Keep you in the loop. I'll keep you in the loop, you fucking douchebag," said Tynan as he slammed down the phone. It was

Klein's attitude that annoyed Tynan the most. Klein believed he was the smartest man in the department. *It's always a problem when you start believing your own bullshit*, thought Tynan.

The phone rang again. Before Tynan could even speak the voice on the phone said, "Lou, you know what they say about pictures and a thousand words. We got a positive ID on the shooter. We're coming back to the office with the witness. He's got a lot to tell you."

"That's good, I'll be here." The voice on the phone hung up without identifying himself. It was one of Russell's guys. Good thing Tynan stayed around. He pushed the thoughts about his two kids to the back of his mind. He missed them but he needed to stay focused. This was going to be a long night. He looked at his watch. He still had plenty of time to get a line on this suspect before he met with McCarthy.

Tynan had the CI moved to another office. He didn't want the witness seeing the CI. The less each one knew, the better. Tynan was pacing back and forth by the time his star witness arrived. Patience was not one of his virtues. Sometimes Tynan wondered if he had any virtues at all.

Russell stuck his head in the door, "I put the witness in the interview room."

"Good," said Tynan. "As for our witness, be polite but let's not forget what he really is."

"What's that, Lou?"

"A drug dealing piece of shit," said Tynan. "Let's go see what he has to say. Can you gather up Linda and Joe?"

"Sure boss," said Russell as he disappeared from the doorway. Tynan made his way down the hallway to the interview room. Like all interview rooms it was bare bones. Table, chairs, blank walls, and the chair being used by the witness or subject was a little shorter than the others. Tynan wasn't sure if that trick made people feel inferior or if they even noticed.

As he put his hand on the door, he was joined by Linda, Joe, and Russell. He opened the door and saw Jaime sitting in the short chair. He was talking with one of Russell's guys. The detective was doing his best to keep Jaime entertained.

Russell walked over and placed his hand on the detective's shoulder, "Thanks Felix, why don't you give us some room in here?" The detective nodded, and walked out. Linda and Joe pulled up the two chairs and sat down across from the witness. Russell and Tynan remained standing with their backs to the door.

Tynan started. "I heard you identified the shooter. How sure are you?"

"Totally. He's the guy. I don't forget a face. I saw him when he pulled up in the car and then I saw him from the apartment window. Besides, I've seen him around. I don't know his name but I know who he works for."

"It was pretty dark," said Tynan. "Maybe you didn't get a good view of him."

"Are you shitting me?" scoffed Jaime. "The dude killed my boss right in front of me. I don't forget something like that. There's plenty of light there. The light in the apartment was off, so I could see everything from the lights on the street."

"Okay," said Linda. "Where have you seen him before?"

"You know. He works for your boy."

"What boy?" asked Joe sharply.

"You know, Warren, the cop?"

"How do you know that?" asked Tynan.

Jaime, sat back in the chair and held his hands out in front of him. "Come on man, what is this? Some fucking game? You know. I didn't want to bring it up at first but this guy who did the shooting works for Warren."

"You said he had a shield, a badge. Is he a cop?" asked Linda.

"No, I think maybe he was a cop once. I asked Santos about him and he just laughed and said something like 'he thinks he's a cop' or 'he was a cop' something like that."

"Tell us what you know about Lugo and Warren?" said Linda.

"Why am I telling you shit that you already know?"

"Just do it for my sake," said Linda softly.

Jaime let out a long sigh and rubbed his hands through his hair. "Okay, I'll tell you what I know. Santos was in the game a long time. Sometimes he does business with Lugo. They are not working together all the time but Lugo will sell stuff to Santos if he's short. Now, according to Santos, he told me Warren caught Lugo with a couple of keys of coke a few years ago. Lugo had it in his car and

Warren and his partner jumped him. But instead of arresting him, they let Lugo keep the coke and Warren took the money. That's how the two cops started in the business."

"What business?" asked Linda as she scratched out some notes on a pad.

"The coke business. What do you think? It all started from that one time. After that day, Lugo and Warren were in it together. Warren helps Lugo move his drugs. They follow Lugo or one of his guys from one place to another if they got money or coke to move. This way Lugo doesn't get hassled by the cops and nobody is going to rip him off with a police car behind him."

Joe leaned over and put his face right up to Jaime's. "You mean Warren is working in uniform in a police car, escorting Lugo when he moves his drugs?"

"You got that right. That's not all he does. He gets a cut of what Lugo makes, and from what Santos said, sometimes Warren gives him stuff to sell. He also runs off anybody who wants to compete with Lugo, takes their drugs and gives it to Lugo."

Joe sat back in his chair. "How do you know all this?"

"Because Santos told me and I know the guy who shot my boss worked with Lugo and Warren."

Linda stopped writing. "Who's in charge?" she asked. "Does Lugo work for Warren or does Lugo pay Warren?"

"Hey, Lugo definitely pays Warren, but I don't know if I would say he is in charge. They just got a thing going. They both make money, so they are cool with it."

"Did your boss, Santos, pay off Warren?" asked Tynan as he folded his arms.

"My boss was smart. Warren gave Lugo some stuff to move and Lugo dumped it off on Santos. He sold it and paid Lugo but wouldn't give Warren his cut. That's when Warren came around asking for his share. Santos told him to fuck off. I know that for a fact because Santos told me Lugo was an asshole for paying Warren."

Linda started writing again. "Why was he an asshole?"

"Simple. Lugo had as much shit on Warren as Warren had on him. If Warren busted Lugo all he had to do was tell his lawyer that Warren was dirty. That's why Santos thought Lugo was dumb. When Warren came around asking for his share, Santos told him no. Warren didn't like that."

Joe stood up. "Were you there when Warren asked for his cut?"

"No, Santos told me. But the guy who did the shooting came by a couple of times asking for Warren's money. So, I know that shit is real. Santos told him to get lost. That's when he said something about the guy being an ex-cop or thought he was a cop. Something like that."

"Okay," said Joe. "Did Warren come around asking for money or the guy who shot your boss?"

Jaime shook his head. He cupped both of his ears with his hands and let out a low groan. "I told you that Santos told me that Warren asked him for money but I wasn't there. But I was there when the guy who shot him asked for Warren's money."

Linda tapped her finger on the table. "How do you know he was asking for money for Warren?"

"Because he said so. He said, 'Where's Warren's money?'"

Linda continued. "How long has Santos been refusing to pay Warren?"

"About two weeks or so. That's how I know Santos was going to call you guys. He told the guy who shot him that he'd turn Warren in if he didn't shut up about the money. Like I said, I was there when that happened."

Tynan leaned over and put his hands on the table. He looked at Jaime. "Okay, that's terrific, but we can't do much with that. We need proof. We need you to help us set Warren up. Can you go to Lugo and see if you can find out when they are moving product again and if Warren will be coming along?"

Jaime shrugged. "I'll go to him and tell him I can run Santos' old spot for him. That will get me in tight with him. Then I might be able to set something up. But first, I'd have to go and check Lugo out. See what he's planning to do."

"When can you do that, and where are you going to meet him?" asked Tynan.

"How about tomorrow? I'll go over there and talk about doing business and see what he says. He's usually around Fox and Longwood. He lives right there at 811 Fox Street."

Joe and Linda looked at Tynan. Linda nodded. Joe shrugged and said, "Might as well, got nothing to lose."

"Okay, Jaime. Thanks for your help today. We'll see you back here tomorrow at noon." Tynan opened the door. "Do you need a ride somewhere?"

"Nah, I'm good," said Santos. "I always find my way. See you tomorrow." He got up and Linda followed him to the front door. Tynan heard it slam. When Linda came back in, she looked at Tynan and said, "What do you think about all this?"

Tynan shook his head. "Honestly, I don't know. I don't trust any of these fucks but we got to run with what we got. Hopefully he will be able to slide in with Lugo and link us to Warren. In the meantime, we need to work up this guy that Jaime identified."

Joe said, "Come on Linda, let's get to work on the shooter and see what we come up with. Maybe we'll get lucky and pick him up tonight." He turned to Tynan and asked, "Would that be a problem boss? Overtime-wise, I mean."

"Are you kidding? As they say, money's no object. Until we get this wrapped up the overtime window is open. By the way, one of Russell's guys is babysitting the CI in an office. Peek in on him and see if he's happy. I want to see if we can set up a call at least between the CI and Lugo."

"You going to be hanging out, Lou?" asked Linda.

Tynan sighed. He thought about his wife and kids but knew they would have to wait. Again. "Yeah, I'll be hanging out. You guys work that suspect up and I'll meet with Bronx Narcotics to see what they can do for us."

"What can I do, Lou?" asked Russell.

"Before narco gets here, bring that CI, Angel, down to the hello phone. Hook it up and we'll see about him making a call to Lugo."

Russell hurried to the door, saying, "You got it."

Tynan stood there for a moment, thinking to himself. He felt alert and refreshed, the thrill of the chase was kicking in. He hoped it would carry him through the night. They had a lot of plates in the air but it was better than a bunch of dead ends.

It didn't take Russell long to set things up. He yelled down the hallway to Tynan, letting him know they were ready. Tynan entered the room. Angel was sitting there smoking. Tynan thought he looked a little nervous.

"He's got something to tell you," said Russell.

"What's up?" asked Tynan.

"Listen bro, I am down with helping you out but I don't like this call thing. I want to meet with Lugo first and feel him out. I think me calling would make him suspicious."

"You've called him before, what's the problem with one more phone call?" asked Tynan.

Angel took a deep drag on his cigarette. "I don't know. I would just feel better if I did it in person, you know and no wire."

Tynan wasn't sure why Angel was suddenly nervous. He said he had called earlier. Now, it looked like he was backing off. Tynan had worked with CIs and undercovers before. Usually, he sent them out wired. The wire was good because you had the perp's own words on tape, but sometimes the subject was raised up, nervous, and looking for a wire. In those cases, Tynan wouldn't push it. If the subject found the wire, things could get ugly fast. He looked at Angel. Was he for real or was he playing a game? Tynan wasn't sure.

"So, when do you want to meet him?"

"Tomorrow, I'll just run into him on the street. If he gets suspicious, he'll look for a wire but if I don't have one, then everything's good. I think it will work better that way. He doesn't say much on the phone anyway. You've heard him. He's slick. He doesn't trust the phone."

Tynan wasn't sure. If he pushed the phone call and Lugo became suspicious, then the CI was useless to him. If he let Angel do it his way, then Tynan felt like he was losing control. He was letting the CI call the shots, something Tynan didn't believe in. Having Angel walk up on Lugo without a wire might work to their advantage if Lugo gave him a toss. Maybe, Angel was right.

"Okay, we'll do it your way for now. But we're going to put you up in an apartment we have. Then tomorrow, we're going to drop you off to meet Lugo."

"I can find Lugo on my own. He's over on Fox Street. I don't need you guys to bring me there."

"We're not going to drop you off in front of his house in a marked police car. We'll let you out a couple of blocks away. We want to be nearby if something goes wrong."

"What are you going to do if something goes wrong? Call an ambulance? If something goes wrong, I'm dead whether you're there or not."

"We're looking out for you. That's why I want to put you up in one of our places and we'll drive you back and forth," said Tynan sharply. He was losing patience with Angel.

Angel took one last puff on his cigarette and stomped it out on the linoleum floor. He looked at Tynan with tired eyes. "I want some money for this. I'm not working for nothing and I don't need a bunch of cops following me around either. I'll stay with my girlfriend. I'll be fine. I just need you to give me a ride. She lives on Stratford Avenue. You can pick me up there tomorrow with the cash."

"Agreed. I'll get you a thousand when we pick you up tomorrow. If things work out there'll be more money," said Tynan.

Angel stood up and offered Tynan his hand. Tynan shook it and said, "Okay, you got a deal."

Tynan turned to Russell and motioned for Russell to follow him outside. When the door closed, Tynan whispered, "Give him a ride but make sure our witness isn't hanging around in the parking lot before you put him in the car. Tomorrow, you can pick him up. He'll get the money after he meets with Lugo, not before."

"Why is he acting so nervous all of a sudden?" asked Russell.

"I don't know. Maybe after Santos got killed, he realized this isn't a game. The meeting with Lugo might be the last thing he does."

"Is that why you're going to pay him after the meeting?" said Russell with a chuckle.

"The thought didn't cross my mind but now that you mention it." Tynan shrugged. "No sense wasting a thousand dollars."

After Russell left with Angel, Tynan went back to his office. Angel not wanting to talk to Lugo on the phone had let the wind out of his sails. The phone call had a lot of potential and Tynan had an uneasy feeling about Angel becoming nervous. A CI starting to dictate terms was not a good thing. He mulled it over in his mind. Was there something he wasn't seeing?

His thoughts were interrupted when Joe and Linda barged into his office. Joe snickered. "This case just gets weirder and weirder."

"Before you go off on another tangent, I'm having Russell and his guys take the CI down to his girlfriend's apartment on Stratford. We'll pick him up tomorrow to meet Lugo but he won't wear a wire. Plus, he wouldn't make the call to Lugo. He's getting nervous."

"Fuck him," said Linda. "He'll do what he's told."

"Yeah, yeah. Normally I would agree with you but right now he's the only connection we have to Lugo so I'll give him a little play."

"You're the boss," said Linda as she and Joe sat down.

"In the meantime," said Joe, "guess who our shooter is?"

"Come on, I don't have time for forty questions Joe, just tell me."

Joe put a central booking photo of the suspect on Tynan's desk and right next to it, a police identification picture of the same guy. "None other than former police officer Richard Kearns."

"Get the fuck out of here," whispered Tynan. All the doubts about Angel were swept from his mind as Tynan picked up both pictures. The two photos showed a white male in his early twenties, with a clean-shaven, ruddy face and close-cropped brown hair.

Joe laughed. "Yep. Mr. Kearns was for a brief moment one of New York's Finest. He was put into the academy class two years ago. Right after he got his gun and shield, he thought it would be a good idea to get shit-faced in a bar, start a fight, and fire a shot."

Linda sat there, shaking her head. "That's generally frowned upon in the academy."

"Anyway," continued Joe, "he got arrested, charged with assault and reckless endangerment, and was fired from the job. He was about a month from graduating. He never did a day on the street. Turns out he never did a day in jail either. He copped out to simple assault and got probation."

"Looks like Jaime was right," said Tynan. "He's a wannabe cop. I think that best describes Richard's tenure with the PD. Do we have his address?"

"According to his record, he lives with his mom in Woodlawn. Don't know if he's still there but that's the last address," said Linda. "I made a quick phone call to the group in Manhattan that had this case and someone there remembered it. They thought this guy wasn't long for the job anyway. In their words, if it wasn't this it would have been something else. Not the sharpest knife in the drawer."

Joe picked up the photos from Tynan's desk. "What do you want to do boss?"

Tynan thought about it for a moment. He remembered Rogan's advice about taking the fastest route to wrap up the case, but he also remembered the Palace would probably prefer if Warren took a fall for narcotics rather than murder.

"I think we go out tonight and pay him a visit," said Tynan.

"Do you think we should jump on it right away like that?" asked Linda. "Maybe we should wait and see how the CI pans out with Lugo. If Kearns is the shooter, he's not going to be able to walk away from a murder no matter who he gives up."

"True," said Tynan. "But if Warren asked him or, better yet, paid him to do it, I'd bet he'll roll for some time off his sentence."

Linda shifted in her chair. She was trying to get both of her feet to touch the floor but without much success. "He's not going anywhere. We know who he is and right now he doesn't think we're after him. If the CI works his magic with Lugo, we could wrap up Warren that way and then still take this guy later."

"Yeah," said Joe, "I think we play both angles. We get Kearns, and, if he cooperates, fine. If not, then we use the CI to get to Warren through Lugo. Plus, I don't think Warren is going to stop riding shotgun for Lugo's drug shipments just because Kearns gets picked up."

Tynan leaned back in his chair. He wanted to take Kearns tonight. If he cooperated, he might be able to make a phone call to Warren. Get Warren to talk about the hit on Santos, and then the case was over. Warren would be gone and the Santos murder would be solved.

"I don't know," said Tynan as he looked at the ceiling. "I can't see leaving this guy out there if we know who he is and where he lives. If he's capable of killing one guy, who's to say he's not going to shoot someone else? Maybe Santos was just the first of many. We don't know for sure. I say we go out looking for Kearns and if we find him bring him in and take a run at him. If he clams up, we've solved one homicide but keep going after Warren. After all, this case was stopped once already and someone wound up dead."

"All right, Lou," said Joe, "sounds like a plan. Are you ready for an all-nighter, Linda?"

Linda sighed, "At this point, I just want it to go away. Could we talk Lieutenant Sullivan into taking the case back? Just kidding."

Tynan picked up the phone and dialed McCarthy's number. Jimmy picked it up on the first ring.

"Must be a slow night in narco land if you can pick up the phone that quick."

"Ah, it's my favorite Lieutenant," said McCarthy.

"I'm waiting for your arrival with bated breath. I've got a lot to share with you. Can you move things up and come over earlier?"

"I'm on my way," said McCarthy and he hung up.

Tynan turned back to Linda and Joe. "Put some folders together on Kearns. Picture, residence, cars in his name, phone numbers, you know the drill. When Russell gets back, we'll go out looking for Mr. Kearns."

"You got it boss," said Joe. "Come on Linda, let's kill some trees."

"Okay, but I still like my idea better."

SETTING THE STAGE

It was seven o'clock when McCarthy walked into Tynan's office. The brown haired, blue eyed, tall, lanky sergeant looked like he just got out of high school. He could have easily walked around a campus as a student. Tynan thought looking so young was an asset in the narcotics world. McCarthy could stroll onto any drug set, looking like some college student eager to score coke, weed or whatever else was being sold.

"Pull up a chair," said Tynan

McCarthy closed the door and sat down. "This place isn't bad. You have a nice view of the Sound, meanwhile we're stuck in an old phone company building with no windows."

"Yeah, it's one of the many benefits to working the dark side."

"Nice," snickered Jimmy. "Better you than me. So, what do you have in mind. Right up front I have to tell you I can't make any promises. I'll have to run it by my bosses. I'm not sure if they want us spending our time on this. We got a shit-pot full of cases and every Detective Squad in the Bronx is asking us for help on their homicides. I don't think you guys will be high up on the priority list."

"Don't worry about that," said Tynan. "The brass at the Palace can pull a few strings if I ask. Let's say they have a personal interest in this."

"I'll take your word for it."

Tynan was going to take another chance tonight. He didn't like the way he had dealt with the Four-One Detective Squad Lieutenant. That guy gave him all the help he asked for, and in return, Tynan had left him out in the cold. He wasn't going to do that with McCarthy. They had a history together and Tynan trusted him. He decided to let McCarthy in on everything.

Tynan told him about the two cops in the Four-One who might be involved and even rehashed his meeting with the Feds, being thrown off the case, and the shooting of Santos. McCarthy sat there and said nothing. It took Tynan about fifteen minutes to go over everything and lay out his plan to use the CI and the witness. McCarthy nodded as Tynan explained how he wanted to get to Warren through Lugo.

When Tynan finished, he shrugged his shoulders and said, "What do you think?"

"I think it's the most fuck-upped story I've ever heard on this job. Sounds like you got a blank check from the powers that be. That is both good and bad. Good in that whatever you ask for you'll probably get, and bad because if you don't wrap this up in a nice, neat package with a pretty bow, you know you're going under the bus."

"That goes without saying. I think I have a few enemies down in the Palace."

"I can work with you on trying to buy into Lugo. Either the CI or the witness could make an intro for one of our undercovers and we'd go from there. Once we have his confidence, we can order a lot of coke and see if Warren provides the escort. Lot of possibilities with using those two. The only question is how reliable are they."

"The CI is good, according to the Feds," said Tynan. "I can't say he's done anything on his own to steer us wrong. Him refusing to make the call to Lugo is the first time he's balked. As for the witness," said Tynan with a sigh, "he's your typical drug guy, but he thinks he can meet up with Lugo at Fox and Longwood."

McCarthy tapped his fingers on the arm of the chair. "How about we go with the intro into Lugo using the CI? If we could get that off the ground tomorrow, it would be good. I'd rather work with him."

"We'll have to wait and see how the meeting between Lugo and Jaime goes tomorrow. Like I said, he won't wear a wire and he wants the first meeting to be solo. Neither the CI nor Jaime will be wired for their first meeting. The up side is, if we send Jaime in first, he might get a feeling if the federal CI is compromised. No sense getting the Fed's CI blown away by sending him into a meeting that's destined to go bad."

McCarthy nodded. "That's not a bad idea. Jaime's meeting would give us an idea of where they both stand. Having Santos out of the picture might actually help us make a drug deal."

"How so?"

"Look at it from Lugo's angle. Santos was an occasional, half-assed business partner. He wasn't competition. Now he's dead and that spot is open. If Lugo doesn't jump in to fill that void with someone, there are plenty of others who will. Then Lugo is shut out. If he's smart, he could take over that spot and put your witness, Jaime, in there to run it for him. If he doesn't act someone else will. It's a tough world out there."

"Yeah, I can see that. I wonder if Lugo has other people on his hit list."

"How fast can you get those pole cameras up if we need them?" asked McCarthy.

"I can get it done within a day. Last resort we can park a vehicle on the street with a camera in it. I wouldn't want to use a surveillance van at that location because they'd probably spot it right away."

McCarthy shook his head from side to side. "Definitely not a surveillance van. How about you call me tomorrow, right after he meets with Lugo, and we'll set something up? I'll let my lieutenant and captain know and get back to you."

Tynan stood up. He walked McCarthy to the door and stuck his hand out, "I really appreciate this, Jimmy. I need someone I can trust." They walked down the hallway towards the front door, in silence. Tynan held the door open and, as McCarthy stepped through, he patted Tynan on the shoulder.

"Don't worry, this will work out. Besides, what's the worst that can happen? You get thrown out of this place."

Tynan smirked, "Worst? Nah, getting thrown out of here is on the list of good things that can happen. You don't want to see the list with the bad things." The door closed as McCarthy disappeared down the stairs.

LOOKING FOR A WANNABE

Tynan decided it was time to bring in some other units in IAB to help out with this case. Up until now, his group had been a one-man band. He called Tech Services. They would be the first group to help share the pain. The sergeant at Tech Services told him they could have a camera at Fox and Longwood operational within twenty-four hours. Deputy Chief Klein had called them personally and told them that Tynan's case was a top priority.

His next call was to IAB's surveillance unit. They had the personnel and vehicles to do long term surveillance on the targets without being made. It might not be bad to have them available for the meetings tomorrow, just in case things went sour. Klein had called there too and the lieutenant who answered the phone was eager to help. *Having chiefs in your corner sure makes things go smoother,* thought Tynan. The surveillance unit would provide whatever units he needed.

The worst of the calls he saved for last. He had to update Klein and Calhoun. He figured he'd make the call to Klein first and maybe, being the professional suck ass that he was, Klein would insist on making the call to Chief Calhoun himself. It was worth a shot.

Tynan reluctantly dialed Klein. "Chief Klein," came the voice on the other end of the phone. From the noise in the background, it was obvious he was home. *That's where I'd like to be,* thought Tynan.

"Hi chief. Tynan with an update."

"Go ahead," said Klein as the sound of the television in the background dropped off.

"We're taking a run at Lugo tomorrow using the CI and the witness. The witness picked out the shooter who is an ex-cop named Richie Kearns. Kearns was fired when he was still in the academy after getting into a bar room brawl where he fired a shot. We're going out to pick him up tonight and see if he's interested in cooperating."

Tynan waited for a reaction from Klein. Nothing happened. Tynan continued. "If Kearns won't help, then maybe either the CI or the witness can get Lugo to implicate himself or Warren. If he doesn't say anything, then the CI can introduce an undercover from Bronx Narcotics to make cocaine buys from Lugo. Tomorrow, we'll have Tech Services do a site survey for cameras, and the surveillance unit will help us out with the Lugo meetings."

There was a long pause on the phone. Finally, Klein let out a sigh. "I told you I wasn't a fan of bringing in Narcotics on this."

Tynan wanted to slam the phone down. All that work and the only thing Klein could say was that he wasn't a fan. *Fuck you,* thought Tynan as he tapped his pen on the desk.

"Do you want to update Chief Calhoun or should I?"

"No," said Klein. "I'll do it. I can explain it better." Klein hung up the phone without waiting for a response from Tynan.

Tynan went over his plan for tomorrow. He wanted to be sure he wasn't missing anything. There were a lot of things that could go wrong, and he knew Klein was waiting in the wings, hoping Tynan screwed it up. It was nearly eight o'clock by the time Linda and Joe came back into his office with folders on Kearns.

"How many people are we going to use on this?" asked Joe.

"I figure it will be you two, me, and Russell. Speaking of Russell," Tynan reached picked up the phone and buzzed his office. "Hey Russ, come down here. You're going to help find the shooter."

When Russell walked into the office, Tynan asked, "What did you do with your guys?"

"I sent them home, Lou. I figured we're going to need some well rested people out there tomorrow."

"Good," said Tynan. "While you were out dropping off the CI, Joe and Linda came up with some interesting information on the shooter. Why don't you fill him in, Joe?"

"Before you start," said Russell, "Angel said he didn't need a ride tomorrow, he'd get here on his own. He swore he'd be here because he needs the money. He told me to tell you that you better have the grand."

They all laughed. "I better have the money? This guy has got some balls. He better be here!"

"I think for a grand he'll definitely be here," chuckled Joe.

Tynan nodded. "Hopefully, we pick this guy up tonight. We'll take two cars. Russ, you are with me and the dynamic duo will be by themselves. Got his info, Linda?"

"Yep." She handed Russell a folder with Kearn's information. "We'll head to his mom's house. She lives in the Bronx at 4319 Katonah Avenue."

"Alright, let's go see the wizard," said Tynan.

Traffic was light as they headed out. Tynan drove. It helped keep his mind off things. The two cars turned into the block where Kearns lived. It was quiet. People were either sitting in their living rooms watching TV or getting ready for tomorrow's daily grind. Kearns lived in a red brick private house, jammed between two identical houses.

The four of them got out. "Okay, Russ and Linda, you stay out here," Tynan said. "If our guy starts to run out the back, head down the alley and cut him off. Me and Joe will go in the front. Maybe he's sitting there with his feet up."

Joe and Tynan went up the steps, two at a time, as Linda and Russ positioned themselves to watch the side alleys. Joe knocked on the door and pressed the buzzer. The lights were on and Tynan could see the glow of a TV coming from one of the windows. Joe pressed the buzzer again. "Come on, answer the fucking door," he muttered.

The light on the front porch went on, as well as a hallway light. Tynan saw an older woman trudging towards the door. She looked out one of the side windows framing the door and Tynan flashed his shield at her. A couple of dead bolts later, and the door opened. A woman in her fifties peeked out. She wore a battered blue bathrobe and her hair was wrapped in a towel.

"Hello, Mrs. Kearns. I'm Lieutenant Tynan and this is Sergeant Spano. We were hoping to speak with your son, Richard. Is he at home?"

"No, he's not here. He's at his girlfriend's house. I am not sure when or if he'll be coming home. Why do you want to see him?" asked the woman with a heavy Irish brogue.

"We'd like to talk to him about something he might have witnessed. He might be able to help us with a case."

The woman leaned against the door jamb. She looked sad. "Is he in trouble?"

"Oh, you have nothing to be worried about," said Joe. "We just want to talk to him."

"I hope so. You know he's been trying to keep on the straight and narrow after he got thrown out of the cops. That wasn't him doing those things. It was the drink. If he stayed away from the booze, he'd be fine. That's what causes it."

"Isn't that true for us all?" said Tynan with a smile.

"He's been listening to his cousin. He's kept him under his wing since that time two years ago."

"That's good. Good to have a role model," said Joe as he looked around. Tynan could see Joe was getting impatient.

"Yes, he wanted to be like his cousin. He's a cop too."

Tynan shifted his weight, hoping to ease the pain in his back. "Where does his cousin work?"

"He works here in the Bronx. Not here, but down in the Forty-First precinct."

He forgot about his back pain. "Really, in the Forty-First? Isn't that something?"

"Yes, he's been there for several years now."

"I know a lot of cops in the Forty-First," lied Tynan. "What's his cousin's name?"

"Peter Warren. Do you know Peter? He's the nicest young man."

It was all Tynan could do to not yell out, 'Are you shitting me?!' Instead, he just smiled and shook his head "No, it doesn't ring a bell."

Joe looked at Tynan. He turned back to the woman in the doorway. "Do you know where his girlfriend lives? What's her name? Anything like that?"

"Oh, let me see." She pulled her bathrobe tighter and adjusted the towel on her head. "Her name is Sarah. I don't know her last name. Let me think. I'm not positive, but she lives at either 3200 or 3300 Bainbridge Avenue. I'm pretty sure. Maybe apartment 4. It used to be a nice neighborhood, not so much anymore. Richie called me around seven and said he was going over there right after work."

"Where does he work?" asked Joe.

"It's a terrible job," said the woman, and she shook her head so hard, Tynan thought her towel would fall off. "He works in one of those scrap-yard places on Garrison Avenue. You know, where they take cars apart. Terrible work. But he makes good money at it."

"Do you know the name of the place?"

"I think it's called 'Vic's.' I know it's down on Garrison Avenue. He works long hours. He's there all hours of the day and night. Tonight, when he called, he said he was leaving soon, so I'm sure he's out of there by now."

"Well, we're sorry to bother you, and we'll go see if we can find Rich at his girlfriend's." Tynan turned and bounded down the steps. "Thanks for your help, it's been nice meeting you. Take care," he called out over his shoulder. Joe followed on his heels. When they reached the sidewalk, Linda and Russell approached.

"Come on," motioned Joe. "Hurry, get in the car." Linda jumped into the car.

Russell stood alongside Tynan. "What gives, Lou?"

"Get in the car and I'll tell you. You're not going to believe it."

As soon as the car doors slammed shut, Tynan turned to Russell and said, "This fuck is cousins with Warren."

"Whoa, this is beginning to fall into place, Lou."

Tynan started the engine and pulled his car up alongside Joe's. As Joe slid his window down, he giggled, "Can you believe this shit? The shooter is cousins with our subject and he works in a place that deals in cars. I don't know, but it sounds like we're forging some links here. Cousins, works with cars? Sounds suspicious."

Linda, leaned her head forward to look around Joe. "What are we going to do now? Are we going to sit here and see if he comes home?"

"We don't know for sure if he's coming home. She gave us a possible address over on Bainbridge Avenue. That's not that far from here. Does he own a car? Is that in the folder?" asked Tynan.

Linda nodded. "He has a black Pontiac Firebird. The plate is in the folder."

"Alright, let's see," said Tynan as he tapped on the steering wheel and let out a low whistle. "Why don't you guys head over to Bainbridge Avenue and see if you can locate his car. If you do, let me know on the radio and we'll head over. If he comes out and gets in the car before we get there, jump him. We're going to sit on this place in case he shows up here."

"Should we get a warrant for the mom's house and hit it in the morning? Maybe we'll get lucky and find the gun or some drugs," said Joe.

Tynan shook his head. "No, right now all mom knows is that we want to talk to her son. If we come back with a warrant, she'll definitely call Warren. Then we're not going to be able to use Kearns to put in a call to Warren or anything like that. Warren will know what the warrant is for and why we're picking up Kearns. He won't talk to Kearns after that. Besides, I'm not so sure that Kearns is going to keep the gun he used to hit Santos."

"Yeah, but Warren is likely going to know that we were here," said Linda. "Mom still might call him."

"She might, after our little knock and talk, but even if she does, what's she going to say? The cops want to talk to Richard about something?"

"I don't know. I think he'll be raised up no matter what we do. We've got to find Kearns tonight," said Linda as she slid back in her seat.

"Maybe we'll get lucky. Head over to Bainbridge and see if you can locate him. We'll be here."

Tynan moved his car back so they could get on their way. Doubts about his plan were starting to creep into his head. Maybe letting the other guys go home was a bad idea. Instead of four against one, it was now two against one, and Kearns had already killed once. Perhaps it was a mistake going after Kearns this quickly.

Tynan could have let Kearns sit out there and see if anything developed between Lugo and the CI or the witness but he was worried about Kearns hitting someone else. If he sat back and another body was linked to Kearns or Warren, he'd look like a bigger fool than Klein and the stooges in the Palace. Tynan let out a long sigh.

He pulled over down the block. They watched the front of the house. There weren't many cars driving by and Tynan tensed up every time a set of headlights drove down the street. He didn't like sitting and waiting, but at this point they didn't have a choice. He was getting tired. As long as things were moving along, Tynan had no problem staying alert, but sitting there in the car with the air conditioner blowing on him, he felt like nodding out. A soft snoring sound coming from Russell told him, he wasn't the only guy running out of gas.

That's okay, thought Tynan. *Let him sleep. That way at least one of them might be able to think clearly.* The minutes dragged by as they sat in the car with the lights out, engine running, and the air conditioner on high. Tynan adjusted the vents so the cold air was hitting him in the face. Maybe it would keep him awake. The ringing of the cell phone woke up Russell with a start.

Tynan picked it up. "Hey, did I wake you up?" It was McCarthy.

"I'm awake," said Tynan. "Isn't it past your bedtime?"

"Not quite. Almost, though. I talked with my boss and he doesn't have a problem with running an operation with you. Although he did say 'keep those cheese eating rats out of my office.' So, I guess we'll be doing most of our meetings at your place."

"Did he really say that?"

"He did," laughed McCarthy. "Don't worry. He's a good guy. Hey, let's face it, you're not in the most popular unit in the Department. I took a look at the spots in that area. From talking to some of the undercovers and the other teams, it looks like Lugo definitely runs the spot over by Fox and Longwood. He is also connected to two other spots. One over on Hoe and the other one on Garrison. They're not as hot as Fox but he does a pretty good business. The other thing I came up with is that nobody thinks Lugo is working for anyone. The other teams think that area is strictly Lugo's. He gets his coke from Washington Heights, cuts it, and puts it out on the street. That seems to be the general consensus."

"What about this Jaime character?"

"Don't know much about him. Santos ran that spot, so it does look like your star witness was probably his right-hand man. My team is coming in early tomorrow. We'll be available if you want to get any buys into that spot or you need a hand with anything. You can always reach me by beeper or cell."

"Thanks a lot, Jimmy. I owe you big time."

"Okay, take it easy and I'll see you tomorrow. Be careful. Your team isn't dealing with cops taking free coffee anymore. Things could get hairy."

"You bet," said Tynan as he hung up.

"Good news?" asked Russell.

"Yeah. Bronx Narcotics is on board. They're willing to help us. We might get this thing into high gear a lot sooner than I thought."

"That's good."

The radio came to life. It was Joe. His voice sounded excited.

"Hey Lou, we found the car. I think you need to get over here right away. We're at Oval and Bainbridge. Can't talk on the radio."

"We're on our way," responded Russell.

Tynan put the car in gear and sped off towards Bainbridge Avenue. He could tell by Joe's voice that there was more to this than just finding the car. Joe sounded too excited. Tynan's mind started to race. Why didn't Joe want to go over the air with what they found? The car sped up as he pushed the accelerator to the floor. It bounced over the poorly paved street and the tires squealed as he rounded the corner. The metal fence and white headstones of Woodlawn Cemetery flew by on his left.

Tynan raced through the streets doing sixty. There weren't many cars on the road. A banged-up city bus struggled down the street in front of them, belching black smoke. Tynan cut into the other lane to get around it. Barely checking for traffic, he leaned on the horn as he blew through a red light. Finally, a block away, he saw Joe and Linda standing beside their car.

They were parked directly behind a black Firebird. The Firebird was pulled into the curb opposite a tunnel leading to the park. He could see someone sitting in the front seat. "There's our guy," said Tynan. He pulled in at an angle to Kearn's car.

Something wasn't right. Joe and Linda were both standing towards the back of the Firebird. They weren't even paying attention to the driver. They stared at Tynan's car as it rolled to a stop.

Tynan got out and approached the car. The driver didn't turn his head to look at him. He just sat back in the driver's seat with the window down and his head resting on the headrest like he didn't have a care in the world. Joe and Linda walked towards Tynan not saying a word.

It was then that Tynan realized Kearns wouldn't be talking to anyone. He was dead.

Tynan looked into the car. A trickle of blood came from Kearn's mouth. The front of his T shirt had a wide red stain from top to bottom. The right eye bulged from its socket and the left one, had clouded over never to see anything again.

"He was like this when we pulled up," said Joe.

Tynan let out a low whistle. "Okay, let's start doing the basics. Call for an ambulance and get patrol to show up."

Joe nodded, pulled the radio out of his jacket pocket, and switched over to a citywide frequency. "Portable to central."

The dispatcher answered with a slightly inquisitive tone. "Portable?"

"I need a 'bus' to respond to Oval and Bainbridge on a man shot. I also need a sector car and the patrol supervisor to respond to this location. Possible DOA."

"What unit is this?" asked the dispatcher.

Joe looked at Tynan. "Just tell them it's Department Auto 1510. We don't need the whole Department knowing we're here," said Tynan.

"Department Auto 1510," said Joe into the radio.

Tynan went back to his car and fumbled around in the glove box for a flashlight. He heard the short, sharp, yelp of a police siren off in the distance. Walking over to the passenger side of Kearn's car he shined the light inside. There was a pool of blood on the front passenger seat. Kearns had been shot in the head. The passenger door was unlocked and the window was down.

With the blood that poured out of the entrance wound, it was hard to tell if he had been hit more than once. It didn't matter. The head shot had done its work. On the floor, by the passenger's seat, was a 9-millimeter pistol. Tynan could see it was a Beretta. Outside the passenger door, laying in the gutter was a shiny brass shell casing. He leaned down to get a closer look. It was definitely a 9-millimeter.

"I can't believe nobody called 911," said Linda. "There's an apartment building right there."

"Who knows?" said Tynan. "The shooter could easily run into the tunnel entrance to the park and be out of sight in seconds. I don't think the shooter was in the car. There's a shell casing laying in the street. Lot of blood on the front passenger seat. The lights and engine are on. Looks like he was either just pulling in or trying to park."

"He definitely got shot from the right side," said Joe. "Maybe he pulled over to talk to someone and they lit him up."

Two marked police cars rolled up and came to a stop as the steady blast of an ambulance siren announced that the "bus" was almost there. Tynan turned and motioned to Russell, Linda, and Joe to gather around. Tynan spoke barely above a whisper as he said, "We're going to tell them we are from IAB's Police Impersonation Squad and we were looking for the victim to talk to him about a case we were working on. That's it. Don't mention anything else. I'll talk to the detectives when they get here."

Tynan took out his shield, holding it up and shining his small flashlight on it. The patrol sergeant walked up to him, "Hey, what do you got?"

"We're from the Police Impersonation Squad. We were looking for this guy and found him here. Looks like he's been shot at least once. Is the detective squad responding?"

The sergeant looked at them and nodded slowly. The Police Impersonation Squad was considered the least offensive part of IAB to most cops. Tynan knew that once you put those letters, 'I-A-B', out there, everything changed.

"I'm going to call them now, along with crime scene and the Medical Examiner. You have anything else on this guy, like his name?" asked the Sergeant.

"Yeah." Tynan turned to Linda. "Could you give the sergeant the victim's pedigree." He then took a few steps away. Joe and Russell followed.

Joe started to snicker. "Lou, this is totally fucked. We go out looking for our shooter, and before we get to him, he shows up dead. Who would believe this?"

"I don't know, Lou," whispered Russell. "This is either revenge or someone tying up loose ends."

"I guess the question we got to ask is who would want him dead the most," said Tynan.

"That could be a pretty long list," Joe responded. "Could be his girlfriend, for all we know."

Russell looked at Joe and whispered out of the corner of his mouth, "You don't believe this was his girlfriend, do you? You're not that crazy."

"No, but I'm just saying. This guy probably had a lot of enemies. Maybe it's got to do with our case but maybe not. It could be something else."

Linda finished talking to the Sergeant and walked over to join them. The ambulance, or "bus," pulled up with flashing lights and two weary looking paramedics got out. They walked over to the car and looked at Kearns. After a quick pulse check and a look at the head wound, the older of the two said to the Sergeant. "He's gone." Looking down at his watch he added, "Time of death 2100."

Tynan looked at the circle of faces gathered around him. "Any thoughts?"

"The most likely suspect is Lugo," said Linda. "The CI said he was afraid Lugo would kill him if he did the job on Santos. Kearns took the CI's place and now he's dead. That's my bet."

Joe and Russell, shook their heads in agreement. "I agree," said Joe. "I'd say it's probably Lugo, but if I had to pick a second choice I'd go with Warren."

Russell's head snapped quickly and looked at Joe. "That's a scary thought, Joe. He whacks his own cousin just to clear up a lose end. That would make him one cold-blooded dude."

Tynan nodded. "If it's revenge, it has to be for the Santos hit. Someone who worked with Santos. But they'd have to know Kearns as well. I'm leaning towards tying up loose ends."

"What makes you think they knew Kearns?" asked Linda.

"How'd they know he was coming here? They would have to be waiting for him or they followed him. But if they followed him, they had to stop their car and then run around to blast him from the sidewalk. I think that's unlikely. That's why I think they were waiting for him," said Tynan.

Tynan started to get an uneasy feeling. Maybe he knew a lot less about this case than he thought. He'd been moving too fast, trusting too many people. The type of people he usually didn't trust. His two main witnesses were a drug dealer and a CI.

Tynan took a deep breath and continued. He wasn't sure if he was talking to the team or out loud to himself. "It's too early to discount either theory. Let's say it's the revenge angle. Then it's someone in Santos' old crew. That would put our star witness, Jaime, in the mix. Does he know more about Kearns than he told us? Did he know Kearns was coming here or where he worked? I think we need to start working a timeline. See if it's possible to go from our office to Garrison Avenue in time to meet Kearns and then ride with him over here."

"We can do that," said Joe.

"While you are at it," added Tynan, "let's get the records on any phones that Kearns or Jaime may have and for good measure throw our CI's phones or beepers in there too. Let's see who they have been talking to. I'd really like to know who Jaime was talking to today."

"They probably have burner phones or extra beepers," said Linda.

"Maybe, but I'd like to get whatever info we can on these guys."

"Who's your money on for doing this?" asked Russell.

"I don't know what to think. All I know is I got more questions now than I did this morning and that's never good," muttered Tynan.

"Do you want us to see if we can track down the girlfriend?" asked Linda. "She lives right down the block. Maybe she knows something."

"Yeah, that's a good idea. Remember, before you head back to the office, you two take a drive by Garrison Avenue and see how long it takes you to get there from our office."

"Hell, if we get lucky, maybe she'll say she did it," chuckled Joe. He and Linda started walking down the block.

Tynan stood there with Russell, watching the uniformed cops take out the yellow crime scene tape and rope off the area. This was not how Tynan thought the night was going to go. He looked at Russell and said, "I wonder what they are going to say at the Palace."

Russell shrugged. "Look at the bright side, Lou. At least they can't say we did it."

FRIENDS AND ENEMIES

Tynan and Russell stood around watching the usual homicide ritual as the cops strung up the yellow and black crime scene tape. When the detective squad showed up, Tynan decided it was time to drop the charade that they were from the Police Impersonation Squad. He grabbed the detective sergeant by the sleeve and said, "Could I talk to you for a minute?" Tynan walked twenty feet from the crime scene and the uniformed cops. The detective sergeant was an old timer, probably with a year or two to go before mandatory retirement. *Anyone who's been around that long deserves at least some of the truth*, thought Tynan.

"What's up?" asked the Sergeant, as he used a wrinkled white handkerchief to wipe the sweat off his brow.

"A couple of things," said Tynan. "We're from IAB but not the Police Impersonation Squad. The victim here was a person of interest in one of our cases. The second thing is that I have two of my people looking for the victim's girlfriend who lives down the block. They are going to interview her and see if she can shed any light on this mess."

The sergeant continued wiping his face. "God, I hate the summer. Give me a homicide in the winter anytime. I appreciate you sharing that info. Do you have anything else you can tell me?"

"Not right now. I will say this," Tynan said, pointing to the corpse in the car, "he was a former cop. He got thrown out of the academy and according to our information, he is involved in the drug business and who knows what else. We think he might be a shooter in a drug- related homicide."

"Ah, I see. Maybe a little tit for tat going on here."

"Could be. We're going to stick around and see what happens when the body is searched."

"Sounds good," said the sergeant as he pushed his handkerchief back into his pocket.

Tynan stood there waiting for Linda and Joe. He watched as the Crime Scene Unit laid out evidence markers, measured distances, and took pictures. Everyone else stood around waiting for the ME.

It must have been a busy night for the ME because when he arrived, he didn't make any small talk. He walked straight over to the Pontiac, looked inside and examined the body. "I'd say it's a homicide. Let's get him out and see if there are any other wounds. You got your pictures, right?"

A crime scene detective nodded. The two uniformed cops who had the "job" dragged Kearns out. Everyone heard, before anyone saw, the 9mm pistol that fell out on the ground. It had either been under the victim or tucked in the back of his waistband. The detective sergeant looked at Tynan. "Interesting, two pistols. One on the victim and the other laying on the floor of the car."

The ME had the cops roll the body over. He looked around at the small circle of cops that surrounded him. "Looks like one to the head. From where the shell casing is and the gunpowder residue on the headliner in the car, I'd say he was shot by someone standing right beside the car, but that's just a preliminary."

The detective sergeant motioned to the two uniformed cops and said, "Okay guys, give him a toss and see what else we got." The cops went through Kearns' pockets. A wad of cash came out of one pocket, a beeper was removed from his belt, and what looked like a small black wallet came out of his other pocket. The cop opened it. It was a shield case, the kind that every cop carried when either off duty or in plain-clothes, and inside was a bright, shiny, silver cop's shield.

The other part of the case contained a police identification card. "He's a cop," said the officer.

Tynan stepped forward. "Can I see that for a minute?" The cop handed it over. Tynan peered at it and the detective sergeant came over and shined a flashlight on it. It was indeed a police officer shield but Tynan could see it was a "dupe." Most cops had one, once they got their shield. It was almost the same size as a regular shield, just slightly smaller, but the bottom of the shield was thicker than usual, giving away that it wasn't real. "It's a dupe," said Tynan. He pulled the identification card out. Looking it over, he could see the ID card was genuine.

"Are you sure this guy *used* to be a cop?" asked the detective sergeant.

"Yeah, I'm sure. Not sure why he has an identification card if he was fired. Maybe he kept it and said it was lost. If he was getting fired, I'm sure he didn't care if they wrote him up for losing his ID card."

"True enough," said the sergeant. He was back to wiping his face with the handkerchief. "We're going to need that back."

"Yeah, sure," said Tynan as he handed it over. "What kind of gun is that?"

The cop looked at it. "It's a nine."

"What make?" asked Tynan.

"A Taurus. He had two guns, plus he's got about six hundred bucks in cash."

"If there isn't anything else, I'm off to another one in Manhattan," sighed the ME. "Alright then, have a good night and have the first officer on the scene report to the morgue tomorrow to ID the body."

As the Medical Examiner got back in his car, Tynan noticed Linda and Joe coming up the street. They were walking fast. Tynan wasn't sure what that meant. They came up to Tynan and the detective Sergeant.

"Sorry it took so long, but the girlfriend was a wreck. She said that he called her a little after seven from his job at the junkyard and said he was coming over to see her but first he had to give a friend a ride. She never hears from him again and didn't know what happened until we knocked on the door."

"Who's the friend?" asked Tynan.

"She didn't know. We asked her about any enemies and she said he didn't have any."

"Works in a junkyard?" asked the detective sergeant. "Maybe I'll go work in a junkyard. I ain't got six hundred in cash on me."

"Did she have anything else to say?" asked Tynan.

"She was shaken up. I didn't push it. I think she'd be worth another visit tomorrow," said Linda.

Tynan turned to the detective sergeant. "Do you need anything else from us?"

"Nope, you're free to go," laughed the sergeant.

"Alright, let's get the fuck out of here. Joe and Linda, do that drive from Garrison, and while we're wasting the city's gas, see how long it takes to drive from the CI's girlfriend's house on Stratford Avenue. What's the address, Russ?"

"Southeast corner of Stratford and Watson," said Russell.

"We'll meet you back at the barn," said Tynan. "Come on Russ, let's go."

"Stratford too?" asked Joe, shrugging his shoulders.

"Yeah, both locations. Just humor me. I'll get coffee and donuts for everyone."

Tynan and Russell got back in the car and headed off looking for a coffee shop. He needed time to think about what he was going to tell the chief. His mind wandered as he drove. He felt like he was falling further and further behind on this case no matter how fast he moved. Maybe it was time to do more thinking and less moving.

Tynan picked up coffee and donuts. It wasn't much but at least it was a small gesture for the work the team was doing. When he got back to his office, he opened the box of donuts and started munching on one. Russell joined him. Maybe the sugar rush would overcome the fatigue for at least a little while. He couldn't see the bobbing white sail boats out of his window. It was just a black picture, punctuated with small dots of white light from distant street lights. He sat down heavily in his chair and holding a donut in one hand, grabbed a yellow legal pad to scratch out a new list of things to do.

"Okay, Russ, time for some ideas. Let's see if we can get this wreck back on the road."

"We're not dead in the water yet," said Russell as he bit into a jelly donut. He dusted off the white powdered sugar that fell on his pants. "We've still got options."

Tynan nodded, and started writing out a list on the pad. He went through all the things he could think of, calling them out to Russell as he wrote them. "Check with the surveillance team, pole cameras, check with narcotics about doing buy operations in the neighborhood, see if they got any prints out of Kearns' car, check on the ballistics, get the witness and the CI to meet Lugo at different times, canvass the building again opposite Kearns' shooting, talk to the girlfriend, get beeper and phone records on the witness, CI, and the two victims."

Tynan looked up. "Anything else you can think of?"

"Yeah, you got to tell the bosses what's going on. That's the real wild card right now."

"It is, isn't it?" Tynan threw his pen down. "I wonder if they are going to want us to take the Kearns case too. There's a real good chance they're connected."

"Do you think IAB is going to take over another homicide case? I'm surprised they gave you the Santos case," said Russell.

Tynan finished his donut. He didn't get the rush he was hoping for. He just felt tired. He went over what had happened. Could Kearns' murder just be a coincidence? He doubted it. Kearns was involved in drugs and who knows what else and maybe he made enemies, but the timing screamed that this was related to the Santos' hit.

To Tynan it followed that people on the street knew Kearns had killed Santos and someone was out to exact revenge. It was the logical explanation. In that scenario, Jaime loomed larger than life. If it was someone tying up loose ends, he was leaning towards Lugo. The CI was sure Lugo would not let whoever shot Santos live. That meant Warren was involved. Warren probably knew all about Kearns' girlfriend and where she lived.

Russell finished his donut and stood up. "Okay. I'll be in my office, Lou."

Tynan hung his "to-do" list on the bulletin board. He rearranged the photos of the subjects that Linda had taped on the whiteboard. Picking up a sharpie, he drew an "X" through Kearns' picture and another through Santos. The other photos of Jaime, Lugo, and Warren stared back at him. He chuckled to himself. *The body count is climbing,* he thought. *How high will it go? At this rate, in a week, there will be nobody left.*

He sat back down, put his feet up on the desk, and clasped his hands behind his head. The case spun around in his mind. Had he made mistakes here? Could he have acted faster on getting to Kearns? He didn't think so. Kearns had been the solution to the case and now he was gone. They were back to relying on a questionable witness and a CI.

Tynan heard the heavy metal door open and slam shut. Linda's and Joe's footsteps echoed down the hall. They walked in, looking as tired as Tynan felt.

"Donuts?!" exclaimed Joe. "Alright, you're okay, Lou. Have one Linda. I'm going to give you this big bear claw. It's got your name on it. Here eat."

Linda took it. "Be careful you don't get a claw across your face."

"Anything of note?" asked Tynan.

"From here to the junk-yard on Garrison would take about twenty minutes. From Stratford to the junkyard, would be ten. You can get to where Kearns was shot in twenty-five minutes from any of those spots, including here. We drove the routes and it's possible that either Jaime or the CI could have gotten to the junkyard before Kearns left for the day, if the mom is right about when she got Kearns' phone call."

Tynan pointed to the list on the bulletin board, "Add interviewing the boss at the junkyard to the list of things to do today."

Joe grasped the half-eaten donut between his teeth and wrote down "junkyard" on the list.

"Do you think Angel, the CI, did this?" asked Linda.

"Like I said, I don't know. I doubt it, but at this point, I'm not giving any of these assholes a pass. I just know they all had the opportunity to do it. We'll find out if they have alibis. The CI said he's with his girlfriend and we can check on that, but what about Jaime? What was he up to?"

Linda sat down and slowly picked apart the enormous bear claw, daintily placing small pieces in her mouth. Between bites, she said, "But neither the CI nor Jaime, had a car. Our records check doesn't show either of them owning a car."

"They could take a livery, easy enough. They're all over the place or maybe someone was waiting to pick them up."

"I don't know, Lou," said Joe. "They're going to take a livery to a shooting. How does that work? 'Hey, I'll be right back, buddy, stay here, I just got to go and kill someone.' I don't see that."

Tynan laughed, visualizing the conversation between the shooter and a cab driver. "No, but they could take the ride to the junkyard and meet Kearns there. Ride back with him and then pop him. They could also get someone to give them a ride to Bainbridge."

"Yeah, but then they would have to know where Kearns was going," said Linda.

"I agree with you Lou. If the shooter knew Kearns was going to be there, they had to know him well," said Joe. "That's what keeps rolling around in my head. The only one who would know him that well is Warren. I agree that Lugo is the primary suspect to be the shooter but I think Warren put him up to it. Just like he probably put Kearns up to killing Santos."

Tynan went over to the box of donuts, picked up another, and studied it before taking a bite. "That sounds believable, but maybe Jaime wants his revenge on Kearns for killing Santos."

"I still think Lugo doing it makes the most sense," said Linda.

Tynan looked at the clock. It would be another long day. "If you want, you can try and catch some sleep in your offices or the lunchroom but at eight we got to get rolling again. I'm going to call my boss and the chief at seven. I'm sure they'll be thrilled."

Joe and Linda got up and shuffled out of the office.

"Good luck with the calls, Lou," called Linda as she headed to her office.

Tynan watched them leave. He jotted down some notes to make sure he covered the highlights when he made his calls. As tired as he was, he knew he wouldn't be able to nap. Instead, he grabbed a handful of worksheets from his in box and started reviewing them.

Ey the time the sun shone on the anchored boats, Tynan was no closer to answers on the case, but he had waded through a pile of paperwork, slowly transferring it over to his out box.

If he had picked up Kearns, Tynan was sure he would have flipped. But now, he would never be able to get Kearns in a room and question him. That opportunity was gone forever. Instead, he had a CI who suddenly seemed reluctant and a witness he didn't trust. Not to mention Warren's role in all of this was still floating out there like mist on a lake. As the cheap plastic clock on the dirty walls of his office hit seven, he picked up the phone to give Rogan the bad news.

Rogan answered like he had been up for hours. "Hi Captain," Tynan said. "I got a lot of updates for you."

"Oh good," chuckled Rogan. "Tell me you got the shooter and Warren in the interrogation room and you can't stop them from talking."

"Not quite. The shooter was an ex-cop named Kearns who got thrown out of the academy and who also happens to be cousins with Warren. According to Kearns' mom, Warren had taken him under his wing after he got kicked off the job. But when we went to pick up Kearns we were a little late."

"Late?"

"Yeah, we found him in his car by his girlfriend's house but he wasn't talking due to the bullet in his head."

Rogan took all the news in stride. "Was it a suicide?"

"Hardly, it looks like he pulled into the curb and somebody blasted him, so we never got a chance to talk. Him being the shooter is all based on the ID by Santos' bodyguard. Kearns had a gun on him and there was another gun on the floor of the car. We'll see if either comes back from ballistics as the gun that shot Santos. If it does, that makes things a little more solid."

"Any connection to Warren with this latest shooting?"

"Nope, we don't have anything leading that way. The consensus seems to be either this is in retaliation for the killing of Santos or it's someone tying up loose ends."

"What do you think?" asked Rogan.

"To be honest, I go back and forth between the two. I think whoever got to Kearns knew him well, because it was done by his girlfriend's house. That kind of leans towards tying up loose ends and for that I'd take a look at Lugo."

"Why wouldn't it be Warren?" asked Rogan.

"Because that would leave Lugo as a loose end and he's still walking around."

"At this rate, pretty soon you guys are going to be a satellite office for Bronx Homicide," laughed Rogan. "Have you told the brain trust yet?"

"No, I'm going to give them a call now. I've been behind on keeping you informed. Sorry about that but I've had Klein breathing down my neck."

"Don't worry about it. I don't talk to Klein very much. You let me know what's going on when you can. You did a lot of work in a short period of time, and talking to me isn't going to get the case closed."

Tynan looked up at the clock. "Do you think we should take over the Kearns case too?"

"Yes. I don't see how you can't. Warren was supposedly behind the hit on Santos. This guy Kearns was the shooter, and he's related to Warren. That's got to be checked out. Maybe either the CI or the witness can get Lugo to spill the beans."

"Yep, I'll run it by the chief to see if we can take the Kearns' case as well. It happened in a different precinct, so that's good and bad. Good in that we don't have to step on the toes of the same precinct detective squad but bad because it's going to spread like wildfire that IAB is looking into two homicides."

"If it spreads, it spreads. Who cares, and there is nothing you can do about it anyway. I wouldn't worry. Look, I'm going to let you go so you can get back to work. If there's anything you need just reach out. Thanks for calling."

With that, Rogan was gone. He was one of the few decent guys that Tynan had met in the organization, at least at the higher ranks. Rogan didn't appear to care about being promoted. He just did his job, and whatever happened, happened. He was the complete opposite of the guys he was about to call. Tynan dialed Klein's number. It rang about five times before he picked up. Tynan was hoping he could just leave a message but Klein's grating voice came on the line.

"Hello?"

"It's Lieutenant Tynan. Calling with an update."

"What is it?" snapped Klein.

"We found the shooter but he's not going to do us any good."

"And why not?" asked Klein. Tynan sensed Klein was annoyed by being called so early. He was in full obnoxious asshole mode.

"Because he's dead. We found him shot dead sitting in his car. He was parked near Oval Park and Bainbridge Avenue in the Five-Two Precinct. The interesting thing is this guy is cousins with Warren. In fact, his mom said that Warren took him under his wing after he was thrown off the job."

"He's dead? Cousins with Warren? Hmm that's interesting. Anything else I should know?"

"Kearns had a gun on him. A nine-millimeter, same caliber that was used on Santos. We'll check with the lab and see if it's the same gun. If it is, that pretty much locks it in that he's the shooter. Then the only question is who shot Kearns."

There was no response from Klein. Tynan wasn't sure if he had hung up. "Are you there, chief?"

"I'm here. I'm just thinking. I'll update the chief on the case."

"We're going ahead with Bronx Narcotics to try and build a case against Lugo. We also have more interviews to do. My people have to check back in with Kearns' mom and girlfriend. Maybe they can add something. The CI and the witness are both supposed to make contact with Lugo later today. If things go well, we'll wire them up and see if we can get Lugo to say something incriminating on tape."

"Yeah, yeah, yeah," said Klein dismissively. "I have to go."

Klein hung up. "What a dick," Tynan muttered to himself. He got up and wandered over to the donut box, looking over the remains. Another donut fell into Tynan's grasp and he started eating it absentmindedly as he walked over to the window. Normally, he enjoyed looking at the boats. Today, he was too tired. He turned away and went over to his list. His first stop was going to be the junkyard. Maybe somebody there could shed some light on whether Kearns left alone or with someone else.

He wasn't too sure how much information he'd get out of them. Junkyards moved a lot of stolen autos and parts and the Feds were convinced Warren was involved in stolen cars. If this one was like others Tynan had dealt with, they'd be pretty tight with info. *Worth a shot,* he thought. He was figuring out what else he could do when his phone rang.

Tynan picked it up. "Group 41, Lieutenant Tynan."

"Chief wants you down in his office, forthwith. Bring the case folder with you," said Klein. Before Tynan could say anything, Klein hung up. *Forthwith?* thought Tynan. That was police slang for ASAP. The last thing he wanted to do was fight rush hour traffic. He threw the donut in the wastepaper basket and went looking for Joe and Linda.

Linda was in her office, asleep in a chair with her feet up on the desk, a jacket pulled over her. Tynan couldn't believe anyone could sleep in such an uncomfortable position but she was sleeping like a log. He knocked on the door jam and she stirred. "What's up?" she said as she squinted at Tynan.

"I got to go down to Headquarters to talk with the chief about this case. They want me to bring the case folder. Could you put it together? There's a bunch of worksheets we need to put in there but just give me whatever we have."

She slowly took her feet off the desk. "Yeah, sure. Do you want us to come with you?" she asked as she let out a big yawn.

"No, that's okay. I'm not sure what kind of a meeting this is going to be, so it's best if I go alone. While I'm gone, go out and talk to the junkyard owner, see what he can tell us. If I'm not back by then, go see the girlfriend and the mom. Maybe they can add something. Russell can stay here and meet with the witness. I'll definitely be back by the time the CI shows up."

Linda gathered the scattered pieces of the folder together and slowly handed it to Tynan. "You're going to bring this back, right Lou?"

"Of course. Don't you trust me?"

"I trust you. I'm not sure I trust the people you're meeting with."

"Don't worry. They are not going to take this away from us now. To the untrained eye it looks like a case folder but to those of us in the know, it's a big leaking bag of shit. They don't want it."

Tynan looked at his watch, trying to figure out how long this would take. "Between morning traffic and hobnobbing with the big shots, I should be back by noon at the latest."

The drive into Manhattan was pretty much what Tynan expected. A stop and go slog all the way down the East Side. He stepped off the elevator on the fourteenth floor and straightened his tie, trying to look presentable despite being unshaven. The receptionist seemed to be expecting him as she held up her hand and buzzed the chief on the intercom. "Lieutenant Tynan is here." She hung up, smiled, and gestured towards the conference room. "They're in there."

Tynan walked in. He felt like he had been transported back in time to a week earlier. All the usual players were sitting in the exact same spots as the last time. Tynan took the hint, dropped the case folder on the table and sat down at the end of the conference table. Lieutenant Sullivan was there, checking her watch and already writing something. Klein sat there and never acknowledged his presence. Riordan nodded but only the chief spoke. "Good morning, Lieutenant. I've heard there have been some major developments in the case."

Major developments? thought Tynan. *That's one way to say it.* "Yes sir, the alleged shooter in the Santos' case is dead. He is also the cousin of the cop who was the initial subject in this case."

Calhoun nodded impatiently and leaned back in his high back, leather chair. He folded his hands across his stomach, took a deep breath, and started talking. "First of all, I would like to commend you and your staff on the fine work you have done with this case up to this point and so quickly. Truly commendable. Excellent work, you did a good job. I think we can all agree on that."

Everyone around the table nodded, as if on cue. Tynan was waiting for the other shoe to drop. *This is a unique experience*, he thought. *They are all so complimentary. Something's up.*

Calhoun continued. "Now it's time to put this entire affair to bed. You identified the shooter, he's dead. The shooter is not the cop, although he is related to him. So that aspect of the case is also closed. The crisis has passed. We can now take a more methodical and long-term strategic approach to find out what Warren is up to."

Klein nodded and shifted in his chair. "Exactly chief, that's what we're all thinking. I believe at this point it would pay to let our federal colleagues continue to work the stolen car ring angle and take care of Warren that way. As we know, Lieutenant Tynan does not have a working relationship with the US Attorney's office; therefore, it is necessary to put this case back in the capable hands of Lieutenant Sullivan."

Tynan was stunned. He thought he might be in for an ass-chewing about not getting Kearns sooner but he didn't see this coming. He was out of his league in this office.

Calhoun pointed to Klein. "Exactly, I think that is the best solution to this."

Tynan flipped open the case. "What about the Santos' homicide? Do I give that back to the Detective Squad?"

"No need," said Klein. He continued looking at Calhoun as he talked. "That case is solved. You can close it."

"How is it solved? How can I close it?"

"Do you know what an exceptional clearance is Lieutenant?" asked Klein as he shifted his gaze towards Tynan for the first time.

"Yeah, I know what it is. It's when you know who the subject is but you can't advance the case any further because of extenuating circumstances. Something other than closing a case with an arrest."

"More or less," snorted Klein. "Are you planning on arresting a corpse?"

Tynan couldn't help but roll his eyes. "No chief, actually I wasn't, but I don't think we have enough evidence to say conclusively that Kearns was the shooter."

"Are you for real, Lieutenant?"

Tynan could feel his blood pressure rising. He was tired of being talked to like a child by some chief who couldn't find a bass drum in a phone booth. "Yes, I'm for real. First of all, we haven't compared the gun found on Kearns or the other gun in the car with the ballistics from the Santos homicide. Second, we don't know for a fact that

Warren wasn't involved in killing Santos. For that matter, he may be involved in killing Kearns as well. Plus, what about the driver?"

Klein raised his hand, as if to tell Tynan to stop. "The original case was that Warren was going to kill Santos. We have Warren's cousin identified as the shooter and he's dead. There is no sense in going down some rabbit hole to make a link with Warren. That type of investigation could take forever and there's no guarantee it would lead to him. The Feds case on Warren is the way to go. As for the driver? You would never be able to prove they knew they were driving someone to a shooting."

Once again, everyone nodded except Tynan. "Well put," said Calhoun.

Klein turned his head and stared at Tynan. "At this point, we want you to hand the case over to Lieutenant Sullivan. The Santos' homicide is closed by exceptional clearance. That's done. Whatever worksheets or other evidence that belongs in that case folder, have it sent down to this office. We're going to give the US Attorney a green light for their auto theft case."

Tynan was almost speechless. On his drive down, he thought he was going to leave with two murder cases. Instead, he was walking out with none. He slid the case folder across the polished wood table to Sullivan. "What about the Kearns' case?"

"What about it?" asked Calhoun.

"Should we ask to have that case taken from the Five-Two Detective Squad and given to us?" Tynan knew the answer before he even got the words out of his mouth.

"Of course not," said Calhoun. "It's their case. It was unusual for us to take the Santos case. I had to pull strings to make that happen. We're not in the business of investigating drug-related homicides. Leave that to the Detective Bureau. We have plenty of work to do."

"Okay," said Tynan. "Is there anything else?"

The chief shook his head no. "Not about this. Where would you like to go after your stint in Internal Affairs?"

"I would prefer to go to the Detective Bureau," answered Tynan. "But I still have about eighteen months left in IAB."

"Maybe not," smiled Calhoun. "I always believe that good work should be rewarded, and you have done some very good work, especially this last week. You never know, sometimes spots open up early, and I would be the last person to stand in the way of rewarding someone for doing a good job. Doing two years in Internal Affairs is not engraved in stone."

Tynan nodded and pointed at the door. "Can I go now?"

"Absolutely. Have a good ride back to the Bronx and make sure Lieutenant Sullivan gets any additional paperwork for this case. I just want to shake your hand." Calhoun got up and came around the table. As Tynan stood, the chief grasped his hand and shook it. "I appreciate all that you've done." The chief let go and opened the door for Tynan. "Good luck, Lieutenant." The door closed softly behind him.

Tynan's anger had subsided. It had started to disappear once Klein had shut up. Maybe he was too tired or maybe he just didn't care anymore. He wondered what Linda and Joe would say. Would they be mad or relieved? *I'll find out soon enough,* he thought.

Tynan glanced at his watch as he walked through the heavy metal door to the offices of Bronx Internal Affairs. It was twelve noon. He'd been up for thirty hours; he felt exhausted.

Russell came from around the corner of the hallway. "Hey Lou. How's it going?"

"You wouldn't believe it if I told you. Did the witness show up yet?"

"No, not yet. My guys are ready to go as soon as he gets here."

"Fucking guy is late," mumbled Tynan as he walked down the hallway towards his office. Russell followed. They both sat down and Tynan looked out at his boats. "I came back a little lighter than I left. They have the case again."

"I don't believe it. Why do they have it again?"

"According to the powers that be," said Tynan, "the homicide case on Santos is closed. We know who the shooter is and he's dead. So that's that. As for Warren, they think it's better if the Feds handle it, since they are so far along on their mysterious auto theft case."

"What about the Kearns' case? Are we going to take it?"

"No," sighed Tynan. "The Five-Two squad is going to handle it. At some point, I'm going to tell the Five-Two detectives what we have as far as Kearns is concerned. What's going on here?"

"We're waiting on the witness. Meanwhile, I reached out to a person I know down at the lab and asked them to do a rush job on the guns found on Kearns. They checked. The gun on the floor of the car was the one used to kill Santos. The gun Kearns was carrying hadn't been fired. That makes the evidence against Kearns pretty solid."

Tynan sighed. "Anything else?"

"There is, and this is weird. The gun found on the floor of the car had no prints on it, not even partials or smudges. It had been wiped clean."

"Wiped clean?" asked Tynan. "What was it doing laying on the floor of the car? That is weird."

"By the way, Linda and Joe went out to check on the junkyard, the girlfriend, and Kearns' mom. They left right after you headed out for the Puzzle Palace. They should be back soon. What do you want me to do?"

"Uh," said Tynan as he tapped his fingers on the desk. "Let's see. If any of your guys have any outstanding worksheets on the Warren case finish them and hand them in. After I sign off on them, they have to go downtown to be put in the rest of the folder. I'm sure Lieutenant Sullivan is anxiously waiting for it, so she can put it in her desk drawer, where it won't see the light of day for who knows how many months."

"What about narcotics? Are we still going to work with them?"

"That's a good question. If they want to move ahead with the witness and the CI to see if they can get a case going on Lugo, I'm not going to tell them no. They can work any narcotics case they want. You never know, they might come up with something themselves."

Russell got up and headed to the door. "Okay, I'll get those worksheets together."

Tynan was about to nod off when the phone rang. He answered it. "Kids need hugs, not drugs or is it the other way around. I forget. Hey Lou, it's your buddy Sergeant McCarthy. We're raring to go. Have either one of your players arrived?"

"Speaking of drugs, I think I might need some after this morning. We no longer have the case, according to the geniuses downtown."

"What do you mean, you don't have the case? You don't have the case on the cop or you don't have the homicide?" asked McCarthy.

"You can make that, homicides, as in more than one and we don't have anything to do with the cop either."

"Whoa, I must be missing something," said McCarthy.

"Yep. If you go to sleep for an hour, you can miss a whole lot on this case. The shooter in the Santos case was killed last night, so that's one case. The Santos case is now closed because the alleged shooter is dead and the Feds are going to handle the Warren case."

"I don't believe it," laughed McCarthy. "What a shit show."

Tynan was interested in McCarthy's reaction to the news, so he laid out what had happened overnight and the meeting he had at headquarters with the chief. When he wrapped the story up, there was a long pause.

"Listen Lou, do you mind if we go ahead and run with this case? It might turn into a major case if we can get either the witness or the CI to introduce one of our undercovers to Lugo. This guy Lugo deals in some weight. It'd be worth our while."

"Be my guest," said Tynan. "I was kind of hoping you'd say that. Of course, you're going to keep me in the loop on anything to do with Lugo and company, right?"

"Absolutely. We're a team, Lou, even if you do play for the dark side."

"I would be willing to bet they've already pulled our surveillance unit and there won't be any pole cameras or any tech support from our end. But if you need bodies or anything, I can help you from my office as long as we keep it a secret. That witness is supposed to get back to us today and so is the CI. They'll be making a run at Lugo. No wire, etcetera. We'll just be hanging back in the area in case something goes wrong."

"What could possibly go wrong with this case?" chuckled McCarthy. "Okay, we're going to do some 'buy and bust' in the area, just to see what the traffic is like. Who knows, maybe we'll catch someone who has something worthwhile to tell us."

"Okay, be good. I'll be in touch," said Tynan as he hung.

"Buy and bust" was Narcotics' bread and butter, thought Tynan. They did hundreds every week throughout the city. An undercover cop bought drugs, radioed in the description, and a back-up team arrested anyone involved in the sale. It was tried and true enforcement that netted low-level dealers, but often enough, these same street dealers had valuable information.

He knew Klein and Calhoun would probably not be happy with that last phone call but Tynan didn't care. He'd lost the case twice, and each time, it didn't make any sense. The first time they took the case, Klein told Tynan to keep his hands off. This time they didn't seem concerned. Besides, McCarthy didn't work for IAB. He worked for Narcotics and had a lead on a possible player. He wouldn't be doing his job if he didn't pick up the ball and run with it.

Tynan stood up and looked at the boats in the water. The door slammed at the end of the hallway, announcing that someone was coming. He heard the shuffling footsteps of leather shoes heading towards his office. Rogan stood in the doorway. "Don't jump!" he said with a laugh.

"I guess you heard," said Tynan.

"Yeah, I heard." Rogan slumped into a chair. "What are you going to do? I wouldn't worry about it. Plus, from what I'm hearing, you may not be long for the world of IAB."

"Really?"

"That's right. The chief is looking around for a spot in the Detective Bureau, and if he finds one, you are gone."

"Why, because I did such a good job?"

Rogan threw his head back and laughed. "I don't think that's it. You're a liability, son. They look at you and realize you know too much. You know how they fucked this case up. The sooner you are gone the sooner they can end this. What's bothering them is you know they knew about the Santos hit and did nothing. Now the shooter is dead. They don't want you out there flipping over rocks looking to solve this. For them, it is solved. Case closed."

"What about them closing the Santos case and giving Warren's case back to the Feds?"

"Of course they are going to do that," said Rogan with a shrug. "Much better to have Warren take a fall for a bunch of stolen cars."

"I guess."

"Makes sense or not, that's what's going on here." Rogan pointed at Tynan. "You are trouble."

"Well, it's not dead yet. Narcotics is going to keep running with the drug angle."

"Of course they are," said Rogan. "Why not? Sounds like it could be a good case. Plus, they can't really control Narcotics. What are they going to say, 'Stop that drug case because we are afraid of what you might come up with?' Bottom line, what do you care? You'll probably be out of here in a month. Go work on real cases in the Detective Bureau. Enough of this bullshit."

Rogan jumped up. "Listen, just do whatever time you have left. You did what you were supposed to do and have nothing to apologize for. I'll call you if I hear anything."

"Thanks for stopping by," said Tynan.

"I'm off to Belmont Avenue to get some Italian food. Take care." Rogan's footsteps echoed down the hall and then the door slammed shut.

What Tynan wanted to do more than anything was go home and go to sleep but he had to wait around for the witness and the CI to show up. He could call off the two meetings with Lugo. What did he care? It wasn't his case. But he didn't want to leave McCarthy hanging. He had gone out of his way to help Tynan and helping McCarthy build the narcotics case was the right thing to do.

As he wandered down towards the breakroom for some coffee, he saw Linda and Joe coming in through the front door. They seemed surprised to see him.

"Look what the cat dragged in," said Joe.

"You don't look much better. Meet me in my office. I have to get some coffee," said Tynan as he ducked into the breakroom. He filled his coffee cup to the brim with the stale but hot coffee. He'd need every ounce of caffeine he could get. Blowing on it, he took a sip, hoping it would instantly revive his foggy brain. "Oh, this is terrible," he moaned.

He carefully balanced the cup as he walked down the hallway, not wanting to add more coffee stains to the old dried ones that decorated the worn-out tile. When he arrived at his office, Joe and Linda were already seated, both of them finishing off the last of the doughnuts.

"What do you got?" asked Tynan.

"That was the worst, Lou," mumbled Linda through a mouthful of doughnut. "Talking to that mom was so sad. It was all I could do to not cry. I'm not going back to see her."

"Did she have anything interesting to say?"

Linda shook her head. "No, just more of the same but now her son is dead. It was awful."

"What about the girlfriend?"

"She was a little bit more interesting. She was upset but she managed to say she knew Kearns was involved with drugs and stolen car parts. That's how he made his money. She didn't know anyone who would want to hurt him. I asked her to come in and look at pictures to see if she could identify anyone he hangs with. She agreed, but said she couldn't do it today."

"And the junkyard?"

"It is one shady place. A typical Hunts Point junkyard. It's called 'Vic's Auto Parts and Salvage,' owned by Vic Grossi. Loads of everything and probably most of it stolen," said Joe. "In fact, when we were there his crew was taking apart a BMW 3 Series. Didn't take them long to strip it down to the frame. I wanted to get a look at the VIN but I didn't want to make him suspicious, since I was hoping for a little cooperation."

"Did you get any?"

"Kind of," said Linda. She had wolfed down the doughnut and was back to her usual assertive tone. "He said that Kearns left the junkyard between seven and eight. We found Kearns at 2050 hours. We just missed him getting shot. Even more interesting is he said that there was a guy waiting for him out front and Kearns gave him a ride when he left."

"Did he happen to get a good look at this guy?"

"He just said that it was a guy. He didn't provide any specifics. He said he might be willing to help us identify the guy but he has to make sure that it doesn't hurt his business."

Tynan winced as he sipped from his cup. "Hurt his business how?"

Joe laughed. "He's got partners and he has to check with them." Joe made finger quotes around the word partners. "This guy is a half-assed wise guy. He's afraid he might bring heat down on his yard."

"Hmmm," said Tynan. "Afraid of a little heat? It could get really hot if he doesn't help us. I think he'll cooperate, if we use the right mix of carrot and stick."

Tynan put the cup down on his desk. He bit his lower lip and wiped his hand across the stubble on his face. *Lot of interesting pieces there,* he thought. They'd already chased down a lot of promising leads that blew up in their faces but the junkyard might be different.

"I think we might have to pay the junkyard another visit. I'd be curious as to what the Auto Crime Division has on that place and what they know about Vic. Maybe tomorrow we can see if his partners are okay with talking to us. By the way, I think you missed your true calling, Linda. You should have been a psychic. You were right about what was going to happen at the Palace."

Her eyes opened wide and her mouth dropped. "Get out of here! We're off the case again?"

Tynan nodded. He told them about his meeting at headquarters. He left out the part about his possible sudden departure to the Detective Bureau. As much as he wanted to get out of IAB, he would miss working with people like Joe and Linda. They had been good soldiers.

Joe shook his head. "You mean all this running around this morning was a waste of time?"

"No, not really. It may still come in handy. While you guys were out, Russell talked to the lab and they say the gun on the floor of the car was used to kill Santos. The other gun was not fired."

"Case closed," chuckled Joe as he pumped his fist.

Tynan raised his eyebrows. "That's what everyone seems to think. I find it odd the gun was laying there to begin with and, to top it off, there were no prints on it. No partials, not even smudges. It was wiped clean. Who did that?"

"Big deal," said Joe. "He used it and wiped it down. That sounds like a smart perp to me."

"Could be. But then if he's so smart why does he wipe it down and leave it laying on the floor of his car for anyone to see? Anyway, it doesn't make a difference as far as Narcotics is concerned. They are going full steam ahead with the investigation into Lugo. This thing still has legs."

Linda frowned. "Did they say we're to have nothing to do with this anymore Lou?"

"As a matter of fact, they didn't. All they said was that Lieutenant Sullivan was going to handle the case, which is Palace speak for saying she's going to do nothing. Our friends over at the US

Attorney's office are going to keep running with their stolen car caper on Warren. Unlike the last time, they didn't say we're to have absolutely nothing to do with the CI or any of the subjects. I'm going to provide whatever support we can to Narcotics and I'm going to talk with this junkyard guy and see what he knows. I'm not disobeying orders. I'm just helping the Narcotics Division and the Detective Bureau solve some open cases."

Linda stopped frowning but she didn't seem thrilled. "But the Santos homicide is closed. Just because there were no prints on the gun doesn't mean anything," she said.

"All very true. Even if the Santos case is closed, the Kearns' case isn't, and whatever we find gets passed along to the Detective Squad. Between us, I don't think Kearns killed Santos. Closing that case is just a matter of convenience."

"So, you don't believe our witness anymore?" she asked.

"Not sure I ever believed him. Let's just say I'd like to have more evidence."

"As long as they didn't give direct orders to drop our investigations, I'm fine with it, I guess" said Linda as she looked down at the floor. "Besides, I know you two can't solve it by yourselves."

Joe laughed. "Yes, it requires a woman's touch." Looking back at Tynan he asked, "What do you want us to do now?"

"We'll wait for our witness to show up then take him to meet Lugo. Maybe something will pan out with that. Then, after that's done, we'll get in touch with our CI and do the same thing. Between the two of them, they should be able to find something out."

Before either of them could get up, the buzzer rang. They didn't get many outside visitors at their office. Tynan wondered if it was Jaime, the witness.

"Joe, do me a favor and see who that is."

"Sure." Joe was up and out of the office in a flash. Tynan looked at Linda. "What's the matter Linda? You don't look happy. You don't have to do anything else with these cases if you don't want to."

Linda took in a deep breath and let out a long sigh. "Look. Lou, I appreciate what you are doing here and I understand that the bosses downtown can be assholes. But I've been in IAB a long time, back to when it was IAD. This has been pretty much my whole career. If you leave here and go somewhere else, people are just going to look at you and say to themselves that you were drafted here and you had no choice. When you go to your next assignment, they'll accept you, but I'm different."

She looked back down at her shoes. "If I get thrown out of here, no matter where I go, they'll say I'm a career IAB rat. And they'll never trust me. I'll never be accepted. I don't want that. I have a long way to go before I can retire and I'm happy spending it here. I don't want to go to the Detective Bureau or, worse, Patrol, and have people hanging dead rats on my locker every day. I couldn't deal with that."

Tynan nodded. He felt sorry for her. "Look, you don't have to do anything with this case, but I promise you that if they try and take it out on you, I'll go to bat for you. Even if I have to go to the Commissioner himself. Shit, even if I have to go to the press. I won't let you take a fall."

Linda looked up. "I know. I trust you." She got up and went to the window. "I hope things work out okay."

Before Tynan could answer, Joe ran into the office. "It's the fucking witness. I put him in the interview room. He's already met with Lugo and he's got some shit you won't believe."

A LOT OF ANSWERS

Tynan rushed down to the interview room. The sleepiness that had been creeping into his brain vanished. When the three of them entered the small room, Jaime was sitting down, smoking a cigarette. He blew a long stream up at the ceiling. "Hey guys, I've got a lot to tell you."

Tynan held his hand up to stop him. "Before you start, didn't I tell you to come here first before you went over there?"

"I know, man, but I just figured why waste time. Besides, I can take care of myself."

"Let's get something straight," said Tynan as he pointed his finger at Jaime. "When I tell you to do something, you do it. Okay? There's no freelancing around here."

"Yeah, yeah." Jaime took another puff. "But wait until you hear what I got. You're going to be very glad I did it."

"Okay, let's hear it." Tynan stood up against the door as Joe and Linda pulled up chairs across from the witness.

"I go up there to find Lugo and sure enough, he's hanging out in front of his building. I talked to him about how we can do business if I step right into Santos' spot. He tells me that I can keep Santos' spot if I give him twenty percent of what I sell. I told him that twenty percent is too high. That's when he says that unless I want to end up like Santos, it's going to be twenty. He also tells me that he's doing me a favor because he had to talk Warren out of killing me."

Jaime put his cigarette out on the floor and reached for another. He lit it up and looked around at the three of them. He took a puff. Smoke cascaded out of his mouth as he spoke. "Then he tells me it was Warren's idea to have Santos killed. Lugo said he told Kearns to carry it out, and after it was done, Lugo killed Kearns because he didn't want any witnesses."

Tynan left his spot at the door and put both hands on the table, leaning over Jaime. "Why would he tell you all this? He kills Kearns because he's a witness and then he tells you? He had to know you were there that night. Why doesn't he kill you? That makes no sense."

"Yeah, but both Lugo and Warren know I can run Santos' spot and make them more money than if they try and run it. Kearns can't do that. I can make them money. That's what it's all about."

Tynan felt himself losing patience with Jaime. "Still, what's his advantage for telling you he shot Kearns?"

"Lugo told me because he wants to show me that he's the man. Warren knew that Kearns had to go but he didn't want to do it himself. It's simple. They are getting rid of anyone who can be linked to them."

Linda looked up at Tynan. She had a slight frown on her face. Tynan was sure she was thinking something wasn't right or maybe Tynan was just projecting his own thoughts. Joe just sat there, staring at the witness. Not moving, not showing any emotion.

Linda turned to Jaime. "Are you willing to go back and wear a wire?"

"You know that. I'll go back today. Not a problem. He's still going to be up there."

"What time did you go see him?" asked Joe.

"Oh, I guess about ten, something like that."

"You're willing to go right back up there and get all of this on tape?" Tynan asked. "You don't think he'll get suspicious?"

"Nah, we're tight now. He knows he can make money with me. I'll get it all on tape and you'll be the big hero. Then Warren's gone. I can get back to my life, and no disrespect, man, but I don't want to see you guys again."

Tynan nodded. "Okay. Let's get him wired up. Grab Russell and his guys and we'll head out as soon as we can." Tynan opened the door and walked out. He went down to his office. After locking the witness room, Linda and Joe followed him.

"Wow, if this is true," said Joe, "we got this thing wrapped up."

"Yeah, if it's true," said Linda. "She shook her head. I don't know. I don't get it. The whole thing doesn't make sense. I'm not buying Lugo telling him that he killed Kearns, just to give himself street credits. I don't buy it."

Tynan nodded. "We're going to find out real soon just how much sense this makes. Wire him up and I'm going to get someone out on that set to keep eyes on him as he talks to Lugo. It won't take us long to find out if he's full of shit or not."

"I believe him," said Joe. "I'll bet a hundred bucks he's for real."

Tynan stuck his hand out, "Hundred? You're on. But there's one thing I want to know."

"What's that?" asked Linda.

"If Warren gave the order to kill Santos and Lugo passed it on to Kearns, then who was driving the car? Was it Lugo? If it was someone else, who are they and are they still alive? We never found out who was behind the wheel of that black Lincoln."

"Simple," said Joe. "I'll tell the witness to get that out of Lugo when he goes to talk to him."

"What happens if we get this all on tape?" asked Linda. "Do we grab Lugo right away?"

Tynan shrugged his shoulders. "As long as we got it on tape, we'll wait for Jaime to get off the set. We'll take him back here and call the District Attorney. If they give the green light, we scoop up Lugo. Then we'll see if Lugo is interested in doing fifteen years instead of life. If he cooperates, we grab Warren right after that. Sweet and simple."

"What about downtown?" asked Linda.

Tynan could see she looked worried. "Don't sweat downtown. I'll take care of that. It may not have ended the way they wanted but the case on Warren is over. I'll convince them it's a feather in their cap."

"I hope so," said Linda as she and Joe walked out of the office. Tynan looked out the window at the boats. *She isn't the only one hoping,* thought Tynan.

TECHNICAL DIFFICULTIES

Tynan decided to make a few phone calls while the witness was being wired. When he contacted Tech Services, they told him they had been pulled off the Bronx assignment that morning. The surveillance unit told him the same thing. Just as he thought, Klein had wasted no time in pulling all the resources he had given Tynan. Klein was eager to end Tynan's involvement with the Warren case.

Tynan was so tired now, he felt like his hair hurt. He'd give anything to just lay down for an hour, but he couldn't rest until he had Jaime wired up and sent out to talk to Lugo. That might put the whole case back on track. *Case? What case?* he thought. There was no case anymore. The bosses down in the Palace wanted the Feds to grab Warren. As far as they were concerned, the Santos case was solved and the Kearns' case was the responsibility of the Detective Bureau. *That was it*! *That was his way out!* thought Tynan. He'd get the Detective Bureau to make the arrests. Then downtown couldn't say they were disobeying orders. "What a fucking place," he said out loud.

Just as he got up to go back to see how Linda and Joe were doing, the phone rang. "Lieutenant Tynan, Group Forty-One."

"Hey, it's Kurt. How are you doing?"

Tynan had to think a moment. Kurt? He'd almost forgotten about his ATF contact. "Fine. How are you?"

"Great. I just wanted to call and let you know that my CI is now working with the US Attorney on their case so he won't be available anymore."

"That didn't take long," said Tynan. "Any chance we could use him just for this afternoon?"

"No way. Sorry. I picked him up this morning and dropped him off at their office."

"Well, thanks for the call. We could have really used him this afternoon but I get it."

"You wouldn't have been able to use him anyway. When we picked him up, he had a broken wrist," said Kurt. "I had to take him to the hospital first."

"By the way, where did you pick him up at?" asked Tynan.

"On Southern Boulevard and Longwood around ten. He called from a pay phone. Why?"

"Nothing, just curious. Thanks for the heads up. Take care of yourself." Tynan hung up. On the wall outside his office hung a large street map of the Bronx. He went over and looked for Southern Boulevard and Longwood Avenue. It was a block from Fox and Longwood. The CI had been within a block of where the witness had met Lugo, and at the same time no less. "Another coincidence," mumbled Tynan to himself.

Joe and Linda came walking down the hall as he was staring at the map. "Are you having a vision, Lou?" asked Joe.

"In fact, I think so. I just got a call from our ATF agent and he said that we're no longer able to work with the CI. But what's really interesting is that he picked the CI up at Longwood and Southern Boulevard, exactly one block from where our star witness met Lugo. How do you like that?"

Joe raised his eyebrows. "I don't. What the fuck is going on here? Why do I get the feeling we're the odd man out on everything in this case?"

"I don't know. I couldn't have used him anyway. Kurt said Angel broke his wrist. When he picked him up, he had to take him to the hospital. We'll have to rely on Jaime, the witness."

He continued. "Tell Russ to use the pickup instead of the surveillance van. It's got a cap on it. He can put two of his guys in the bed of the truck, under the cap, and take pictures with the camera out the back. The truck will be less noticeable than the van. Have one of his guys park it near Lugo's spot and walk off. The guys in the back can try and film from there. They can put a repeater in the truck and we'll monitor Jaime's conversation with Lugo from one of our cars."

"Okay, Lou. We should have everything set up in about an hour. I'll draw up a tactical plan and give the briefing," said Joe.

"Sounds good. In the meantime, I want to check on our junkyard. Maybe I'll head back there after the Lugo meet."

Linda let out a sigh. "How about you just go home, Lou? We can get in touch with the junkyard tomorrow. Remember, this isn't our case anymore."

Tynan nodded. "We'll see." He patted Linda on the shoulder and went back to his office.

Tynan called home, but nobody answered. He looked up at the clock and realized his wife and kids were probably out at the park. That's where he should be, not sitting here playing hide and seek with drug dealers for bosses who didn't care. He thumbed through his department phone book looking for the Auto Crime Division number.

If anyone knew anything about junkyards in the Bronx it would be them. He dialed the number and after being transferred around from one office to another he finally got in touch with a Detective Alvarez. According to the last person to transfer Tynan's phone call, Alvarez knew more about Bronx junkyards and auto salvage than any normal human would want to know.

Tynan grabbed his pen and turned over a new sheet on his legal pad. "Hi detective, I'm told you are a walking encyclopedia when it comes to auto salvage in the Bronx."

The detective laughed. "I don't know about that. What do you want to know?"

"How about Vic's Auto Salvage on Garrison Avenue? Run by a guy named Vic Grossi."

"Ah, old Vic. Haven't seen him in some time. He's a player. Says he's legit now. In reality, he deals mostly in stolen parts. We don't have anything on him right now but he's been collared in the past for running chop shops. He's not a 'made guy' but he's an associate for organized crime. Do you have anything on him?"

"No. I think he might be able to help us on a case but he seems reluctant. He says he has to talk to his partners."

"I'll bet. His partners are probably all wise guys. He's taken a lot of pinches for stolen car parts but he's no cowboy. Whenever he's been arrested, he's been the perfect gentleman. He knows he's not going to do any real time. If you can convince him you're not looking at him for stolen parts he might help you. He's just a little nervous. Anything else I can do for you?"

"No. In fact, you've been a big help. If I need something, I'll call back. Take care."

Interesting, thought Tynan. *Vic would definitely be worth talking to again.* Linda stuck her head in the door. "Do you want to do the tactical plan in here?"

"Yeah, time to get the show on the road."

It was one o'clock in the afternoon by the time the tac plan was finished and the group headed out the door. Tynan knew that a lot depended on the pickup truck getting a good spot to film the witness talking to Lugo. He wanted to be able to see, not just hear, the meeting. If nothing else they would have the audio but Tynan wanted to keep a close eye on Jaime. There were too many gaps in this case and he wasn't a big fan of the witness taking matters into his own hands by meeting Lugo earlier.

As they headed over to Fox Street, the group tuned in the frequency for the Four-One. It didn't seem too busy. At one time, that precinct had been the busiest in the city. A real bucket of blood. Its nickname was Fort Apache. After the abandoned buildings were burnt to the ground, it was known as the Little House on the Prairie. A pretty good swath of it looked like Berlin at the end of World War Two. Although things had calmed down, the drug business was still going strong.

The pickup truck with its lone driver and the two detectives laying down in the bed under the cargo cap headed out before everyone else. They wanted to be able to search for the best spot before the witness was turned loose. It was the driver of the pickup that came over the IAB frequency to the rest of the group. "Something is going on at Fox. Three patrol cars, Crime Scene and the Detective Squad."

Tynan picked up the radio. "Are they on the street or at a building? Do you see our subject hanging out?"

"The patrol cars are empty. It looks like everyone is in one of the apartment buildings. We're going to do a drive by to get a closer look."

Tynan went over the air to the other cars. "Everyone, stay put and let the surveillance truck see what's going on first. Just pull over and wait until we get the all clear."

The surveillance truck came back on the air. "Don't see the subject standing around. There's a crowd outside 811 Fox Street and the cops are in the subject's building. We're going to find a spot to pull over and let you know what's going on."

Tynan acknowledged. *Something else to screw things up,* he thought to himself. *Why can't anything go smooth with this case?* Linda was sitting in the front passenger seat and Joe was sitting in the back, checking the equipment for the recording device. "We'll just sit tight," said Tynan.

Linda looked at Tynan. "Maybe we should send the witness out and he can let us know what's going on. Lugo could be in the crowd and our guys missed him."

Tynan nodded. "Not a bad idea." Tynan looked at the tac plan and picked up the IAB radio, "Hey Russ, get Jaime to walk onto the set and see if he can spot our subject. Maybe he can find out what the commotion is all about. Let's do a sound check before he steps out."

"Ten-four, Lou," said Russell. Joe turned up the volume on the receiver for the witness's wire. "One, two, three, four." Jaime's voice came in loud and clear.

Joe got on the radio, "He's loud and clear. All set to have him step out."

"He's out of the car. He'll be at Fox and Longwood in about five minutes," said Russ.

Tynan yawned. He drummed his fingers on the steering wheel. "Let's hope this goes okay."

"You are an optimist," said Joe. "It already isn't going according to plan."

The minutes went by. They could hear the sound of the witness walking as his clothes brushed against the mike on his wire.

"Surveillance truck to Group leader, we got the witness in sight and he's walking toward the location. By the way, Sergeant McCarthy from Narcotics just pulled up. He's going inside."

"Detective squad and narco? That ain't good," said Tynan.

Joe adjusted the volume on the receiver. They could clearly hear the witness talking to people. "Hey, what's going on?" asked Jaime of someone in the crowd.

"I don't know. They say some guy got shot in an apartment."

There were more swishing sounds as Jaime's clothes rubbed against the wire. He talked to more people but they were of no help.

"This sucks," said Tynan. "A shooting. Shit, it's got to be a DOA. He's not going to meet up with Lugo. That drug spot is going to be shut down until they get the body out of there. Can you believe this?"

"Actually, I can," chuckled Linda. "Are we going to stay or call it off?"

"I don't know, we'll give it a few minutes and see what happens."

Tynan's cell phone started ringing. "What now, something else going wrong?" said Tynan before he grabbed the phone. He was running out of patience. "Lieutenant Tynan."

"Hi Lou," said Sergeant McCarthy on the other end of the cell. "Guess where I am?"

"Let me see, I'd say you are at 811 Fox Street staring at a dead body."

"What the fuck? How'd you know that? Do you have a pole camera up?"

"Nope, we got eyes on the location."

"Do you know the rest of it?" asked McCarthy.

"No. What's the rest of it?"

"I came down because we got a call from the detectives that it might be a drug related homicide. Right now, I'm staring at Lugo. He's lying on the floor of his apartment. Dead as a doornail."

"Get the fuck out of here."

"Nope. Honest to God truth."

Tynan almost found it hard to breathe. "Just him. Any other victims? Any witnesses? Any idea who the shooter is?"

"Just him. Looks like one shot to the face. They're doing a canvass now to see if anyone heard anything. There was an anonymous call made to 911. The caller said he was a friend of the victim and discovered his body. Do you want me to tell the squad anything?"

"Do they know when this happened?"

"Sometime earlier this morning. He hasn't been dead long. Looks like he answered the door and got popped. There's two guns laying here. Both nines. One in Lugo's hand and the other lying next to him, along with a big bag of money."

"Alright, thanks. We're going to wrap up our surveillance here. I'll come over once we get our guy off the set. Looks like you're not going to have a case on Lugo after all."

"That's the way it goes. We've been doing some 'buy and busts' in the area. It's not a major case but good for the neighborhood and gives us overtime, so not a total loss. You never know, we may still come up with something."

"Okay, I might be seeing you in a few if you're hanging out there."

"Nah, I'm going to give the squad what we know and then head back to the office. We got more 'buy and busts' later."

"Take care," said Tynan as he clicked off the phone.

"Are you going to fill us in Lou?" asked Linda.

"Yeah, just give me a minute." He picked up the radio. "Russ, see if you can get one of your guys to go into the crowd and tell Jaime to head back to your car. Let me know when he's back in the auto. We're going to wrap this up."

"Ten-four," said Russell.

"It turns out we're not going to need Jaime to talk to Lugo."

"What?" said Linda and Joe together.

"Lugo is dead. Someone put an end to his promising career as the King of Fox Street."

"Right after he talked to Jaime?" asked Linda.

"It's one of three options," said Tynan. "One, this guy was dead before Jaime said he talked to him and he made the whole thing up. Two, he got popped after Jaime talked to him." Tynan took a deep breath.

"What's three?" asked Joe.

"Jaime did it."

It took about fifteen minutes to round up Jaime. Tynan told the rest of the group to head back to the office and he'd meet them there. Then he drove over to Fox Street. The crowd had started to thin out. Tynan found out, over the years, that a dead body on the street was like having a free movie. Everyone wanted to see what was going on. But if the body was inside and the building had been roped off for a crime scene, people lost interest. If there was no excitement, people went back to their dull lives.

Tynan tinned the cop guarding the entrance to the building, who let the three of them pass. Inside they saw the detectives gathered in the doorway to Lugo's apartment. Lieutenant Morris from the Four-One Squad looked up and laughed. "Tell me, you're here to take this case too."

"Not quite. We just happened to be in the neighborhood, as they say."

"Did anything pan out with that case?" Then Morris whispered, "As far as a cop being involved?"

"No. It turned out we were looking for an ex-cop who got fired while in the academy. Supposedly, he's the shooter in the Santos case but he turned up dead too." Tynan wasn't sure if he was telling Morris a lie or not.

Morris nodded. "I get it. That's why the Santos case is closed."

"We found a witness who said the ex-cop did it but I'm beginning to have my doubts."

"Doubts? Who cares? It's closed. What about this case right here? Got anything," asked Morris.

"This dead guy was involved in the Santos murder too, and our witness in the Santos murder talked to Lugo about ten o'clock this morning. He might be the last person to see this guy alive."

Morris snorted. "That's some coincidence, ain't it?"

"Well, if you think that's a coincidence, I got another one. At just about the same time, a confidential informant for the Feds, who also knew Lugo, was being picked up about a block from here."

"You think they might be involved?"

"I don't know," shrugged Tynan. "It's possible. The witness will be over at our office if you're interested."

"What's the story with the informant?" asked Morris.

"He's a federal CI that we thought might have some information. Feds swear by him. I just know he was very cooperative until he suddenly wasn't. Then he gets picked up by his handler a block from here. Do you have an idea as to when this guy got killed?"

"Nah, looks fairly fresh. The door was closed but not locked. Supposedly, a friend found the body and called anonymously to 911. The patrol car responded. The door still had the security chain on it and they had to bust it off. I know this guy is a player according to Narcotics. An initial canvass didn't turn up anything. Nobody heard anything. Want to go and take a look?"

"Sure, why not?" shrugged Tynan. He motioned Linda and Joe to follow him. Lugo was laying right inside the apartment door. He had taken one round in the face. The bullet had lodged in the wall and the bullet hole was surrounded by blood spatter and brain matter. Off to Lugo's right was a clear plastic bag. Inside were rolls of twenty-dollar bills, tightly wrapped with rubber bands. Lugo was wearing a T shirt, blue sweat pants, and lime green flip flops. He didn't look like someone who was dressed for company.

Lugo wasn't taking any chances when he answered the door. He had a nine-millimeter in his right hand. *While he might have been prepared, he wasn't fast enough,* thought Tynan. *Or maybe he decided the guy at the door wasn't a threat.* That decision was a mistake. Another semi-automatic pistol lay at Lugo's feet. "What's with the two guns?" asked Tynan. "Every time I see a dead body these days, there's two guns with it."

"Beats me," said Morris. "Maybe he had the gun in his waist-band and it fell out. Could be the shooter's gun and they left it. We'll send it to the lab for ballistics. We're not going to disturb anything until the Crime Scene Unit is finished. The apartment is empty. He has a girlfriend but she left early this morning to visit her mother. That was around eight-thirty. She says he was alive then and your guy says he was still alive at ten. He gets found here by his friend and the call comes in at eleven-thirty."

Tynan thought it seemed pretty straight-forward except for the second gun. He turned to Morris. "Looks like Lugo was ready. He's got a pistol in his hand. What if Lugo opened the door, saw trouble, and tried to slam the door shut? The shooter fired but dropped the gun."

Morris shrugged and said, "Hey, I'll buy it. Just as good a theory as any other."

"Okay, we'll leave you to it," said Tynan. "How about if we bring our witness over to your office and your guys can talk to him? I'd like to watch the interview if you don't mind."

"No problem," said Morris. "Bring your witness over. My guys will give him the once over."

"You got it." He turned to Joe and Linda, and said, "Come on, let's get out of here."

The three of them were silent as they walked back to the car. Tynan wanted to take a moment to clear his head. He had been up for too long. He wasn't thinking clearly anymore. Before Tynan started the car, he turned and looked at Joe and Linda. "What do you think?"

Joe pulled himself up from the back seat, putting his head in between Linda and Tynan. "I don't know about you two but I think this whole think stinks. We got two guys dead in as many days, and both of them are wacked before we're about to talk to them. Why do I have the feeling someone doesn't want us to ask them too many questions?"

Tynan nodded. "Yeah, but who doesn't want us to talk to them?"

"Warren," said Linda.

MORE QUESTIONS THAN ANSWERS

Tynan wanted to go down to the junkyard and talk to the owner. Maybe that guy could shed some light on who had talked to Kearns last. He started the car, picked up the phone, and dialed Russell's cell. "Hey Russ, I want you to take the witness over to the Four-One Squad. They have some questions for him. I'll meet you there. While you're driving him over, you might want to ask him who would have a reason for killing Lugo."

"Are you kidding?"

"No, that mess back on Fox Street was a crime scene for Lugo."

"Great," said Russell. "I'll ask him and see what he says."

Tynan hung up and put the car in drive. "Let's go visit the junkyard."

It didn't take long to get to the yard. It sat on a dirty street, lined with machine shops, empty buildings, and stripped, abandoned cars. The junkyard was surrounded by an eight-foot, battleship gray, corrugated metal fence, the lower half of which was filled with faded graffiti. Inside the yard, there were several piles of what had once been the pride and joy of new car owners but now sat in depressing heaps of rusting auto bodies.

A large metal gate was opened barely a foot. Looming over the front entrance was a tall scaffold holding an old Chevy Impala, with the business name sprayed along the sides in red paint. "Vic's Auto Parts & Salvage" looked like it was open for business. Tynan pulled into the driveway and stopped in front of the gate. "I wonder if this guy is still alive."

"Hey, don't joke like that, Lou. Not the way things have been going," said Joe.

Tynan slipped through the narrow opening into the yard. It looked worse inside. The lot was strewn with car parts, used tires, and shells of old cars. Two men stood at the back of the yard next to a car crusher. Tynan started to head that way but stopped when a heavy-set balding man with glasses, appeared in the doorway of a trailer.

"Can I help you?" he barked.

"That's Vic," said Linda.

Tynan ambled over towards the trailer. The uneven dirt floor of the lot was almost black from oil. The aroma of gasoline hung in the air. Tynan flashed his shield at the owner. "I'd like to talk to you about Kearns."

"Yeah, I talked to those other two already. I don't really have anything to say."

"I was hoping that talking to your partners might have refreshed your memory," said Tynan.

Vic hopped down the trailer's oil-stained wooden steps. He was dressed in grease-stained blue overalls. *He moves fast for a middle-aged fat guy,* thought Tynan. Vic wiped his hands on his coveralls and stuck his right hand out to Tynan. "I'm Vic, the owner. I'd love to help you but I don't know what I can add."

"What can you tell me about Kearns?" said Tynan as he shook Vic's hand.

"He was a good worker. Hung out with some shit-heads but when he was here, he was top shelf. I'm going to have a hard time replacing him."

"What kind of friends? Do you know their names?"

"Listen, detective, I mind my own business. I don't get involved in other people's lives. If you come here and do your job, what you do outside of here is not my concern. Got it?"

"Yeah, I got it. But maybe you know their names, or nicknames, maybe a description. You know, something like that."

Vic pointed at Linda and Joe. "I told you guys; I really don't have anything. I can't afford to have the police hanging around. You know what I mean."

On another day, Tynan might have played along with Vic but he was way too tired and felt like he was walking in a fog. He didn't like playing the heavy but had no problem doing it if it got him what he wanted. He decided to go straight at Vic.

"Listen, Vic. You look like a nice guy, just trying to run a business and I'm sure your partners are all nice guys too. But you see my problem is that I got a dead body and every time I try and find out why he's dead, I get this run-around. You don't want the police around here, I understand. But what you don't get is that if I walk out of here with no more information than I came in with, I guarantee you that you're going to have cops crawling all over this place. Like maybe cops from the Auto Crime Division." Tynan looked at the dirt and drew a line in the oily soil with his shoe. "Like maybe the Environmental Protection people. Would you like me to do that, Vic?"

Vic held up his hands in front of him. "Easy, easy. I understand. I might be able to help but are you interested in anything else other than who killed Kearns?"

"Vic, I don't give a shit about whatever it is you are supposedly doing here. I know that probably fifty percent, nah, ninety percent of the stuff that rolls in here is probably stolen. I don't care. I want to know what you can tell me about Kearns and who his friends were and what happened the day he left here for the last time. Get it?"

"Alright. I know of one name. It's a guy named Angel. That's all I know. He was here on Kearns' last day. He came by and asked to speak with him. I told Kearns to make it snappy. I'm not paying people to yap with their friends."

"Did he drive up? What kind of car?"

"He walked in here, just like you did. He didn't have a car because he was asking Kearns to give him a ride. I don't know how he got here. He wanted to hang out in the yard but I told him to wait outside. You know, I ain't getting sued if something falls on his head."

"What did he look like?"

"He was short. Fair skinned. Had a goatee, kind of blond."

As Vic described the guy who came to see Kearns, both Linda and Joe edged closer. Tynan could sense their interest was picking up.

"What kind of hair did he have?" asked Linda.

"I don't really know. It looked light brown, hard to say. He was wearing a Yankee baseball cap."

"What about his eyes?" asked Joe.

"Oh yeah, that was the funny part. He was wearing sunglasses. When I told him to wait outside, he pulled them down to look over his glasses at me. Like he was trying to act like a tough guy. That's when I saw he had blue eyes. He wasn't dressed like you would think for someone coming to this yard. Leather jacket, and it was kind of warm for a leather jacket, shiny shoes, regular pants. Just different."

Tynan nodded. His stomach was starting to tighten. "If you saw a picture of him, would you recognize him?"

"Yeah, I'm pretty sure," said Vic.

"Anything else you could add?" asked Joe.

"He used my phone in the trailer. After I told him to wait outside the lot, he came back in and helped himself to my phone. The guy's got some balls."

"Do you know who he called?" asked Tynan.

"No. When I came back into my office, he was using the phone. I told him to get the fuck out. He comes here, talking to Kearns when he's supposed to be working. Kearns uses my phone, then this loser uses my phone. Hey, I'm trying to run a business. That was it."

"What time did Richie Kearns leave?" said Linda.

"Like I said before, Richie left between seven and eight. He was going to see his girl. I guess after he dropped this guy off. I know Richie called his mom and the girlfriend. Then he left."

"Okay, I appreciate it," said Tynan.

"It's a shame," said Vic. "Hard to find someone who worked like him. Not a lot of guys interested in doing this kind of work anymore."

"Yeah, I'll bet. Take care," said Tynan as he walked to the car.

As they backed out of the driveway, Linda said, "I think we got a problem with our CI."

"We sure do," said Tynan. "We need Vic to see a picture of the CI and see if our Angel is the same Angel he's talking about. It sounds like the same guy. We also need to find out if the Crime Scene Unit lifted any prints from Kearns' car."

"At least we're getting somewhere," said Joe.

Tynan gunned the car as they headed towards the Precinct. "Maybe. I still have a lot of questions."

Tynan didn't have to drive far to get to the precinct. He was too tired to talk anymore. Linda and Joe must have felt the same way because they just sat there staring out at the drab brick buildings they passed along the way. Tynan double parked in front of the precinct. The three of them trudged up the stairs. Tynan flashed his shield at the desk officer, yelled out "squad," and went up to the Precinct Detective Squad's office.

Lieutenant Morris was standing in the squad room talking to the detectives. He nodded to Tynan and pointed towards the interrogation room. "They're in there. Do you want to watch from the observation room?"

"Yeah, I don't want to interrupt anything. Who's in there?"

"One of your guys and one of mine. The guy seems pretty cool and collected."

They went into the adjoining observation room with a two-way mirror. Jaime was seated at the table in the interrogation room. One of Morris' detectives sat opposite him and Russell was leaning against a wall in the corner. Jaime sat there and calmly blew streams of smoke from his cigarette.

"Okay, let's go over this again," said the detective. "Start at the top and tell us about your day."

"Sure. I was supposed to go over to the Internal Affairs office at noon. I got up around eight, took a shower, got dressed, and then around nine o'clock I headed towards Lugo's spot."

Russell interrupted. "Why did you go there when you were supposed to come to our office?"

Jaime shook his head disapprovingly. "I told you. There was no sense in going to your office when Lugo was closer. I wasn't going to wear a wire, so what did I need to go to your place for? For protection? Like the kind you gave Santos?"

Jaime flicked the ash off his cigarette and pushed back in his chair. "I went over to Lugo's spot, on Fox and talked to him. He said I could keep Santos' spot and pay a tax to him. He also told me Kearns killed Santos. Lugo told Kearns to do the hit and Warren wanted Kearns killed so there wouldn't be any way it could come back to him."

"That doesn't make any sense," said the detective. "If Warren was going to get rid of Kearns, why would Lugo believe he was safe?"

"I guess Lugo thought that Warren needed him to run the operation. Looks like he was wrong. Now Warren has two spots that are wide open. Anyway, Warren is getting rid of everyone who can link him to the murder."

"Why isn't he getting rid of you?" asked Russell.

Jaime, leaned forward and raised his voice. "Because, he doesn't know I'm the witness. But he might now, after you brought me in here. This is the fucking precinct he works in."

Russell laughed. "Are you kidding? How could Warren not know you're a witness. Kearns had to have told Lugo you were there when he shot Santos. Don't you think Kearns told Lugo about you and he passed that on to Warren?"

"How should I know? Remember, I was there when Kearns showed up in the Lincoln but Santos sent me inside. Kearns didn't know I saw him from the window."

"Where did you talk to Lugo?" asked the detective.

"Right there on the street in front of his house. I made it quick because I don't want to be hanging out at his spot. I got there around ten and left after five minutes at the most. Just ask people up there. They must have seen me. I went right to your office after he told me that shit."

The detective leaned over the desk towards Lugo. "You see, that's a problem because we did ask people and nobody saw Lugo that morning. We even talked to his girlfriend and she said that when she left, Lugo was still in bed."

Jaime crossed his arms and legs, shook his head no, and looked down at his feet. "I don't care what she said or what anyone else said. They're not telling you the truth, anyway. He wasn't in bed when I got there. He was out on the street."

Russell cracked his knuckles. "He was out on the street by himself?"

"No, there were people there but they ain't going to tell you anything. They're smart. They know the score. They know that Warren works here and they probably think you and Warren are working together."

"Your story isn't adding up," said Russell.

"Did I go over to your office and tell you what he said to me or didn't I? Why would I run over to your office and tell you this shit and agree to wear a wire if it wasn't true?"

Russell smiled. "Pretty simple. You knew Lugo was dead."

"Oh man, this is bullshit." Jaime stood up. "Am I under arrest?"

"Not right now," said the detective.

"Good, then I'm walking. I ain't putting up with this shit. I try and help you and now you are trying to lay this off on me. Next thing, you'll be saying that I killed Santos. You guys are fucked up. You just don't want to arrest Warren. That's what this is all about."

Russell opened the door for Jaime. "Before you go, you might want to think about how many enemies you have out there on the street. Right now, we could be your only friends."

Jaime sucked his teeth. "I'll keep that in mind." The detective escorted Jaime out.

Tynan looked at Morris. "Let's go to your office."

The four of them went into Morris' office and he closed the door. "Is Warren dirty? Was he the cop you were looking for originally?" asked Morris.

"Keep that between us. It's just an allegation. I'm hoping your detective won't go blabbing that all over the precinct."

Morris shook his head. "He won't. He's a pro. What about this guy, Jaime, and the CI you have?" asked Morris.

Tynan raised his eyebrows. "I don't like the fact they were within a block of each other around the same time the victim gets killed."

Morris nodded. "Maybe Narcotics will come up with some information."

Tynan stuck his hand out and shook Morris' hand. "Alright, we're out of here. Us being here will probably bring you bad luck anyway."

Tynan felt dejected. He had lots of theories but no proof. The ride to the office was as quiet as the ride to the precinct. Tynan didn't trust Jaime anymore. He knew he should just let the case go and forget about it. Kearns, Lugo, and Santos were just three more drug related homicides. Warren was a problem for the Feds.

When Tynan got back to the office, he called the Five-Two detective squad. They had not come up with any witnesses to the Kearns shooting and there were no usable prints lifted from inside Kearns' car. He couldn't deal with anymore strikeouts. It was time to go home.

He tried to put the case out of his mind on the ride home. He wanted to see his wife and kids. This case had just pulled him down one rabbit hole after another and he'd forgotten about what was important. *How is my family doing?* he thought. *Who cares about Santos, Kearns and Lugo. They're nothing to him. Two weeks ago, he didn't even know they existed.* As he walked in the front door to his house, he heard his kid's voices. He felt happy for the first time in days.

The next day, Tynan was heading back to the office. He felt refreshed. Even though he was exhausted when he got home, he managed to play with his kids and listen to their stories about what they did while he was missing in action. After some sleep, he found himself at peace with the idea that the cases were no longer his. In a few weeks, or maybe a month, he'd probably be transferred to the Detective Bureau.

As he walked back into IAB, he stuck his head in the administrative office and said hello to the staff. The past few days he had forgotten they existed. The two detectives that kept the paperwork flowing in and out of the Group didn't have any urgent messages. Tynan felt lighter on his feet as he grabbed a cup of coffee from the breakroom and strode down the hall to his office. Even his back wasn't bothering him. His boats were waiting, nodding hello in the gentle waves and early morning sunshine.

As he went behind his desk, he noticed he hadn't updated his calendar. He smiled and thought to himself there might not be much of a future for that timekeeper. He made his diagonals, and let out a low whistle. Grabbing a stack of worksheets, he started reading and signing off on them. Today would be a normal day, and for once, the dull routine did not bother him.

Joe came in first, holding a cup of coffee in his hand and nodding to Tynan. "You look a lot better, Lou."

"Feel a lot better too," said Tynan. "How about you?"

"No complaints. I'm going to check and see if they got any ballistics back on Lugo."

"Don't bother. Let's just put that to rest. Let the detective squad handle it."

"It's no problem," said Joe. "I'll do that and then me and Linda are going to show the CI's picture to Vic."

"Alright. Then, after that, we're just going to move on. Let's stick to free French fry cases."

The metal door slammed, followed by Linda's footsteps and she came to a stop in the doorway. "Good morning, you two."

Joe said, "I got good news for you Linda. We're putting the Santos-Lugo-Kearns-Warren mess to bed. We'll show Vic the picture, get the ballistics and that's it. Heard it from the Lou just now."

A smile lit up Linda's face. "Yes," she said as she slapped her hands together. "I'm glad that's over with. I was getting tired of people dying on us all the time. The body count was too high."

Tynan chuckled. "Okay, get back to work. I've got a lot of crap to sign."

They disappeared to their offices and Tynan went back to reading. The Warren case had chewed up everyone's time and newly arrived cases were sitting in his basket unassigned. He glanced at all of them. They were all pretty routine and uninteresting. *Just as well,* he thought.

The morning seemed to sweep by as Tynan slowly transferred the pile of papers to the out box. For lunch, he decided he was going to walk along the water. By the time the wall clock showed noon, he was ready for it. When he got to the door, the phone started to ring. He was going to go back and pick it up but decided not to. *Today, they can leave a message,* he thought.

Tynan enjoyed the walk along the waterfront. *This wasn't really that bad of a place as far as location,* he thought. He'd miss some of the people when he was transferred but he knew he wouldn't miss the work. Too much drama and politics for his taste. His beeper went off. It annoyed him. He looked down and saw that it was a call from McCarthy, followed by 911.

McCarthy never put the universal sign for an emergency after his beeps. "Shit," Tynan said out loud. He didn't want to head back to the office just yet, but it was McCarthy calling. He turned and headed back to the building. As he passed the administrative office, "Bronx Narcotics is burning up the phones for you," one of the detectives yelled.

Tynan picked up the phone on his desk, and without sitting down, dialed McCarthy's number.

"Sergeant McCarthy."

"What's up? Sounds like something urgent," said Tynan. He was hoping it wasn't.

"I'll say," said McCarthy. "We're out doing 'buy and bust' this morning down in the Four-One and we pick up a guy on Fox Street. We got him doing a hand to hand with one of our undercovers. Not a big deal by itself. He sold him two tins. When we're processing the arrest, we ask the guy if he knows anything about the Lugo or Santos murders, and this guy decides to take a chance and talk."

Tynan wasn't sure if he wanted to hear the rest. He felt like someone was waking him from a pleasant dream. A dream where everything was calm and peaceful. He was afraid the dream was about to end. Tynan sighed. "What did he have to say?"

"This guy told us that he knows a guy who is willing to identify the shooters in both cases."

"Shooters?"

"Yep, as in more than one. According to him, this guy not only knows who popped Santos and Kearns but also Lugo. He says this witness wants to talk because he's afraid he'll be next. If you want, we can pick him up. It's your call but I figured I'd give you first dibs on it."

Tynan didn't have to think long. The need to get to the bottom of the old case came rushing into his head like an express train in the subway. "Yeah, we'll take it. Give me the name and address and we'll pick him up." Tynan wrote the information down. "Thanks, buddy. Once again, I owe you one."

He rushed down the hall to Linda and Joe. "Let's mount up, we have to roll on something right away. I'll fill you in on the way."

The three of them rushed down the hallway and out of the building. Tynan had the car in motion before Linda and Joe closed their doors.

"What's going on Lou?" asked Linda.

Tynan told them about the phone call from McCarthy. Linda just shook her head and Joe laughed. "Wait a minute. What happened to letting the detective squad handle it? Did I imagine that?" he said.

Tynan looked at Joe in the mirror. His smile looked genuine. Linda, just looked out the window. He couldn't see her expression but he was sure it was very different from Joe's.

Tynan reached over and lightly pushed Linda. "Come on! You guys want to know what happened as much as anyone else involved in this mess. You mean you don't want to get to the bottom of this?"

"No, I do Lou," said Linda in a low, tired voice. "But I'm just fed up with getting jerked around on this case. This is going to be another load of bullshit and we're going to wind up back here twelve hours from now, looking like a bunch of idiots."

"Not me," laughed Joe. "I like looking like an idiot. I can't wait to get there. Doesn't this crate go any faster?"

"As a matter of fact, it does," said Tynan as he hit the gas.

Their new witness lived on Aldus Street in a dreary brick apartment building. Fortunately, it was on the first floor. *At least he won't have to climb up five flights of stairs to listen to a bunch of lies,* thought Tynan. The door to the lobby was locked. Tynan looked for the buzzer to the apartment and pressed it three times. A man's voice came over the speaker, "Who's there?"

"Police," said Tynan. There was a long buzz and they pushed the door open. They walked up to the apartment door. Joe and Linda took their positions on either side. Tynan knocked, stepped to Joe's side, and stuck his shield in front of the peep hole.

A man's voice, yelled through the door, "I'm not opening up until I see your face."

"Okay," said Tynan as he stepped from the side of the door and stood squarely in front of the peep-hole.

A series of dead bolts snapped open and the door opened a crack. The man kept the chain on it. A pale man with black hair, brown eyes, and a moustache peered out. "Who else is with you?"

"Just my buddies." Linda and Joe both thrust their hands out holding their shield cases open so the man could see their identification cards.

"Okay, just a minute." The door closed and the chain came off. "Come in," whispered the man as he opened the door. The man was of medium build. He wore a blue denim shirt, black jeans and black sneakers. He had a two-day stubble on his face. His darting eyes were blood shot.

"We're from Internal Affairs. What's your name?"

"Tony. Tony Defede."

"You're just the guy we're looking for," said Tynan as he walked into the living room. It was small, with beat-up furniture. A TV sat in the corner. Defede walked over to the worn couch and sat down. Tynan thought he looked tired and scared.

Tynan stood in the middle of the room as Linda and Joe watched from the foyer. Tynan folded his arms across his chest. "A friend of yours says you have a big problem. There might be people looking to kill you. But he also says you have some information that we might be interested in. Maybe we can help each other out. What can you tell me about that?"

Defede sat back in the couch. He looked back and forth from Tynan to Linda and Joe. He licked his lips and put his hands on his knees. "I can tell you a lot. But I need to know what you can do for me."

"Like what?" asked Linda from the foyer.

"First of all, I need to know that I'm going to be protected and second, you're not going to lock me up on some bullshit that I say."

"We can manage that," said Tynan. "As long as you're not going to tell me that you killed someone or something crazy like that. We're not the drug police. We're interested in some murders and crooked cops. That's what we want. And if you tell us the truth, I guarantee you will be safe and you won't wind up in a cell on Rikers Island for some bullshit. But your information has got to be good."

Defede nodded. He jumped up from his seat. "Do I have your word?"

Tynan stepped towards him and stuck his hand out. "You got my word." As Tynan shook Defede's hand, he hoped this wasn't another wild goose chase, but deep down he felt that this guy was going to be different.

"Okay," said Defede. "Let's get the fuck out of here."

The new witness took a seat in the back of the car and looked out the window. Nobody spoke. They drove straight back to the office. Tynan felt excited. He'd been willing to walk away from the whole mess but McCarthy's call brought the thrill of the chase back to him. He still felt like he had a score to settle with downtown. Them pulling him off the case a second time was a real slap in the face. This witness might make it possible to pay back Klein and the others at the Palace.

He glanced occasionally in the rearview mirror to keep an eye on Defede. He seemed nervous. Even though he was sitting in a police car with three cops, he looked like a man who spent a lot of time looking over his shoulder. Tynan didn't blame him, considering the number of bodies piling up.

The four of them went up the stairs to the office. Tynan took the steps two at a time. He opened the door with his card and held it for the other three. "Go into the interview room." As Linda passed, he grabbed her by the arm and whispered in her ear, "Do me a favor and run this guy and see what type of record he has. I want it in front of us when we talk to him. And put together some photo arrays with Angel and Jaime in them." Linda nodded and went down the hallway.

Defede, took a seat at the table and pulled out a pack of cigarettes and a lighter. Joe took the chair opposite him. "Do you mind if I smoke?" asked Defede.

"No, knock yourself out," said Joe. "Do you want something to eat or drink?"

Defede shook his head. "No, I'm good." He shook out a cigarette, put it in his mouth and lit it. He took a long drag. The tension seemed to leave his body along with the smoke.

"Okay, Tony. Do you mind if I call you Tony?" asked Tynan. "Why don't we start out with you telling us about yourself."

"Like what?" asked Tony.

"Like how you know what you know. What do you do to make money, that kind of thing."

Tony closed his eyes and took another drag on his cigarette. "Look, I'm not saying I'm some kind of good guy. I make my living on the street. I work for Sammy Lugo. I guess I should say *worked* for Lugo. I was one of his boys, part of his crew. We'd been together a couple of years. I also knew a guy named Richie Kearns. We we're friends. I brought Richie in with me to work for Lugo. Richie was a good guy."

A long stream of smoke came out of Tony's mouth. "And I also knew Santos. I didn't work with him but I knew him through Lugo. We did business together. I know those three people and they're all dead."

Joe frowned. "Anything else you can tell us? Because we already know that. Anyone who reads the papers knows that."

Tony leaned back and tilted his chair up against the wall. "I know something you don't know and it ain't in no paper. I know who killed all three of them."

"I'm all ears," said Joe as he leaned forward.

Linda opened the door and handed Defede's rap sheet to Tynan. She dropped a legal pad on the table, along with a folder with some photo arrays, and sat down next to Joe. "Did I miss anything?"

Tynan glanced down at the rap sheet then looked back at Defede. "No, we're just getting to the good part. Why don't you tell us what you know, Tony? Start at the beginning."

"I worked for Lugo but was friends with Richie. We met right after he got busted out of the police. He was into the coke a little, not bad, but that's how we met. I sold him some stuff, and when I found out about him once being a cop, I mentioned it to Lugo, and he thought that maybe Kearns could be a good guy for the crew. Having been a cop and all, maybe he might come in handy. That's how it started."

"I used to move stuff around for Lugo. Kearns had a cop badge, so we worked together. I drive a livery cab. He sits in the back with the stuff and if we get stopped by the police, he shows them his badge. That was our system and how we used to move stuff around. We got pulled over a couple of times, but he'd whip out the badge and the cops thought everything was cool so they left us alone."

Tony rubbed his hand across his face and yawned. "It was a good plan. Things kind of got going from there. We were a team. We rode around, made deliveries, picked up cash, and did whatever Lugo wanted us to do."

"Okay," said Linda, "So, how did everyone wind up dead?"

"Sheesh," said Tony. "That's a good question. Part of the problem was Kearns was always looking to make a buck. He always wanted to do things on the side. Richie should have been happy with what we had. We made money and it was simple. Richie started to get too greedy."

"How did he get greedy?" asked Joe.

"First off, he was working in that junkyard. I understood that, because he was on probation and needed a job. But he got carried away with it. He started getting into the stolen car business with that guy." Tony snapped his fingers, "What's his name? An old guy who owns a junkyard on Garrison."

"Vic?" offered Tynan.

"Yeah, that's it. He started getting into stolen cars and taking them there. I thought it was dumb but he swore he made good money, and if he got caught, he wouldn't do any time. Nobody cares about stripping stolen cars. Then he starts bringing this guy Angel around. Richie gives Angel small amounts of coke to sell and he gets a piece. He made extra money that way. Lugo wasn't happy about that but he let it go because Richie was a big help moving the coke around."

"Angel? Who is Angel?" asked Tynan. "What's his real name?"

"Angel Lopez. Lugo knew Angel too, but he never really trusted him. They grew up together. Lugo didn't like Angel. He thought he asked too many questions. Lugo would give him small jobs to do but nothing big. He would never let him know where we kept our stash. Right before Santos got killed, Lugo was going to give Angel a job, dropping off some money to a guy in Washington Heights. It was going to be like a test, to see if he could be trusted, but it never happened."

"What's this guy look like?" asked Linda as she opened the folder with the photo arrays.

"He's not a big guy. Kind of blondish hair. He's got blue eyes. Talks a lot about guns and always asking who's selling guns, all sorts of shit. That was one of the reasons Lugo didn't trust him. This guy Angel also knew Santos. Angel wanted to become a regular part of a crew. I don't think he cared if he worked for Lugo or Santos."

Linda flipped one of the photo arrays over and pushed it towards Defede. "Do you see anyone you recognize among these pictures?"

Defede pulled the array closer and quickly pointed out Angel. "That's him, that's Angel."

Linda slid a pen over to Defede. "Could you circle that picture and sign your name?"

Defede quickly circled Angel's picture and scratched out his signature.

Tynan was getting impatient. "Okay, what else?"

"Things were fine. We're doing our business but sometimes we get hassled by Kearns' cousin. That was another problem."

"His cousin?" asked Linda as she placed the pictures back in the folder. "What about his cousin? What's his name?"

"Warren. He's a cop. Right there in the same precinct where we are doing business. He's always pestering Kearns. Wants him to get straight, stop hanging out with me, get out of the junkyard. Like non-stop."

Defede shook his head. "Shit, Warren even pulled us over once when we had a shitload of coke in the car. I thought we were done. But Kearns was smart on that one. He didn't argue. He just got out of my car and jumped into the police car with Warren. That was a close one. Lugo was in the car with us that day, which was unusual when we were carrying stuff. I thought Lugo was going to shit but it all turned out okay. Warren never searched the car. He just wanted his cousin, and once he got in the police car, they took off."

"Nobody got arrested?" asked Joe.

"No, it went smooth. Warren was just looking to keep his cousin out of trouble. He didn't search my car or anything. Aside from Richie getting hassled by his cousin, dealing in stolen cars, and bringing that asshole Angel around, things were okay."

Defede drew one more puff, then put the cigarette out on the floor. "Yeah, things were pretty good, but Angel starts pushing Lugo to give more coke to Santos to sell. I guess Angel wanted to get in tight with Santos." Defede shook his head. "That should have tipped me off that this Angel guy was up to something."

"Santos is getting the stuff up front from Lugo and paying off after he sells it. They'd done it before, but Angel wants Lugo to give Santos bigger amounts, and he does, but this time Santos doesn't want to pay up. He keeps stalling. So, Lugo sends me and Kearns over to put things straight with Santos. I don't know what Santos thought he was doing. Maybe he had spent the money, and didn't have it or maybe he was testing Lugo, I don't know. But after me and Richie talked to him, he agreed to pay up."

"When was this?" asked Tynan.

"Oh, I don't know. About two or three weeks ago. This was the first time we had a hard time getting money out of someone. I started to think maybe we were being tested. Santos agreed to pay us the twenty grand he owed, and me and Richie were supposed to go pick it up."

"Yeah, that was the plan. Me and Richie go over and pick up the money and everything is back to normal. I'm driving my livery and Richie is in the back seat as usual. We go to Santos and he's sitting at his spot with his guy, Jaime. He's like his right-hand man. We pull up and Richie rolls the window down and sticks his badge out."

"Why did he do that?" asked Linda.

"Richie thought they might think someone was going to shoot them if we just rolled up on them. That's why he stuck the badge out the window. He wanted to put them at ease."

Defede took out another cigarette, and lit it. He took another deep drag then blew the stream of smoke up in the air. "That's when shit got crazy. Santos has a plastic bag and lifts it up as Defede is coming near him. Just when I think the handoff is going to happen, the fucking guy, Jaime, whips out a pistol and starts blasting."

"Blasting who?" asked Joe.

"Santos. His own fucking guy." Defede held both of his hands up to his head. "I couldn't believe it. He shot his own fucking boss, right there in front of us."

"What did Kearns do?" asked Tynan.

"What did he do? What the fuck do you think? He runs back and gets in the car and we get the hell out of there. We're not hanging around for that."

"Did you think you were next?" asked Linda.

"All I know is Richie jumps back in the car and I'm in motion. I heard another shot and I think it was at us. He must have missed because when I checked my car later, there were no holes in it."

"What kind of car were you in?" asked Joe.

"My livery. A black Lincoln with heavy tint. My usual ride."

"Okay, what did you do next?"

"We went back to Lugo and told him what happened. I was afraid he'd think we took the money, but he must have seen we were for real. Richie was shook-up. He'd been standing right there when it happened."

Linda took another photo array out of her folder. "How many shots did Jaime fire?"

"Like, bam, bam, bam. Three and then later a fourth shot but I think that was at us."

Linda pushed the photo array across the table. "Anyone you recognize in these pictures?"

Defede tapped on Jaime's picture. "That's him. That's Santos' guy, Jaime. He shot Santos."

"Are you sure?" asked Linda.

"No doubt about it," said Defede. He grabbed the pen, drew a circle around Jaime's picture and signed his name. "That's the fucking guy."

Linda took the array back and without looking up, asked, "Did Lugo tell anyone else about what happened?"

"No way. We kept that to ourselves. He told us to keep our mouth shut. He didn't want the cops snooping around screwing up our business and he definitely didn't want people to think someone was holding out payment on him. He didn't tell anyone. I'm sure of that."

"Why do you think Jaime shot Santos?" asked Linda.

"I don't know for sure but I think he wanted the spot. He wanted to be the boss."

"Did he think your guy was going to forget about the money?" said Joe.

"Maybe he thought, if he killed Santos, Lugo would forget about the money, because the money was owed by Santos. But he didn't know Lugo. Lugo wasn't going to forget. Not after Santos had said he was going to pay. You can't let someone rip you off for twenty grand. If that got out on the street, you'd be known as a punk. Nobody would pay you. Someone would come and take your spot. Can't have that."

Tynan wanted to speed up the interview. "Why don't you tell us about the other two murders?"

"After Santos was shot, we weren't too sure what was going to happen next. Lugo wanted to see what Jaime would do. He could wait a couple of days to see if Jaime would contact him about the money, but if he didn't then Lugo would have to make a move. We went about our normal business. Richie was still at the junkyard and then Angel shows up asking a lot of questions."

"What do you mean?" asked Tynan.

"He went by the junkyard looking for Richie. He was there the day Richie got killed."

"How do you know that?" asked Linda without looking up from writing her notes.

"Because Richie called me and Lugo that same day. He wanted to go see his girl and he beeped Lugo to see if he needed him that night. He beeped me too. I called him back at the yard and he said this guy Angel was there asking a lot of questions about why Santos was killed, and he was still asking about the stolen cars."

Linda stopped writing suddenly and looked up quickly at Defede. "Stolen cars? Why was he asking Richie about stolen cars?"

Defede laughed and shook his head as he puffed on his cigarette. "Oh man, Richie was such a crazy guy. One time when Angel was around, we went for a ride, and Angel was talking about how he needed money, and Richie told him there's a lot of money in stealing cars."

The smile melted from his face. "Richie was a good guy but besides being greedy, he liked to talk a lot of shit. When Angel started talking about money, Richie said he was into stolen cars. He didn't want to tell Angel that all he was doing was chopping cars, so he started talking a line of shit."

"Like what?" asked Linda.

Defede chuckled again. "Like he told Angel that he was involved in some stolen car ring and he was stealing Mercedes and BMWs. Then he'd ship them over to the Middle East and make all sorts of money. He told Angel he wasn't worried about being arrested because his cousin was a cop in the precinct and he would protect him."

Defede started laughing, "Angel was really interested. After he heard about this stolen car ring, he'd bring it up every time he saw Richie. He wanted to get in on the deal."

Joe tapped his finger on the table. "I don't get it, what's so funny?"

"Don't you see, it was all bullshit. Richie wanted to pretend like he was some high roller. Yeah, he dealt in stolen cars alright. He took them apart for Vic in the junkyard. That's what they do. They chop up cars. Richie told Angel about stealing cars and sending them overseas because he wanted to be a big man, but he did none of that."

Linda looked at Tynan then back at Defede. "Okay, what about his cousin protecting him?"

"It was all bullshit. His cousin wouldn't do that. If Richie had asked him to do that, he would have kicked his ass. His cousin was trying to get Richie out of the life. He'd never help with that kind of shit. Besides, if Angel knew anything about stolen cars, he should have known it was all bullshit."

"Why would he know that?" asked Tynan.

"Because," chuckled Defede, "you make more money stripping a car for parts than selling it. Don't get me wrong, his idea sounds good and you could make money that way for sure, but why would you do that when you can rip off cars and strip them for parts?

Any stolen car is worth more in parts than in one piece. Plus, he was talking about shipping them overseas. He didn't have any connections for that. Richie was a good guy but he was strictly small time. We're all small time. I know that."

Joe and Linda were looking at Tynan, and he knew what they were thinking. This was the great mystery case the Feds were working on. *A mystery case involving cops that was turning out to be total bullshit,* thought Tynan.

"But how do you know for sure Richie wasn't involved in that?" asked Tynan

"Because, man, he told Angel that shit when we were riding around that one day. We dropped Angel off and Richie was laughing his ass off about how Angel had fallen for his line of shit. He couldn't believe Angel fell for it. He even told me that if his cousin knew about half the shit he did, Warren would beat the crap out of him."

"It was like the day Warren pulled Richie out of the car. He didn't search my car because he was just interested in protecting his cousin and getting him away from me and Lugo. That was it."

Defede seemed to drift off for a moment. He shook his head again. Tynan thought Defede was genuinely upset that Kearns had been killed. He didn't say it, but Tynan could feel it.

Defede nodded and put his elbows on the table. He held his head in his hands. He looked sad, thought Tynan. Maybe this was a good time for a break.

"How about we get you a burger and a soda," asked Tynan. "Let's take a break."

"Sure, okay."

Joe, Linda, and Tynan walked out of the interview room, leaving Defede to wrestle with his thoughts. Tynan was sure Defede was scared of getting killed but he was also mad. Defede wanted revenge on the people who killed his friend and who were probably out there looking for him. Tynan knew that people became informants for different reasons but the best informants were the ones who did it for revenge.

The three of them walked down the hall. Tynan turned to Joe. "Get him something to eat and then we'll go back in and see what he has to say about those other murders. Right now, I want him to think for a while. I want him thinking about everything he has lost in the last few days."

"I think this guy is solid," said Linda. "Everything he said makes sense. He had the right number of shots fired that night but he thought one of them was fired at his car. He doesn't know that Jaime shot Santos in the head to finish him off, but that makes him more believable."

Joe tugged on Tynan's sleeve. "How can you stand there like a statue? This shit is great. Did you see him explain the stolen car ring. It's the stuff the Feds were so hot on. They didn't tell us what was going on because the Feds had nothing to tell. The whole story was bullshit and this CI who they thought was golden was chasing smoke rings."

"It looks that way. Linda, call Russell's friend at the lab and see if they have any ballistics back on the Lugo case. Then ask one of Russell's guys to go over and show some pictures to Kearns' girlfriend? See if she recognizes anybody. Show them pictures of this guy, the CI, and Jaime. Throw Vic into the mix as well. Then have them go down to Vic's junkyard and show a photo array with the CI's picture in it."

Tynan turned to Joe. "Fill Russell in on what our new witness is telling us. Then ask him if he can go to the Crime Scene Unit and get copies of the photos from Lugo's scene."

"Do you guys want anything to eat?" asked Joe.

Linda was already walking down the hallway to find one of Russell's guys and yelled, "Nope," over her shoulder. Tynan shook his head no. He wanted to stay sharp for the interview. After listening to lies on top of lies from bosses, perps, witnesses and informants, he finally had someone who seemed to be telling the truth. *The rest of the afternoon was going to be very interesting,* he thought.

Tynan went back into the interview room. Defede sat in the chair, leaning back against the wall, smoking another cigarette. A thin layer of cigarette smoke hung in the air. Tynan made small talk with Defede, asking him about how he got involved with Lugo. His life story was not unusual. Tynan had heard similar tales before. Defede's dad died when he was six years old. He and his brother were raised by his mom. He turned to drugs while in high school and was thrown out of the house when he was sixteen.

He hung out with some junky friends, sharing an apartment. Finally, Defede straightened up enough to start working for the same people who sold him coke. He stayed loyal and slowly moved up. Defede started out as a lookout, then to doing hand-to-hand sales on the street. He had been arrested three times.

He never did state prison time, but whenever he was arrested, he kept his mouth shut and eventually Lugo brought him into his inner circle. As others in the crew were either arrested or killed, Defede became a courier, acting as a buffer between Lugo and his suppliers. Lugo trusted him enough to allow him to bring Kearns into the fold. It looked like they both had a future; if selling drugs was a future. Tynan could tell Defede was smart. Smart enough to know that his future was in jeopardy.

Joe arrived with the food. Defede wolfed the burger down, like he had not eaten in a day or two. He scarfed up the greasy fries in his fingers, three and four at a time. Linda opened the door and motioned to Tynan to come outside.

"What do you got?" asked Tynan.

Linda whispered as she read from her notebook. "According to Russ' friend at the lab, Lugo was killed by a different gun than Kearns. Lugo was killed by the gun that was dropped at his feet and the gun in his hand was not used to shoot either Santos or Kearns."

Tynan slowly nodded his head. "So, the shooter dropped the gun."

Linda raised her eyebrows, "It looks that way. They're still doing prints on it. Two of Russell's guys went out to show pictures to the girlfriend and Vic."

Tynan rubbed his chin. "The hit on Lugo didn't go so smooth. The shooter drops his gun at the scene, very sloppy. Sounds like amateur night."

Tynan grabbed another chair to bring into the room. He put it in the corner and sat down as he half-listened to Joe and Defede talk about baseball. Tynan's mind was going a hundred miles an hour, and baseball was the last thing he cared about. Up to now, the case was like looking through an out of focus telescope, but since he started listening to Defede things were becoming clearer. Just a few more adjustments and Tynan was sure they'd start to see everything razor sharp.

Linda interrupted the baseball chatter. "Alright, how about you tell us what happened the day Richie was killed?"

Defede seemed more relaxed after eating. He burped, reached for another cigarette, and lit up.

"Richie checked in with me and Lugo about whether or not he was needed that night and he told me Angel was hanging around the yard. He said he was going to his girlfriend, but he was going to give Angel a ride."

"How did he get in touch with you and Lugo?" asked Linda.

"The usual way. He beeped us and I called him back from the phone on the corner. Those phones on the corner of Fox are our phones."

"What do you mean, they're *your* phones?"

"Everyone in the neighborhood knows they can't use those phones on the corner. We have someone standing there when we're doing business. They won't let anyone use the phone. When a beep comes in, we pick up one of those phones and call. We know it's harder for the cops to put a tap on a pay phone. Lugo was standing right there when I called Richie back at the junkyard. That's how we found out he was going to his girlfriend's house. I told him that there was nothing going on and he should meet up with me tomorrow."

"Do you know his girlfriend?"

"Not really. I mean, I saw her once or twice. Either I was in a car dropping Richie off or he drove by with her in his car. I know her like that but I don't really know her. We didn't party together or anything."

"You know where she lives?" asked Tynan.

"Yeah, it's by the park, on Bainbridge Avenue. That's what I thought was odd."

"What did you think was odd?"

"This guy Angel wanting a ride. Richie told him where he was going and Angel said he was going to the park to do some business, and if he could give him a ride. I wish I had said something," said Defede as he shook his head.

"You think Angel had anything to do with killing Richie?" asked Tynan.

Defede flashed an angry look at Tynan. "Of course he had something to do with it. He set Richie up."

"You're sure he set him up but he didn't kill him?" asked Joe.

"I know he didn't kill him because Jaime told Lugo he killed Kearns. I know that for a fact."

"How?" asked Linda.

The muscles in Defede's jaw tightened. Tynan could see Defede was getting mad. Was he mad because he was being challenged or because of what happened to Ritchie?

"How?" asked Defede. "Because I was there when Lugo got the call from Jaime. I showed up at Lugo's house in the morning to drop off some coke for our guys. Ritchie was supposed to be working with me but he didn't show up. I wasn't happy but I figured he was with his girl. Usually, when we dropped stuff off, we would wait in the car by Lugo's house, and his street dealers would show up and pick it up from us. Then Lugo would come out later. He was never there when we gave the stuff out."

Linda let out a low sigh. "What stuff? Just say what it is."

"The coke. Me and Richie always picked it up from a place where we packaged it for the street. Then we would bring it over to Fox Street. That morning it was just me. Richie didn't show up. What I didn't know was that Richie was already dead."

"Where was he supposed to meet you?" asked Joe.

"Don't ask me where we package the stuff because I'm not saying. I'm not giving up any of my people, that's part of the deal." Defede shot Tynan another angry look. "I thought you gave me your word about this."

Tynan put out both of his large hands and motioned Defede to stop. "Relax, we're not interested in anything other than the murders. That's it. We're just trying to get an idea as to how all of this went down. Take it easy. We're good."

Defede grabbed his can of Coke. He tilted the soda up and noisily drained the last drops. Another burp came out of him. "The morning after Richie was killed, Lugo comes out of his house. He's not even dressed. He's wearing sweats and flip flops. He comes over to the car and jumps in and tells me to drive him up to the pay phones on the corner. I asked him what's up, and he said that he had a beep."

"Did he say who the beep was from?"

Defede crushed the soda can with his hand. "No. The whole thing was weird. Usually, he didn't get in the car like that with all the stuff packaged for the street sitting right there. He didn't want the stuff around him. When he jumped in the car, I knew something was up. He just said he got beeped and it was a 911. He didn't know who it was. That's why I think he was nervous. It could have been a warning from someone. He was very careful after Santos got killed. He wasn't going to take chances. He had to find out what the beep was about."

"Okay," said Joe, motioning Defede with his hand to speed things up. "He jumps in the car and you get to the corner and what?"

"He tells me to get out of the car with him while he makes the phone call. He wants me to watch his back while he's on the phone. He makes the call and it's this guy, Jaime. Jaime tells him that he took care of Santos but that he is still willing to do business and give him the money he owes."

"Why would he tell him that?" said Joe.

Defede put his hand up. "Wait. You'll see. He tells Lugo he wants to do business with him and that he shot Kearns last night because he doesn't want any witnesses, but he doesn't want a war. I was standing right there when he told Lugo."

Defede stood up and stretched. "As soon as he got off the phone, he told me that Jaime asked who was driving Kearns when Santos got killed. Lugo told him it was me, and then Jaime said that if Lugo killed me, he'd pay him the money and they could do business together."

Linda looked up from her note-pad and tapped her pen on the desk. "Did you think Lugo would do it? Did you think Lugo would kill you?"

Defede sat back down and waved his right hand dismissively. "No way. That's why he told me, but that's not what he told Jaime. He said right on the phone, while I was standing there, 'Don't worry about him, he's gone tonight. You won't see him again.' Those were his exact words. Lugo was playing Jaime. Stalling for time."

Defede pulled his chair in close to the table. He took another long drag. He fiddled with the pack of cigarettes. "Lugo wanted to get his money first. He told Jaime he would get rid of me, so he could get his money and put him at ease. But Lugo had his own plan. He was going to kill Jaime. Lugo was going to pay Jaime back for killing Kearns. When Jaime was dead, I would run Santos' old spot."

"What time was this?" asked Linda.

"It was a little after nine in the morning."

Joe drummed his fingers lightly on the table and shifted in his seat. "Help me make sense of this? Jaime kills Santos to take the spot. Then he gets rid of Kearns because he's a witness. But you're a witness? Why does he trust Lugo to get rid of you? You're Lugo's guy."

Defede put the cigarette in his mouth and mumbled, "Jesus Christ." He rubbed his hands through his hair and looked over at Tynan. "Okay, let me explain it again. Jaime kills Santos. I saw that. He fired a shot at us. I was there. We got away. He knew Kearns but he didn't know for sure who was driving the car. My car has heavy tint on the windows. He had seen me with Kearns before but it could have been some other guy. That's why he checked with Lugo."

"Lugo told Jaime you were driving the car and you trusted this guy?" asked Linda.

Defede glared at Linda. "Yeah, I trusted him. Lugo was no dope. He knew what was coming. He knew that Jaime was going to make a move on his spot too. Jaime just needed my name before he made his next move. Lugo knew Jaime was going to kill us all."

"Alright," said Tynan. "Calm down. What happens after the phone call?"

"Simple. Lugo tells me he's going to kill this guy but he wants his money first. When they were on the phone, Jaime told him he was going to send someone that morning to give him the money. It was supposed to be like a sign of good faith."

"After the phone call, Lugo went back inside. He told me that his wife had left for her mother's house or some shit like that, and he wanted me to stay outside in the car and wait to see who showed up.

If more than one guy entered the building at the same time, I was to come right in as back-up. If it was just one guy, then I was to stay in the car."

"Why didn't he have you stay in the house with him and wait for the guy?" asked Tynan.

Defede's lips tightened. "Because he wasn't a punk. He could handle one guy, and he didn't want me to leave the car with all the stuff in it unless it was absolutely necessary. Lugo was a tough guy but he wanted his money. He wasn't worried about one guy. It was supposed to be a simple handoff. He'd get his money and then he'd move against Jaime. That was his plan."

"That didn't work. Why not?" asked Linda.

"I waited in the car and maybe in thirty or forty minutes here comes Angel. I couldn't believe it. He's carrying a plastic bag. That's when I knew Angel was in tight with Jaime. He's delivering the money. When I saw Angel was delivering the money I started to relax. I thought Angel was a punk. He didn't have the heart to shoot someone. I see him go in, and in a couple of minutes he comes running out, without the bag, and runs right up the street."

Tynan stared at Defede. He was trying to detect any sign of evasiveness or anything that might show this whole story was made up, but Defede talked in a steady pace, like he was reviewing the scene in his mind. "What did you do?" asked Tynan.

"At first, I was going to go in but then I wanted to see where Angel was going. I drove after him but laid back so he wouldn't see me. He wouldn't have seen a garbage truck because he was running so fast. Running and holding his hand. When he gets to the corner he stops and a blue Monte Carlo all dressed out with chrome wheels pulls up and rolls down the window."

Defede shook his head. "I knew that car. It was Jaime's car. I've seen it before. He doesn't use it much but it was his car. I drove by and I could see Jaime at the wheel. He was leaning over, talking to

Angel. I didn't slow down, just made a quick pass. Then I turned at the next corner and watched. Angel started walking away and Jaime hung a U turn and took off."

Tynan nodded. "Okay, then what did you do?"

"I went back to Lugo's house and waited outside. After a couple of minutes, I figured I'd go in and see if everything was cool. I knew Lugo might get mad because I left the stuff in the car." Defede shrugged. "I was worried. I went in and found him there. I could see he was dead."

Tynan leaned in towards Defede. "Why didn't you go in?"

"The chain was on the door. He was laying there dead with the plastic bag, that Angel carried, next to him. It had money in it. Lugo had a gun in his hand but I guess he wasn't quick enough. There was another gun there too. I got the hell out of there. I got back in the car and left."

"Did you call the police?" asked Joe.

"Not right away. I had to get rid of all the shit in my car. I'm not hanging out there. I went back over to the place where we stash our stuff. After that, I went out and made the call."

Defede stomped the cigarette out on the floor, "That was that. Lugo was dead, so was Kearns, and now Jaime knew for sure it was me in the car. A friend of mine said I should go to the cops and I said I'd think about it. I guess he told you guys."

Tynan got up slowly from the chair. "Not that I care, but when Lugo said he was going to kill Jaime, how was he going to do that?"

"I don't know. Maybe he was going to get me to do it along with one of his guys or he might have wanted to do it himself."

"Would you have done it?"

Defede looked him straight in the eyes. "I know what I'm supposed to say. I'm supposed to say that I would never kill someone. To be honest, I never have killed anyone. But I'd kill both of those motherfuckers right now in front of you, and if you don't get those guys, I will go out looking for them myself. I don't have a choice. They will kill me."

"You won't have to do that," said Tynan. "Stick with us and you'll be safe. We're going to put you up somewhere and watch you until they are both off the street." Tynan motioned for Linda and Joe to leave. "We'll be right back. Do you want anything?"

Defede slowly shook his head from side to side. "No, I'm fine."

Tynan joined Linda and Joe in the hallway. "Let's go over this down in my office."

They took their usual spots. Tynan behind his desk. Joe and Linda in the chairs.

"What do you guys think?"

Joe nodded yes. "This guy just wrapped everything up. I think he's believable."

"I do too," said Linda. She glanced down at her notes and scanned the page. "Just about everything he says matches up. His version of the Santos shooting makes sense. The killing of Kearns is a little iffy. As for Lugo getting killed, he is spot on. Not to mention he puts Warren in the clear. It sounds like all that stolen car ring shit is just that. A load of shit."

Tynan put one long leg up on his desk and leaned back in his chair. "I think he's solid. Best of all, he's pissed. Maybe we can use him to reach out to Jaime and put all of this to rest for good."

"Don't you think we have enough to arrest them?" asked Joe.

"Arrest them? We're not arresting anyone." He looked at Linda and winked. "We'll let the Detective Squad do that. All we have to do is hand this to them on a silver platter and step back. We have a lot of little details to stitch together, but I think we're on target."

Tynan looked at his watch. "We're close to wrapping this thing up. We'll give it to the Detective Squad but first I'd like to make the case a little stronger. I don't want any holes in this case."

"What about Angel?" asked Joe.

"I think we've got enough to drag his ass in as well. The story is backed up by the crime scene."

Joe nodded. "Lugo opened the door, with the chain on it. Angel handed him the money, and when Lugo wasn't looking, Angel pulled a gun and shot him. Lugo tried to slam the door and that explains Angel's broken wrist."

The door at the end of the hallway slammed, and the echo of heavy feet told Tynan that Russell was back. Russell strode into the office and dropped a folder on Tynan's desk. "As ordered sir, crime scene pictures."

"Sit down, Russ. Things have taken an unexpected turn," said Tynan as he dumped the pictures out on his desk. He spread them out, looking for closeups of Lugo. "Here we go," said Tynan. He looked at the picture of the dead body then handed it to Joe.

Tynan picked up other pictures and studied them. His stomach tightened as he stared down at a picture of the gun lying beside Lugo. It was a 9mm Colt pistol. What caught Tynan's eye was the Colt emblem on the handle. The horse had a thin scratch coming out of its head, making the horse look like a unicorn. Just like the 9mm Colt that Tynan had picked up in Angel's hotel room. He looked closely. It was the same gun. He was sure of it. He tossed the picture of the gun on the pile of photos. He felt sick.

"What's wrong Lou?" asked Linda.

Tynan didn't answer. His chair squeaked as he turned and looked out the window at his boats. They sat still in the motionless water. Tynan couldn't believe it. He had always doubted the CI's story about throwing the gun away. He might have sold it, even kept it, but Tynan never dreamed he would use it to kill someone. Joe and Linda's voices sounded like they were coming from another room. He heard them saying, "Are you alright Lou?" Tynan turned and looked at them.

He took a deep breath and pursed his lips, letting the air out slowly. Then he spoke. "Yeah, I'm fine. We need to see if the lab is finished dusting those guns in Lugo's apartment for prints, and they need to check the plastic bag with the money. I think it might be time to see just how serious Defede is about taking Jaime and the CI down."

"What did you have in mind?" asked Joe.

"I wonder if he would be willing to call Jaime and set up a meeting. Get him to talk about the three hits. If we have that on tape, we're solid as a rock."

"Do you think Jaime would go for that? Wouldn't he be suspicious at this point?"

"He might be. But I'm betting Jaime wants to know where Defede is bad enough that he'll meet with him. Only one way to find out."

"I don't know," said Linda. "That's really putting Defede at risk. If they meet, what's to stop Jaime from killing him as soon as he shows up?"

Tynan gathered the photos together into a pile. "Nothing. We'll arrange for something in a public place. I don't think Jaime would try it then. We'll pick Defede up right after the meet and bust Jaime as he drives away. It'll all be on tape."

"Worst case scenario, Defede is dead and we still collar Jaime," snickered Joe. He glanced over at Linda. "Win, win."

Tynan stood up. "You guys work on those other things and I'll talk with Defede and see about him putting in a call to Jaime. I hope he doesn't fold up. Russ, have you heard back from your guys on the photo arrays?"

"No, not yet, Lou. Should be soon. I'll tag along with you when you talk to Defede."

Tynan nodded. He and Russell walked back to the interview room. Tynan sat down across from Defede, who was smoking a cigarette. The growing pile of crushed cigarettes was growing. *I really need to get some ashtrays,* thought Tynan.

"How much do you want to put Jaime away?"

"I'll do anything. I only have three choices here. Either I kill him, he kills me, or you guys lock him up. Other than that, what can I do?"

"Okay. I'd like for you to reach out to Jaime. Get him on the phone. Talk to him about Kearns, Santos, and Lugo. If he's willing to talk to you on the phone about the murders, we record it and then go out and lock him up. If he's not going to talk on the phone, then we set up a meeting between you and him. A public place. We'll wire you up and you record him. As he drives away, we lock him up. Is that something you'd be willing to do?"

"What about that fuck Angel? What happens to him?"

"Don't worry about Angel. We'll take care of him. Hopefully, when you are talking to Jaime, he'll drag Angel into it as well."

"Alright. I'll do it," said Defede. "I think I can get Jaime to call me. If I send him a 911 beep, he'll call back. Then I'll get him talking."

Tynan turned to Russell. "Can we set that up? I also want two of our guys to head out to the Castle Hill Diner and sit on that place. That'll be our meeting spot. Make sure they keep a lookout for Jaime or anyone that looks like they're casing the place."

"I'm on it," said Russell and he walked out the door.

Tynan grinned as he looked at Defede. "Things are going to turn out fine." Tynan wasn't sure he believed it himself. Seeing that gun in the photo had shattered his confidence. How could he have been so stupid? Why didn't he just lock Angel up or take the gun? If he had done that, Lugo might still be dead but not with *that* gun. He was glad he remembered to wipe the pistol down.

He tried making small talk with Defede. He didn't want him changing his mind now. He was glad when Russell finally popped his head into the room. "The phone is set up and two guys are on the way to the diner."

Tynan turned to Defede. "Let's go."

They went to the other room and sat down next to the phone and tape recorder.

"Alright, let's get this done," said Tynan. Defede didn't seem nervous. "What we want to happen here is to get Jaime talking about the murders. That's a lot to get done in one phone call, but if you get him talking about doing business together, you can bring in the murders. If he won't talk about any of that, try and set up a meeting with him. Tell him you'll meet him at the Castle Hill Diner on Tremont and Castle Hill Avenue. Pick a time that's two hours after he wants to meet. Tell him you're busy. You think you can remember all that or should I write some of it down?"

Defede frowned and sucked his teeth, "Yeah, I can remember that. Let me beep him and see if he gets back to me. What's the number to this phone?"

Tynan scribbled the number for the phone on a piece of paper. Defede reached into his pocket and took out a wrinkled piece of paper with numbers written on it. He found the number he was looking for and pounded them into the phone. Defede smiled. "Now we'll see just how fast he gets back to me. The faster, the more worried he is."

"Did you deal much with this guy, Jaime?"

"Nah, not really. He was a Santos guy. We had dealings with Santos and he was always around, but he didn't say much. He was there to protect Santos. He was kind of like me with Lugo."

"What about Angel?"

"What about him?" shrugged Defede. "Lugo never trusted him. He'd use him if he was short of guys and he was around but he was never really part of the crew."

Tynan watched Defede. He believed he was telling the truth. His answers never changed, but it never hurt to get more details. "Do you think Santos trusted Angel?"

"He used him more than Lugo did, but I wouldn't say Angel was a Santos guy. I didn't think he was a Jaime guy either but obviously he was. Jaime used Angel to kill Lugo. I'm pretty sure Angel must have told Jaime that I was probably the driver with Kearns the night Santos got killed. That's why when Jaime asked Lugo who was the driver, Lugo gave my name up right away, because he knew Jaime probably knew the answer already. He was asking a question he knew the answer to. Just like you guys do. Jaime was just making sure."

"Yep, just like us," nodded Tynan.

The phone rang. Tynan leaned over and turned the tape recorder on. Tynan gave the signal for Defede to pick up the phone. He lifted the extension in time with Defede. "Hello."

Jaime's familiar voice came through. "Who's this?"

"This is Defede. You know I work for Lugo. I mean I used to work for Lugo. I need to talk to you about doing business now that he's gone."

"Oh yeah. I remember you. You used to ride around with that punk Kearns." Jaime chuckled. "Yeah, he's not with us anymore, just like your boy Lugo."

"Lot of bad shit happening out there. That's why I want to see if we can still do business."

"Do business?" asked Jaime.

"You know, I take over Lugo's spot and give you a piece of the action."

"I don't know. I already got someone in mind for that," said Jaime.

"Like who?" asked Defede.

"Someone you know. You know Angel, right? I think he'll run that spot for me, but maybe you could keep your old job. You know, running things around, pick-ups, that type of stuff."

Defede hesitated before he answered. "You're going to give that spot to Angel? I think you're making a big mistake. I could run it. Everyone knows me and I know how everything works. Angel killed Lugo. Some people might have bad blood for him because of that. They liked Lugo. If you stick the guy who shot him in there, that might not go down too good."

"Hmm," said Jaime. "You think that might be a problem. See, I think differently. People see Angel in there after he killed Lugo, they know not to fuck with him. Besides, he'd be working for me."

Tynan, signaled thumbs up to Defede.

"People don't care about you killing Santos but they liked Lugo and they won't be happy with Angel."

"Hey, you know what? I think maybe we should meet. You can convince me to give you the spot and I can straighten you out about some things. How about we meet today? I can meet you around six. How about Tiffany Street, down by the park?"

"I'm kind of busy around then. I got a lot of stuff to do."

"Don't be selling anything around Fox and Longwood," said Jaime. "That's my spot now. Nobody deals there without me saying so. Got it?"

"No, no, don't worry about that. I'll meet with you but at the Castle Hill Diner. It's right there at Castle Hill and Tremont. I could meet you there, say about eight o'clock," said Defede as he played with his lighter on the table.

There was a long pause. "Okay, I can meet you there but come alone," said Jaime. "I don't want to see anyone else with you."

"No problem. See you then." Defede hung up the phone, smiled and looked at Tynan.

"See, I got him."

"You did good. Very good," said Tynan as he pounded his fist on the table. "You definitely sunk Angel. Now we have to get this guy. Bring up the two shootings when you meet at the diner and he's done." Tynan got up and stretched. "Hey, you want anything else to eat or drink?"

"Yeah, I'll take a soda."

Tynan winked at Defede and walked out the door. The whole thing was finally coming together. Angel was as good as gone. All he had to do was get the District Attorney's office to go along. He thought it was a pretty good case and if Defede could get Jaime to incriminate himself on tape, it was over.

Tynan went to his office and started making up a plan for the meeting at the diner. This was going to be touchy. He didn't think Jaime would walk into a diner and start shooting but it wasn't beyond him to sit down with Defede then kill him as he left. Tynan thought it was an outside possibility. Possible but not probable. To Tynan, the smart way to do it would be to put Defede at ease and then have someone kill him later. Like the way Kearns was probably killed.

Tynan had to set up the meeting in a way that Jaime wouldn't dare think about killing Defede. As he wrote the plan, it struck him. He had the perfect way to protect Defede. Have two uniformed cops sitting in the diner eating while the meeting was taking place.

An hour passed. Tynan got the tactical plan sketched out. He would have enough guys even if Jaime showed up with some muscle. He got up, strode over to the door, and yelled down the hallway, "Joe and Linda in my office in five minutes."

Joe came in and sat down. "Linda is going to check to see if any more info came in. I tracked down a car that belongs to Jaime's mom. I called up Riker's Island and they gave me the scoop on anyone who visited Jaime when he was in jail, and one of his regulars was his mom. I ran her in DMV and bingo, she owns a Monte Carlo. I'll bet she doesn't know she owns it," laughed Joe.

"Nice. Good work."

"What about the phone call?" asked Joe.

"Beautiful. He agreed and made the call. It went better than I could have hoped but we're still going to need a meeting between Defede and Jaime. That's what I'm working on now."

He heard Linda's footsteps hurrying down the hall. She walked in, sat down beside Joe, and took a deep breath, "You won't believe this. They found Angel's prints on the Colt that was used to kill Lugo and some of the rounds. Better yet, they found Jaime and Angel's prints on the plastic bag with the money."

"Shit," said Tynan. "That's a homerun."

"It gets better," said Linda. "Vic from the junkyard identified Angel as the guy who came to see Kearns the day he was killed."

"Did you say homerun?" snickered Joe. "Sounds like a grand slam."

"The girlfriend picked out pictures of Vic, Defede, Lugo, and Warren. She knows Warren is Kearns' cousin and she said the same thing Kearns' mom and Defede said, that Warren was trying to get Kearns back on the straight and narrow. The detective who talked with her said she was believable. The only downside is the detectives never found any witnesses that actually saw Kearns getting shot."

"Anything on the phone records?" asked Tynan.

"No, not yet. But they are working on it. So that's what I found out from Russell's guys and the Four-One and Five-Two Detective Squads." Linda smiled. "Looks pretty good, Lou."

"Fill Linda in on the phone call," said Joe.

Tynan said, "Defede beeped Jaime. He called back. Defede said to Jaime that he knows Angel killed Lugo, and Jaime not only doesn't deny it but says that Angel killing Lugo makes him the top guy to run Lugo's spot. He couldn't get Jaime to admit to killing Santos on the phone but he wants to meet with him."

"We're not going to do that, right?" asked Linda with a frown. "Jaime will kill Defede."

Tynan shrugged. "I don't think he'll kill him right away. He'll talk to him to see what he knows. Then put Defede at ease and kill him later."

"We're not going to do that," said Linda again, as she tilted her head and raised her eyebrows.

"Actually, we are," said Tynan. He held up both his hands as Joe chuckled and Linda gasped. "Hear me out on this. We set up a meeting at the Castle Hill Diner. They meet there, we'll have back up on the street and put guys in the diner. Defede will be wired and we'll have the whole thing filmed and taped."

"Oh boy, here we go," laughed Joe.

Linda sat straight up in her chair and wagged her finger at Joe. "This isn't funny. This is serious. What is to stop Jaime from coming into the restaurant, sitting down, finding out what Defede knows, and then shooting him as he leaves?"

"I figured you'd ask that," said Tynan. "The biggest deterrent to criminals known to man. Two uniformed cops sitting in the diner eating. He's not going to shoot him in front of two uniformed cops."

"Who are we going to get to do that?" asked Linda.

"Simple. We put two of our guys in uniform. We'll have them drive up in our black Crown Victoria and they'll go into the restaurant and order dinner. Everyone will think it's just two cops on their meal break. Then they sit there and keep an eye on our witness to make sure nothing goes wrong."

"Don't you think that Jaime might not want to talk about killing people with two cops in the diner?" asked Joe. "I mean the guy isn't that stupid."

"The cops will be sitting at one end of the diner and Defede will sit at the other. Nobody will know what they are talking about. Even Jaime will feel safe with them sitting there. If it turns out that Jaime gets raised up and won't talk, then we signal the cops to leave and sit in their car in front of the diner like they're watching for someone to run a red light."

"Where are we going to be?" asked Joe.

"The usual. You guys will be with me. Russell's guys will be both back-up and surveillance."

"I don't know," said Joe. "It's crazy enough that it might work."

"I agree with half of that," said Linda. "It's crazy."

"Okay, glad we're all agreed," said Tynan. "We got a lot of work to do." Tynan gave Joe and Linda the Tac Plan. "And Joe, could you let Russ know what we're going to do and have him get the surveillance van ready and wire up Defede? We're going to want Defede in a vest too."

"Won't Jaime get suspicious if he sees that?" asked Linda.

"I don't think so. It won't be the first time a drug dealer wore a vest to a meeting."

Joe and Linda headed for the door. Linda turned back and looked at Tynan. "What are you going to do Lou?"

"Me? I'm going to sit here and think great thoughts."

"Or maybe just nutty thoughts," said Linda with a smirk.

Tynan was psyched about the meeting between Defede and Jaime. It had an element of danger to it but he was confident Jaime was not so stupid as to start a shootout in a diner. Jaime was a ruthless thug but he was also a planner. *He takes risks but he isn't reckless,* thought Tynan. Everything was going Jaime's way, and Tynan saw that as an opening. Jaime was more likely to let his guard down and make a mistake. He had already made a mistake by agreeing to the meeting with Defede.

Tynan called the Four-One Squad. He was surprised that Morris hadn't called him as soon as the prints came back on the gun at Lugo's apartment. "Four-One Squad, Lieutenant Morris."

"Hey, it's Tynan over at IAB."

There was a brief, almost nervous laugh. "I was just about to call you," said Morris.

"I beat you to it. I know the prints came back to the CI but I've got something even better."

"I'm listening," said Morris. "Tell me he confessed and it's all on tape."

"Not quite that good. But I do have one of Lugo's guys sitting here and he is willing to testify that he saw who shot Santos and Lugo."

"Really? I thought you guys had the Santos murder all wrapped up. I thought the ex-cop did it."

"Not according to this witness. He says he and Kearns went to get money from Santos, and when they pulled up, Jaime Aponte shot Santos. He also says that he was sitting outside Lugo's apartment building when the CI waltzed in with a bag of money and shot Lugo. It looks like the CI broke his hand while trying to shoot Lugo."

"And he's willing to testify to this?" asked Morris.

"He certainly is, and to top it off, we have Jaime Aponte on tape admitting the CI killed Lugo. And if that's not enough for you, our witness is going to meet with Aponte today at eight in the Castle Hill Diner. He'll be wired for sound and we'll be there. I'm going to have two guys in uniform sitting in the diner just in case Jaime decides to get frisky."

"Holy shit, that's incredible! We're more than happy to help out. Anything we can do, just ask?"

"First, they meet in the diner. We get Jaime on tape admitting he killed Santos and Kearns, and that he sent Angel to kill Lugo. It looks like Jaime wanted to take over both spots and have the CI work Lugo's spot. Our witness is going to try and talk him out of it because he wants to work the spot for Jaime. That's how the conversation is supposed to go. After we get it on tape, we grab Jaime as soon as they come out of the diner and bring him over to you and your guys make the collar. Arresting the CI is going to be tricky. That's where you guys can come in."

"Sure, what do you want us to do?" Tynan could sense the eagerness in Morris' voice.

"I'm not real popular with the Feds, so if I call up asking for the CI to come and meet us, they'll probably tell me to take a hike. But if you call and say you want the CI to come in and look at some pictures of who might be involved in the Lugo murder, he is more likely to show up. After we get Jaime on tape at the meeting, you can arrest the CI, but I'd like to be there for the interrogation."

"Yeah, we can do that. Give me the number of the handler and we'll see if we can get him in."

"Thanks. We'll deliver Jaime to your office and you can play one guy off against the other. Kearns was killed in the Five-Two so you might want them to send people down."

"This is great," said Morris. "I'll take care of getting the CI."

Tynan gave Morris the number, and hung up. He debated making a call to Rogan to let him know what he was up to. He trusted Rogan but at the same time he didn't want to put him at risk. If things went bad and Rogan knew about the plan but didn't call it off, his head would roll, right along with Tynan's. Tynan decided against it. He was sure Rogan would understand.

Tynan had one more important call to make. He called home. There was no answer. *Everyone must be out,* he thought. Hopefully, they were having fun. After tonight, he'd make it up to them. Tynan looked out the window at his boats. He drifted off into a daydream about how things would be different at home.

Joe knocked on the door. "I'm just about to give the tac plan briefing. Do you want to sit in?"

"Absolutely. I'll be right there."

The meeting was quick. Everyone knew their roles and positions. They also knew there was the potential for violence. Tynan glanced around the room. He didn't detect any doubts. Everyone grabbed their equipment and headed out.

"The witness will ride with us," said Joe. "He's already wired up and raring to go."

"An eager witness. That's refreshing," said Tynan.

It was a short drive to the diner. Tynan watched Defede in the mirror. He seemed relaxed as he sat there looking out the window. Tynan parked the car a block from the restaurant. Linda and Joe checked the wire to make sure it was working, while Tynan called the units on the radio to confirm they were in position.

The two detectives in uniform were sitting in the Crown Vic in the parking lot. They would enter after Defede went in. Besides the two uniformed cops, Russell and two of his guys were across the street from the diner in the surveillance van. Two other detectives, were sitting in a car down the block. They had been keeping an eye on the diner since the call was made to Jaime. Tynan felt confident.

He turned to Defede. "You ready to do this? Do you remember the signals in case something goes wrong?"

Defede nodded.

Tynan got on the radio. "Witness is stepping out."

Linda patted Defede on the arm. "Good luck."

Defede got out and headed towards the diner. Jaime had not shown up yet, and according to Russell's guys, nobody had been hanging around scoping out the place. Everything looked normal. Tynan listened to the soft swishing sound of Defede's clothes rubbing against the wire.

Russell's voice came over the air. "Witness is entering the diner. The two uniforms are getting out of the car and going in after him."

The sounds of dishes clattering and people talking came over the wire. A waitress seated Defede in a booth by the window. The two uniformed cops took a table on the other side of the restaurant where they could watch the door and keep an eye on Defede. Tynan breathed easier. *So far, so good,* he thought.

Now came the hard part. The waiting. Tynan tried to stay focused and push thoughts about things going wrong out of his head. Everything would be fine. He had a lot of guys, more than enough if Jaime decided to show up and do something stupid. He'd done plenty of takedowns in his career with a lot less people. Linda and Joe sat there quietly, listening to the sounds coming over the speaker from the wire.

The radio came to life. It was Russell again. "Blue Monte Carlo with chrome wheels just rolled up with only the driver in the car." There was a pause. "Subject is getting out of the car." It seemed like an eternity before Russell spoke again. "Subject is in the diner."

Joe adjusted the volume on the receiver as they all leaned towards the speaker.

"Hey dude, glad you came," said Defede.

Jaime's voice came over the wire. "Of course, bro, what did you expect? This place isn't bad. I've never been here before. What are you going to get?"

"I'm just getting a burger and fries," said Defede. "What are you getting?"

"Same," said Jaime. "I'm glad to see you came alone. That's a sign of trust, dude. I respect that."

The waitress came over and the two of them placed their orders. Nothing was said until she was out of earshot. Defede opened the meeting. "Speaking about trust, I can't believe you are going to let that guy, Angel, take the spot. That guy is a dumbass. He doesn't know what he's doing. How could you disrespect me and everyone else by putting him there? Nobody likes him. What's he got?"

"Look, Angel helped me put this whole plan in motion. Plus, he knew about Santos and Kearns. He had weight on me. That's why I had him kill Lugo."

Tynan pumped his fist in the air and mouthed the word "YES!"

Jaime continued. "Then we would be even. But I still had to take care of him, because he helped me out. That's why I wanted to give Angel the spot."

"Oh yeah, so what about me?" asked Defede. "I know you killed Santos and I know you put Angel up to killing Lugo. Why aren't you worried about me?"

Jaime laughed. "That's a tough one. To be honest, bro, I thought about it. You were there when I shot Santos and so was Kearns."

"Alright!" whispered Linda. "He's done!"

Jaime spoke without emotion. "That's the reason why I got rid of Kearns. I was thinking about getting rid of you too but things have changed. Now I'm thinking I have a better idea."

"What's your idea?" asked Defede.

"Look, what you said about Angel is true. He's not that bright and he doesn't know anything about the spot. You know everything and can step right in. You have to pay a tax to me but you'd still make money."

"I'd still know that you killed Santos and Kearns and had Angel kill Lugo," said Defede.

"Yeah, but I got that covered dude. You know about me but you won't snitch me out because you are going to do me a favor."

"What favor?"

"You are going to get rid of Angel. Then he's gone. You would be the only one who knows about Santos and those other guys, but then I'd know you did Angel. I got dirt on you too. If you give me up, then I'd have to give you up. See, it's just like the deal I had with Angel except you know the business."

"If I kill Angel, you'll let me have the spot?"

"You got it. Besides, I can't trust Angel anymore. He's got to go. He fucked up."

"How?" asked Defede.

"When he went to kill Lugo, he was supposed to knock on the door, go inside, give Lugo the money, and when he was counting the money, shoot him. But he panicked."

"What do you mean?"

"Lugo answered the door but he had the chain on it and he was holding a gun. Angel handed him the bag of money and when Lugo took his eyes off Angel, he shot him. But Lugo must have seen it coming and tried to slam the door on Angel's hand. The gun went off and killed Lugo but dumb-ass Angel dropped his gun inside the apartment."

"BINGO!" yelled Joe. Linda and Tynan shot him a dirty look.

"Sorry, sorry," said Joe, as he turned up the volume.

"What a stupid fuck," said Defede.

"Yeah, I mean if you have any brains, you don't stick your hand in through the door, you just shoot him, and if you drop the gun, then you have to break the chain off and get it. He not only left the gun he left the money too. Twenty grand," said Jaime.

"Whoa. See, he is a punk and a dumbass."

"His gun is in that apartment. Probably has prints on it. The cops are going to come looking for him and he's going to rat to save his ass. I know it. He has to go."

"Yeah, he definitely has to go," said Defede. There was a pause. Only the clattering of dishes came over the wire. "Okay, I think you got a deal, bro. I never understood why you started working with that asshole Angel."

Jaime laughed. "Angel came to me asking about stolen cars and dirty cops. I knew he was crazy. He told me that he was working with the Feds to get dirty cops, and that's when I had an idea on how to make this all work. I had been planning on moving on Santos but I knew the cops would come looking for me."

"Then when he told me that he was talking to the Feds about dirty cops stealing cars and then, like bang, this plan hit me. I told him that if Santos was gone, we could blame the whole thing on this cop Warren and his cousin. He was already talking to the Feds about them. Now we just had to throw drugs into the mix and make it look like Warren was a player with drugs too."

The loud clattering of glasses and plates almost drowned Jaime out. "I told him to tell the Feds that Warren wanted Santos dead and had asked Lugo to put it together. The cops would look at Warren, and when they came around asking questions, I'd reluctantly say that I saw Kearns shoot Santos. That would get them off my ass."

Jaime let out a loud burp. "See, I knew Angel wanted to move up. I told him that if Kearns got picked up by the cops, he'd have his chance because if Kearns got arrested, he would give up Lugo, and then Angel could run the whole spot. When Angel realized that, with Kearns and Lugo out of the way, he could be the boss for the spot, he was totally down with the plan."

"Not a bad plan, but how'd you know that Kearns was going to get arrested?"

"What I didn't tell Angel was that Kearns was never going to be arrested. Yeah, I was going to eventually tell the cops Kearns did it, but I was planning on getting rid of Kearns before they grabbed him. That was the part Angel didn't count on."

The two of them fell silent as the waitress brought their food. Jaime spoke after the waitress left. "Angel was so stupid. He even helped me set up Kearns without knowing it. I told him to find out where Kearns was going to be, so I could give him the money Santos owed, but not to tell Kearns because he might be nervous about meeting me. Angel found out where Kearns was going and called me. Kearns didn't know I was going to be there. You should have seen Angel's eyes when I popped Kearns. I thought he was going to piss his pants."

Tynan slammed his fist on the dashboard. "Got you."

There was a long pause. Defede finally said, "See, I told you that Angel was a punk. Okay, we have a deal. I just need to know when you want me to do this."

"Like as soon as you can. Tomorrow is good. I'll send Angel over to Fox Street tomorrow night. I'll tell him to go over there and scope out a place for a stash house. It'll be in the same building where Lugo lived. You wait for him and take care of business. There's a catch, though."

"A catch? What's the catch?"

"I'm going to give you a gun. You have to put that gun on Angel. If he's got a gun on him, take that one, and leave the one I give you."

"What for?"

Jaime let out a loud laugh. "Because this is the gun that killed Kearns. You put it on Angel and that's the end of that. The case is solved, the cops won't be looking for anyone. They'll think Kearns killed Santos and that Angel killed Kearns and Lugo."

"But then what weight do I have on you?"

"What? Are you kidding? You know about me doing the hits and I know about you doing Angel. Why would I bring that to the cops? If I tell them that you killed Angel, then you're going to start talking about all this other stuff. Besides, you start running Lugo's old spot and we both make a lot of money together."

"Oh, I get it. Takes the heat off us. I see. But what about Angel? They'll be looking for who killed him?"

"The cops ain't going to give a shit about who killed Angel. They'll be happy knowing that Angel killed Lugo and Kearns and they'll forget about it."

"Okay, where's the gun you want me to put on Angel?"

"I got it in my car outside. I'll give it to you when we're finished."

Tynan looked at Linda and Joe. "We've got this motherfucker. This tape is great."

"I can't believe it," said Linda. "The whole thing was a set-up from the beginning between Angel and Jaime, and we fell for it."

"Not anymore," laughed Joe.

"One problem," said Tynan. "We've got to stop them before they get to the car. Maybe Jaime is going to give him the gun or maybe he's going to shoot him with it. We'll grab him as soon as they step out of the restaurant. Then we'll go get the gun."

Tynan held his finger up in front of his lips and picked up the radio. "Group leader to all units. As soon as they come out of the restaurant, we're going to take them. I don't want the subject getting to his car." Each of the units acknowledged and Tynan put the radio down.

They sat there waiting, listening to Jaime and Defede eating and talking about their trade. Tynan was only half listening. Once he heard the check being paid for, he put the car in gear and started towards the diner.

Russell came over the air. "They're leaving the restaurant."

Tynan stepped on the gas and yelled into the radio, "Take 'em, take 'em, take 'em." He whipped the car into the parking lot as Defede and Jaime came down the diner stairs. Tynan jumped out of the car and pointed his gun at the two of them. "Police, don't move."

Both Defede and Jaime were cuffed. Tynan grabbed Defede and handed him to Linda. "Put him in our car." Russell had Jaime and was frisking him. "He's clean." He had a set of car keys in his hand and threw them at Tynan. "Keys for the Monte."

Tynan trotted over to the car and opened the door. After fumbling around a bit, he finally found what he was looking for. A 9mm pistol was tucked under the front seat. Russell's guys helped toss the rest of the car but came up with nothing.

Russell came over and stuck his hand out to Tynan. "Looks like you finally got your revenge."

Tynan laughed. "I guess that's what it is. Whatever it is, it feels good."

Tynan called Morris on the way to the Four-One Precinct and gave him the details. When Tynan strode into the Four-One Squad, several detectives looked up. He could sense they weren't thrilled that IAB was in their "house." Lieutenant Morris had been friendly but Tynan and his crew had not made any converts among the rest of the Detective Squad.

Tynan went over to one of the detectives. "Is there a place where we can put your witness?" The detective looked surprised and glanced around the squad room. "Sure, there's a small room over there that he can sit in," he said, pointing towards a door.

They led Defede into the room and took the cuffs off. He was all smiles. He asked for a soda and a pack of cigarettes. Joe shrugged. "Why not? You deserve it. Probably deserve a couple of beers, but you'll have to wait on that."

Linda sat with Defede in the cramped room with the dirty, pale green walls. Tynan looked at Joe. "Go ahead and get him what he wants. I'm going to check in with Morris and see what they have so far."

Morris was on the phone in his office. As he saw Tynan approach, he waved him in and gestured to one of the chairs. Morris hung up, and smiled a large toothy grin. "Wow, we've got both of these guys dead to rights. We have the CI in one of the interrogation rooms. We've been showing him pictures of people to pass the time. He's convinced he's here because we need background information on people who hang out at Fox and Longwood. Boy, is he in for a surprise."

"Did the Feds give you a hard time about getting him?" asked Tynan.

"No, not at all. We told them we needed him to identify some people and they dropped him off. They told us to call them when we were finished. How do you want to play these interrogations? I think we let Jaime sit there and simmer for a while. He's already in one of the holding rooms with his head on the table, catching some sleep."

"Asleep in the interrogation room," chuckled Tynan. "You know you got the right guy when he goes to sleep. Let him sit there and relax. He might have a long night ahead of him. I'm thinking I'd like to go in and talk to the CI. Give him the good news that he's being arrested for murder. See how he takes it."

"What do you think? Is he a stand-up guy?" asked Morris.

"He's an informant. If he sees some wiggle room to get out of this, he'll take it. If he balks, I'm going to play the recording for him. He should really like the part where Jaime asks Defede to kill him."

"Beautiful. That's what I'm thinking. See if the CI will roll on Jaime. It doesn't make a difference, but it'd be nice if we could get each of them to make statements against the other." He looked down at his watch and back up at Tynan. "Shall we start?"

Tynan and Morris walked into the interrogation room where the CI was looking at photos with two detectives. The CI looked startled when he saw Tynan. "I don't know if I'm supposed to talk to you anymore," said the CI as he pushed the binder of photographs away from him.

Morris and Tynan ignored him as Morris introduced Tynan to the two detectives. One was in his thirties, balding, with long sideburns. The other was much older with a thick handlebar moustache and a drinker's face. Then Morris turned to Angel. "And I don't have to introduce you two, do I?"

Tynan pointed to Angel's cast. "What happened there, Angel?"

"Oh nothing. I tripped and fell, that's all."

Tynan could feel the CI's nervousness. Angel didn't look at any of them. He pulled the binder with the photographs back towards him and started to flip the pages quickly. *There is no way he is even looking at them,* thought Tynan.

"Is that what happened to your wrist?" asked Tynan. "Because I heard differently. I heard you broke it when Lugo slammed the door on it while you were trying to shoot him. That was a tough break for Lugo. If he had been a little faster with that door, he might still be alive."

Angel stopped looking at the pictures. His eyes darted back and forth between Tynan and Morris. His jaw dropped open and he tensed up as if he was about to try to bolt out of the room.

"It must have been a bitch when you dropped the gun. You lost Jaime's money *and* your gun. Tell me, did it hurt when he slammed the door? You know I hear that when your adrenaline is really pumping, you don't even feel it. Is that true? Did you feel any pain when Lugo broke your wrist? Hmm? Or did you only start to feel the pain as you ran up the street to meet Jaime in his Monte Carlo?"

Angel closed his mouth and licked his lips. "What are you talking about?"

"Jaime must have been pissed when you showed up with no money, no gun, and a broken wrist. You know what they say about getting good help nowadays. I guess he must have realized right then and there that you were a loser. That's probably when he decided to kill you."

"What the fuck are you talking about?" asked Angel as he jumped around in his chair. He looked at the detectives for help. "What the fuck is this?"

"You want me to sign your cast?" asked Tynan. "Because I will. I'll put 'You're going to prison, loser' on it. You want me to do that?"

"I'm leaving," said Angel as he stood up. "I'm calling Kurt."

Angel landed with a thud, when Tynan pushed him back down in his chair. "You're not going anywhere and you're not calling anyone. Kurt can't help you, asshole. Right now, we're the only people who can help you. You're going to prison for a long time for killing Lugo. If you have a brain in your head, now's the time to come clean and tell us about who killed Santos and Kearns. That's the only way you can help yourself."

"Bullshit. This is bullshit. You don't have shit."

"I got Jaime trying to hire someone to kill you. I got that."

"He'd never do that," said Angel, his voice rising. He looked at the floor. "He'd never do that," he repeated.

"Oh yeah, I got that on tape and I'll play it for you. You know what else I got?"

Angel's eyes had that desperate look. They wandered around the room as if he was looking for some way to get out of there.

Tynan leaned down and got in Angel's face. "I got Jaime saying you killed Lugo. I got a witness that saw you. I got your prints on that bag of money and on the pistol that you dropped. Do you want me to go on? If you think you're going to talk you're way out of this, you're dumber than you look. We got Jaime in another room, giving you up. You're sitting here, like some kind of stand-up guy, and he's selling you down the river."

Tynan looked at Morris and the two detectives. "I'll bet that before the night is out, Jaime will pin all three murders on our guy here." He turned back to Angel. "What do you say about that? You got to make a decision right now and if you make the wrong one and play the tough guy, you'll die in prison. And how long do you think you're going to last in there when it gets out that you're an informant? I don't know, Angel, looks to me like you're in a bad spot."

Tynan flashed the CI a brief smile. "You know what? We're going to give you about ten minutes to think it over and then I'm going to come in and play that tape. After you hear it, I'll give you one minute to make up your mind about how much of a good guy you want to be. In the meantime, these two nice gentlemen are going to read you your rights."

The detective with a drinker's face took a small card with the Miranda warning on it out of his shirt pocket and slid it across the table to Angel. The other detective recited it out loud as Angel stared at the card. Tynan and Morris walked out.

They stopped outside the room. "Let him think about that for a couple of minutes," said Morris. Tynan walked over to the room where Linda was sitting with Defede. "You got that tape?"

Linda rummaged through a briefcase and handed it to Tynan. "What did he say?"

"As of now nothing. He's too busy scraping the shit out of his pants. He'll talk. He doesn't believe Jaime would do him in. Of course, he forgot that he told us he doesn't really know Jaime. I think the tape will refresh his memory."

After ten minutes, Tynan got a tape recorder from Morris and cued it up to where Jaime talked about killing Angel. They walked back into the interrogation room. Joe decided to look on from the adjoining observation room. Tynan put the recorder on the table and hit the play button. All eyes were on Angel as he sat there with his elbow on the table propping up his head, staring at the recorder.

The tape played. Angel listened, fiddling with his cast. A low groan came out of Angel when he heard Jaime make the offer to Defede. He pushed his chair back against the wall and leaned forward, clasping his head with both hands, listening to the tape. Tynan let the tape roll for a little bit then turned it off.

He glanced at his watch as the second hand swept by. When a minute had passed, he leaned down and whispered to Angel, "There you go, Angel. He was going to have you killed. You got to make a choice. You can spend the rest of your life in prison or you can try and help yourself and get even with that piece of shit, Jaime. Right now, you're standing up for the guy who lied to you, for the guy who was going to have you killed. It's your call, but when I walk out of here, that's it. You're done. What'll it be?"

Angel sat back up, looked at Tynan then over at the two detectives. "Okay, I'll tell you what happened. It's not like Jaime was saying. What do you want to know?"

Tynan patted Angel on his shoulder. "You made the right choice. Talk to these two detectives. I'll be outside." He turned, leaned over to Morris, and whispered, "I want to bring my two people in on this, if you don't mind."

Morris nodded. "Absolutely. We wouldn't be here if it wasn't for them."

Tynan went right into the observation room where Joe had been standing watching and listening. Joe smiled and gave a thumbs up to Tynan.

Tynan looked through the two-way mirror at Angel. He felt sorry for him, in a way. Here was a guy who thought he had it made and now it was all going to blow up in his face. Even if he cooperated, he would be going away for some time. How much was ultimately up to a judge, but whatever time he got, it would be less than Jaime.

"Why don't you go and get Linda? Have someone else babysit Defede. I want you two in on the interrogation. I want him to tell us how he came to know everyone. He needs to tell us what happened with Kearns, and I want him to nail down what he knows about Warren."

"You got it," said Joe as he stepped out to get Linda.

After a few minutes, Joe and Linda appeared on the other side of the mirror, dragging two more chairs with them. Morris stepped out and joined Tynan in the observation room.

"This should be interesting," said Morris.

Linda had a new legal yellow pad in front of her. She clicked her pen nervously, looked at the other two detectives, then turned her full attention to Angel.

"Angel," said Linda. "I want you to tell us how you came to know Jaime, Lugo, Santos, Kearns, and a cop named Warren, and everything you know about the three murders."

The two detectives threw side glances at each other when she said Warren's name. The one with the handlebar moustache started to take notes while the bald detective bore holes into Angel with his eyes.

Angel moved closer to the table, cleared his throat, and started telling his story. He went over how he had known Lugo and Santos. Tynan thought Angel sat up straighter when he mentioned he was an informant for the Feds. *He was proud of that,* thought Tynan.

He confirmed Defede's account of finding out about a stolen car ring. According to Angel, he pushed for information from Kearns but could never get any. That's why he brought it up to Jaime and asked him if he knew anything about Warren stealing cars. The story about Warren being a drug guy and wanting to kill Santos was all made up. That story took the heat off Jaime, and it almost worked.

Tynan moved closer to the mirror as Angel talked about the night Kearns was killed. He started to pick at his cast. Looking down at the table, Angel let out a loud sigh.

"The night he was killed, I went to the junkyard. Jaime asked me to find out where he was going. He told me that he was going to meet up with Kearns, and give him the money but he wanted to do it someplace where Kearns' wouldn't be suspicious. He thought if I was there Kearns would be relaxed. Jaime was afraid that if I wasn't there and he just walked up, Kearns would whip out a piece and start shooting. It made sense to me."

Angel shook his head again. "I was so stupid. I went down there and asked Kearns' what he was up to. He told me that he was going to see his girlfriend, and I asked him where, and he told me where she lived. I asked him for a ride because I had a friend who lived on the other side of the park and I had to do some business with him."

"Kearns didn't think that was suspicious?" she asked.

"I guess not, he went along with it. He never asked me about what kind of business I was doing. We drove up to the park and I told him to let me out by the tunnel. That's where Jaime said he was going to be waiting with the money. I didn't see Jaime around. I couldn't wait, so I got out of the car, and that's when I see Jaime come from around the corner of the building. He had a gun in his hand and I thought he was going to shoot me, but he walked right past me, and fired into the car. Then he took a gun out from under his shirt. It was wrapped up in a rag and he dropped that gun in the car."

Linda tapped her pen a few times on the yellow pad. "What did you say?"

"Nothing. What could I say? It was over and done with. His car was around the corner by the park and he told me to get in. That's when he tells me there's a change in plans. I was going to have to go see Lugo with the money. Except now, I had to kill him. He uses the same rag to wipe down the gun he just shot Kearns with and says I'm supposed to drop that gun beside Lugo after I kill him and take the money back."

"What did you say?" asked Joe.

"What else?" snorted Angel. "I said sure. I just saw him kill Kearns and I knew he killed Santos. If I say no, he's going to kill me."

The bald detective leaned closer to Angel. "Why didn't you just come to us after he dropped you off?"

Angel laughed. "And what were you going to do? I'd be dead after I walked out of here."

"Then why not go to your federal friends?" asked Joe.

Angel waved his hand dismissively. "Same shit. I'd still be dead."

Linda was busy writing. She stopped and pointed her pen at Angel. "Did he promise you anything if you shot Lugo?"

Angel looked down at the floor. "Yeah. He said I could run Lugo's spot after he was dead. Jaime made it sound pretty simple.

Santos was dead. He threw that gun into Kearns car after he shot him, to make it look like Kearns killed Santos. I was supposed to shoot Lugo and leave the gun that killed Kearns in his apartment. But that's not what happened."

"Okay, then you tell us what happened with Lugo," said Linda.

"I got picked up by Jaime. He said Lugo would be expecting someone to drop off the money. We went early because Lugo would still be in his apartment. Jaime thought if Lugo saw me when he opened the door, he'd be cool and let me in. I knocked on the door and Lugo answered, but he had the chain on. He was definitely surprised when he saw me. I pushed the bag in and he took it. He was looking at the money in the bag and that's when I took my gun out and shot him. I was nervous. I had never shot anyone before. I shoved the gun in through the door but he looked up and tried to slam the door and the gun went off."

Angel, shook his head again. "Oh God. That's when the shot hit him in the head and he fell. The shot was so loud. He really hurt my wrist and I took off. I ran up the block and met up with Jaime and told him what happened. He was pissed. I lost the money, my own gun, and didn't drop the other gun like I was supposed to. Jaime was so mad he told me to take a walk and he'd call me."

"What did you do with the gun he gave you to plant on Lugo?" asked Linda.

"Jaime took it back. I called Kurt and asked for a ride. I figured I could lay low for a while with the Feds."

Tynan felt his body relax. Now he knew what had happened with Kearns. He knew that someone like Angel was smart enough to try to put himself in the best possible light. If he was going to get any kind of a deal, Angel would have to play the unwitting accomplice who was afraid.

Tynan watched Linda and Joe go to work on Angel asking him about Warren and the stolen car ring. The answers never changed.

Everything he knew he had heard from that short ride in the car with Defede and Kearns. If there was a car theft ring, there was no evidence of it. *Warren was not the turncoat after all,* thought Tynan. *It really did look like he was trying to get his misfit cousin on the right path.*

Tynan turned to Morris. "Are you going to call the District Attorney's office and get them over here to put this guy on video?"

Morris nodded. "Yeah, might as well."

"Do you think Jaime will say anything?"

"We'll give it a shot," said Morris. "I don't think he'll budge. He's been around long enough to know talking won't save him."

Tynan followed Morris to the room with Jaime in it. He was cuffed to a metal ring on the top of the table and he was sleeping. Tynan thought he heard a slight snore.

Morris walked up to the table and banged on it with his fist. "Wake up, sleeping beauty. It's time to talk."

Jaime yawned and blinked his eyes a couple of times. He looked at Morris, then over at Tynan. "Fuck you, motherfuckers. I ain't got nothing to say. I want my lawyer."

Morris chuckled. "As you wish asshole." Tynan followed Morris out of the room and looked back at Jaime. Jaime spat on the floor. Tynan flipped him off and closed the door.

ANOTHER OPPORTUNITY

It was after midnight by the time Tynan walked into his office with Linda and Joe. The rest of the group had already gone home. Tynan was tired but pleased with himself. He sat at his desk as Joe and Linda pulled up chairs.

"It looks like your case is finally closed," said Linda.

"My case? Since when did this become my case?"

"Come on, Lou. This was always your case," Linda said, holding up a scolding finger and waving it at Tynan. "You always say don't take a case personally but that's what you did."

"Give it up, Linda," snorted Joe. "You know we wanted this thing just as bad."

Linda smiled. "Maybe. I wonder what they are going to say downtown."

Tynan shrugged. "What can they say? The Detective Bureau made two arrests tonight with the assistance of the Narcotics Division and Internal Affairs. It's a tribute to the professionalism of the men and women working in the NYPD."

"Oh man, you should work in Public Information," laughed Joe.

"I'll find out tomorrow what is going to happen. How can they complain? The lab said the gun in Jaime's car is the gun that killed Kearns. Angel and Defede gave statements. Even the Assistant District Attorney said the case was a slam dunk. All in all, I think you guys did a great job, and it wasn't easy."

"Thanks, Lou," said Linda. "I must admit I had my doubts."

"Not me, I had this whole thing figured out from the beginning," snickered Joe. "Didn't I predict the whole thing, Lou?"

"Maybe in your dreams you did," said Tynan. "Now why don't you two go home? I'll see you in the morning."

"You staying?" asked Linda with a frown.

"No. I just want to let Rogan know. I don't like calling people at night but I think he'd appreciate how it turned out. Unlike some people I could name."

After they left, Tynan called Rogan and told him what happened. Rogan mostly laughed, especially when he found out the auto theft ring was a figment of Kearns' imagination, blown out of proportion by an informant looking to score points with the Feds.

"Should I call Calhoun?" asked Tynan.

"No, I'll do that. I'm going to give him a sketch of what happened, but I think we should go tomorrow morning to tell him in person."

"Really?"

"Yeah," laughed Rogan. "Because I want to see the look on their faces. I'll see you in the lobby of the Palace at nine sharp."

"You got it, Captain." Tynan hung up the phone. He looked out the window. He couldn't see the boats in the darkness but he knew they were out there, nodding approval. He got up and started the drive home.

Once again, he had to sneak into his house in the middle of the night, tiptoeing around in the dark. After four short hours, he was up and out the door again. He left a note saying he loved them and pinned it to the refrigerator with a magnet. Hopefully, there weren't going to be too many of these nights in his future.

Rogan was already standing by the bank of elevators when Tynan pushed his way through the turnstile in the lobby of the Palace. Rogan walked towards him with his hand out, and said, "There he is. Are you ready for this?

"I don't know. That depends on how your call with the chief went last night."

Rogan grabbed Tynan by the arm as they walked into the elevator. "He didn't say much, but I'm sure he's been on the phone with the Feds." He snickered. "We'll find out when we get up there. If we get coffee, they're in a good mood."

They rode the rest of the way up in silence. Rogan strode into the chief's office and stopped in front of the receptionist. Tynan half expected Rogan to click his heels and salute. "Captain Rogan and Lieutenant Tynan to see the chief. He's expecting us."

The receptionist smiled back. "Again," she scoffed, looking directly at Tynan. "You can go into the conference room. They are all waiting for you in there."

"I'll bet they are," whispered Rogan as he poked Tynan with his elbow.

There they were again, thought Tynan. *The four horsemen of the apocalypse.* They were sitting in the same spots as the last two times. He tried to read their faces but drew a blank. Calhoun gestured towards the chairs at the end of the conference table. Tynan sat in the same chair as before and Rogan joined him on the right.

Rogan cleared his voice. "Good morning, chief. There have been several new developments in the Warren case that Lieutenant Tynan can elaborate on."

"Good morning, chief," said Tynan. "I know everyone here is familiar with the case. Yesterday, several new leads were developed which led to two arrests for three homicides by the Detective Bureau."

"Please proceed, Lieutenant," said Calhoun in a low but clipped tone.

Tynan noticed there was no offer of coffee, even though the four of them had cups. He wanted to joke that someone should turn down the air conditioning because it was very frosty, but he decided to just plunge right in.

His briefing was not interrupted. Occasionally, Calhoun would nod or even let a thin smile cross his face. Klein and Riordan sat motionless. Riordan's eyes were riveted on Tynan, and Klein looked off into space. Sullivan scribbled away on her legal pad.

Tynan finished up with "Any questions?" and looked at the faces around the table.

Klein sipped from his coffee then placed the cup slowly on the saucer. "I'm confused, Lieutenant. Perhaps you could help me."

You'll be a lot more confused when I get out of this chair and kick your ass, thought Tynan. But he sat there expressionless and waited for Klein's obnoxious question.

"Did it ever cross your mind that we should have been informed about what was going on?"

Tynan figured he'd go for broke. "Not at all. I was merely assisting the Detective Bureau and Bronx Narcotics with information they had developed. It wasn't our case. I thought that, based on the assistance they gave us in the Warren case, we owed our counterparts in the other bureaus our full cooperation."

Tynan thought he heard Rogan laugh but he covered it up quickly with a fake cough and a brief "Excuse me, I have a cold."

Calhoun smiled. "Of course, that was the correct thing to do, but still it would have been nice if we knew. Then we could have told our federal partners. After all, they are working on a case against Warren."

"Ah, yes, the auto theft ring. I wasn't worried about that because our information proved their case was based on some fiction created by the CI. There's absolutely no evidence to corroborate anything the Feds were doing."

"We'll never know now, will we?" asked Riordan.

"I think we do know," said Tynan. "The witness said it was all bullshit fed to the CI. The junkyard where Kearns works chops cars, according to the Auto Crime Division. Nobody has come up with a shred of evidence that Warren was involved in anything."

Klein picked up his coffee and drained it, putting it back on the saucer with a clatter. "I think Lieutenant Tynan should be commended for his work on this case."

Tynan almost fell off his chair. Klein was giving him a compliment. A minute ago, he was questioning his judgment on failing to notify his superiors. Tynan tried to figure out Klein's angle but couldn't. Out of the corner of his eye, Tynan caught Rogan shifting in his chair. He knew Rogan thought something was amiss.

"I agree," said Calhoun.

Riordan vigorously shook his head up and down, mumbling, "Yes, of course."

"Perhaps it's time to tell the lieutenant of his transfer to the Detective Bureau," said Klein softly as he pushed his cup and saucer away from him.

"Yes," said Calhoun. "It just so happens that I was talking to the Chief of Detectives this morning and effective midnight tonight you are being transferred to the Detective Bureau."

Tynan was stunned. For a moment, he said nothing. "Where in the Detective Bureau?"

"Oh, I don't know. I think they said you would be assigned to the chief's office right here at One Police Plaza. Later, they'd move you to Brooklyn. I'm not sure."

Calhoun stood up and walked down to Tynan's end of the table. He clapped Tynan on the shoulder and put his hand out. "Congratulations. You weren't in Internal Affairs long, but we appreciate all the work you did."

Calhoun turned towards the rest of the table. "Right now, gentlemen and lady," he said, bowing towards Lieutenant Sullivan, "I have to see the Commissioner, so if you'll forgive me." He walked out the door of the conference room and closed it firmly.

Klein said, "You better head back to the Bronx. You have a lot of packing to do. I guess we'll be seeing you in the building. Enjoy your commute from Westchester. I hear the train ride can be beautiful in the fall. It'll probably take about an hour to get from your house to Grand Central Station, then a quick twenty-minute ride on the subway. That'll seem like a short commute after they transfer you to Brooklyn. How long would that commute be? Two hours?"

Tynan and Rogan stood up and walked out. Neither of them said anything until they were out of the building.

"I didn't see that coming," said Tynan. "Assigned to headquarters in the Detective Bureau for who knows how long, and then Brooklyn."

"Don't worry about it," said Rogan. "I'll get the word out that you're a good worker. The Chief of Detectives isn't a dope. I'm sure he knows this is to get you out of Klein's hair. As soon as he can, he'll change it and ship you up to the Bronx. Besides, what difference does it make? You're out of IAB and you're in the Detective Bureau. Congratulations son, you beat them."

"It doesn't feel like I beat them," said Tynan. "But I just want you to know that I appreciate your support through all of this."

Rogan shrugged. "Think nothing of it. Don't be a stranger. I'll see you around." He walked off towards his car. "And when you're in the Detective Bureau, don't take no shit from anyone," called Rogan over his shoulder.

It's too early in the morning to go have a drink, thought Tynan. He might as well go back to his office. Klein was finally right. He did have a lot of packing to do.

THE END